A Taste of Tradition

Mysteries of Sparrow Island®

A TASTE OF TRADITION

Susan Plunkett & Krysteen Seelen

Guideposts Books
CARMEL, NEW YORK

www.guideposts.org
(800) 431-2344
Guideposts Books & Inspirational Media Division

Cover and interior design by Cindy LaBreacht
Cover art by Gail W. Guth
Map by Jim Haynes, represented by Creative Freelancers, Inc.
Typeset by Nancy Tardi
Printed in the United States of America

To our parents, Alexander and Elyce Fassbender.
For the love and traditions they handed down,
we are most grateful.

TO CANADA

SHAW

SAN
JUAN
ISLAND

LOPE

San Juan
ISLANDS

SPARROW
ISLAND*

CHAPTER ❧ ONE

DINNER AND A MYSTERY PARTY

LOCATION: Candace Grover's home
Green Harbor, Sparrow Island, Washington

TIME: Saturday, November 10, 7:00 PM

Bring a dish to share

PLAYERS:
Al Minsky—Gangster
Abby Stanton—Flapper
Bradford Collins—Bouncer
Brandi Phelps—Torch Singer
Candace Grover—Waitress
Donna Morgan—Socialite
Keith Gordon—Gin-Ger-Ale Runner
Laverne Minsky—Chorus Girl
Nathaniel Dawkins—Banker
Sven Dyer—Big Band Leader

D<small>R. ABIGAIL STANTON STOOD</small>
on the footstool and tried to hold still while her sister Mary
Reynolds checked the hemline on her flapper costume. During

Abby's thirty-five years with Cornell University, she'd gone to countless parties. None had had murder as a theme.

"Your dress looks very, very authentic." Mary took a final stitch and reached for the scissors.

Abby looked in the mirror, removed and cleaned her glasses, put them on again, then double-checked her reflection.

A dazzling stranger peered back.

This isn't me. How can it be? I'm a mature and dignified fifty-five-year-old, not a glittery creature in shimmering gold.

The image decked out in feathers and fringe looked nothing at all like the Associate Curator of Sparrow Island's Nature Conservatory. That woman wore hiking boots, denim jeans and multi-pocketed vests, the ultimate in practical attire for a well-seasoned ornithologist.

"Earth to Abby, earth to Abby," Mary called in a teasing tone.

A little embarrassed by her preoccupation, Abby met her sister's curious gaze and explained, "This outfit just doesn't seem real. Oh, Mary, it's ..."

"Adventurous? Sassy? Fun?"

"Ye-e-sss, but Halloween was last month. Don't you think it's a little over the top?" Abby stepped down and pushed the stool aside with her foot.

"No, it's perfect for the 1920s. Besides, you need a change of pace. After the three-sizes-too-big shepherd's outfit you wore to the church's Autumn Festival, it's definitely time for a new fashion statement." The laughter lurking just beneath Mary's words proved she was enjoying herself far too much. "Now get back on the stool and hold still so I can finish the last bit of fringe on your hem."

Obeying the command, Abby let her gaze wander over

spools of ribbons, jars of beads and the assorted boxes of supplies in Mary's craft room. "You know, this seemed like a good place to dress, but it feels like I'm turning into one of your art projects."

"What's wrong with that?" Mary snipped the thread and stabbed the needle into the pincushion on her wrist. Releasing the handbrake on her wheelchair, she rolled back and surveyed her handiwork. "You should consider yourself blessed you have such a talented sister willing to create the dress of the century just for you."

"Oh, I do. I do." Abby turned in a slow circle. "I think I know how the male peacock feels when he spreads his tail feathers." She finished her turn and met Mary's amused gaze. "You ought to be wearing this outfit. It's so much more . . . *you* than it is me."

"Candace said getting the guests to do something different is the whole point of the party. If I were going, I'd want to be one of the bootleggers, one of the gin-ger-ale runners." Mary rolled to the long, low worktable built specifically to accommodate her wheelchair.

Abby chuckled. Her sister's beau, Deputy Sheriff Henry Cobb might find Mary's choice quite interesting.

While transferring her sewing supplies from her lap to the table, Mary continued, "Heaven knows, I'd love to be in two places at once tonight, but the law enforcement awards are a special event for Henry and his men."

"I wish you could make it to Candace's too. If the timing had worked out, I could see you coming to the party as a gin-ger-ale runner and Henry as . . . what?" Abby straightened her flapper headband. "One of Elliot Ness's boys?"

Mary groaned. "I'd rather see Henry have to stretch and do something totally out of character. Maybe a gangster or a numbers runner."

Abby almost choked on her laugh. "Great idea. It'd be a hoot watching him in such an unfamiliar role. I think we'll get the chance eventually. Candace may be starting a new fad with this party. If it works out, everyone will want to have one."

"I hope you're right."

Candace had scheduled the party to coincide with her cousin Brandi's visit, not realizing it was on the same night as the San Juan County Law Enforcement Awards for outstanding performance and service above the call of duty. Henry had nominated two of his deputies, Artie Washburn and Mike Bennett, and they were among the four honorees selected.

"Henry's a great guy, Mary. You always pick such terrific men."

Surprise lit Mary's face. "You know, I think they picked me. I'm just grateful God gave me the good sense to recognize them when He sent them into my life."

"So, Henry isn't receiving an award?"

"Not one actually pinned to his chest. Decorating his men is the honor he prizes."

Abby's admiration for Henry deepened. For Artie and Mike to receive awards in front of an audience of their peers *was* a top honor. It also reflected well on Henry's ability to help them reach their full potential. "I can certainly understand why you're thrilled to be part of this evening."

"Good. I know you'll have a great time at Candace's 'dinner and a mystery party'. It's right up your alley."

Abby couldn't quibble. She loved a good mystery and usually had a stack of whodunits on her nightstand. Lately, several real-life puzzles had come her way. "I'm rather pleased I've been able to solve the mysteries that have cropped up since I came home to Sparrow Island. With each one, I've learned more about God's loving care and the way He blesses us."

Mary opened a box of costume jewelry. "For those who have the eyes to see, He provides lessons and blessings in everything." She smiled at her sister. "Tonight, there's one thing that isn't a mystery. You look absolutely, positively fabulous, Abby." She held up a long strand of fake pearls. "You need one more necklace, one you can tie in a knot and swing."

Lifting the long strand over her head, Abby took great care not to disturb her headband or the ostrich feather rising up from the side. "Are you sure more beads aren't overkill?"

"Not a chance." Mary deftly put a knot in the pearls. "There, that's it. Check it out."

Gazing in the mirror, Abby twirled the necklace. Layer upon layer of gold fringe shimmered down the length of her flapper dress.

Abby was thrilled to see that she totally looked the part. Her short brown hair was just the right length for that era and the little spit curls Mary had formed around her face with hair gel were the perfect touch. "I think I'm going to enjoy being a flapper, but I can't imagine how Candace thought of giving me the role."

Seeing her sister's valiant effort to suppress a smile, Abby's suspicions morphed into certainty. Thirty-five-year-old Candace might have chosen a younger woman as the flapper. No doubt, Mary had helped plan the roles while they were working at the flower shop. "This was your idea, wasn't it?"

"I'm sure she thought you'd enjoy it." Mary's bright blue gaze glided quickly away and she reached for the yellow

Labrador retriever service dog at her side. A gift from her children, Finnegan was a constant companion, faithful friend and impeccably trained helper. "You have to admit, you look great as a 1920s flapper. Besides, it stretches you."

"It does a little more than that." Abby shook herself, much like Finnegan did when he came in out of the rain. The fringe on her dress went wild. The beads jangled and swayed. The long dangling earrings caught the light and sparkled.

Mary laughed. "That's the spirit! Tonight, you're a flapper, not an ornithologist. You're spreading your wings, not studying them. And remember, you have to stay in character for the whole party."

The whole party? Abby gulped. The shimmering fringe and silky texture of the costume made her feel slinky, nervous and special all at the same time. A slow blush crept up her cheeks. Why, she even felt a little flirty. How exciting. Pretending to be a flapper would definitely be an adventure.

"Candace wants all the guests to become their characters," Mary encouraged. "She says you'll all have a lot more fun if you do."

IN HER SPECIALIZED VAN, Mary turned on the overhead map lights, then handed a photograph to her date. "You've got to see this to believe it."

The big engines of the interisland ferry bound for Friday Harbor thrummed as Henry Cobb angled the picture under the bright beam. "Whoa! This is Abby? Watch out, Hugo. Somebody might steal her away."

Wondering if she should show the picture to Abby's boss, Mary bit her lip. At times, she thought that with a little nudge, something more than friendship might develop between her sister and Hugo Baron. Then, again . . . she let out a soft sigh. She knew better than to meddle in that part of Abby's life.

"I presume she's seen this picture?"

"Yes," Mary said and turned off the van's overhead light. "I convinced her to let me take it so Mom and Dad could see her in the costume."

"Uh-huh." Even in the dim lights of the ferry's big parking bay, the smile tugging at the corners of Henry's solemn expression was visible. "You're getting to be quite the shutterbug. What brought this on?"

"My digital camera's so easy to use. I love being able to delete the bad shots. And I can get the pictures I want right away. The photo printer makes copies in no time."

"Uh-oh." Henry handed back the snapshot. "My innocent, little flower seller is turning into a technology junky."

"I'm afraid so." Pretending to wilt like a southern belle, Mary batted her eyelashes. "Is it a crime?"

"*Mmm.*" Immediately catching the cue, Henry lifted her hand, held her fingers to his lips and whispered, "Felonious family photos—we're talking dangerous territory. Very dangerous."

His breath tickled her fingers and she grinned. They were as comfortable together as macaroni and cheese. Making each other laugh was as easy as breathing. "Flowers too," she murmured. "I take pictures of flowers too."

"Why doesn't that surprise me?" Laughing, he released her hand.

"Hey, I'm pretty good at it. Mike Bennett's mom asked me to take pictures of him during the awards ceremony."

"But she's going to be there. I expect she'll take her own

pictures. She's so proud of Mike she practically walks on air." Henry's forehead wrinkled in puzzlement and he sat back. "Did something happen I don't know about? Is she ill?"

"No, no, she's fine," Mary answered quickly. Henry's concern for his men and their families was one of his many endearing, noble traits. "Mrs. Bennett's afraid she'll be too full of emotion to hold the camera steady when you pin the decoration on her boy."

"I see." Henry rubbed his chin and nodded. "I'll do it real slow, so you'll have plenty of time to take pictures. Her *boy* is a fine officer."

"Thanks." Mary leaned over the console and squeezed his arm. "You're the best. Being a mom is sort of like being a law officer. Active duty or retired, you're always a member of an exclusive club and you're always on call."

"I hadn't thought of a mom network like the cop network, but it makes sense. You're an amazing woman, Mary Reynolds. What else have you done I should know about?"

Without hesitation, she said, "I donated the centerpieces for all the tables."

"You did? Why?"

"It's terrific advertising for Island Blooms."

"I don't get it. My guys don't need convincing; they already think you're the greatest."

"Sweet of you to say so, but they'll be on the dais." The ferry docked at Friday Harbor. Mary started the van and prepared to disembark.

"Ahh. The audience will be full of proud families and business owners from all over San Juan County. Besides being beautiful, you are one smart businesswoman."

The compliment warmed her while she drove off the ferry and up the steep hill into town. Two turns and a short distance later, she eased the van into a parking space near the restaurant's entrance.

She didn't like using the blue parking places. With Finnegan's help, she usually didn't need them and preferred to leave the convenience for those who did. Tonight though, she had no choice. The lot was almost full and the hydraulic lift she used to enter and exit the van required the extra room.

Wearing the blue cape identifying him as a service dog, Finnegan trotted around the van and watched attentively as the lift engaged. A moment later, Henry was there too.

In his dress uniform—shades of dark green trimmed in gold—he made her heart beat a little faster. Beneath his dark green campaign hat, a neat fringe of white hair formed a partial halo around his balding pate.

At almost six feet, he commanded subtle authority. When necessary, a word delivered in his low, deep voice reinforced who was in charge.

She smiled up into his warm brown eyes. "Have I told you how handsome you are?"

Standing a bit straighter, he gave her shoulder a gentle squeeze. "Thank you."

Before she could say more, he moved behind her chair, let Finnegan take his customary position and guided her into the restaurant.

Immediately, the artist in her wanted to jump for joy at the elegant displays of Native American baskets. Under discreet spotlights, against a backdrop of washed golden suede, nearly a dozen invisible glass shelves showcased the handmade pieces.

"You were right," Henry said. "This is a great venue for the Washburns' work. Artie considers it a feather in his cap to have his work on display with his Aunt Wilma's."

"Sharing venues didn't turn out quite like I thought it would," Mary said wistfully. She'd introduced Wilma to several of her business contacts. Within a week, the restaurant had called Wilma and Artie with a mutually profitable consignment offer. Mary hadn't stopped to consider that success for the Washburns' work at the restaurant meant there would be fewer pieces available for her display at Island Blooms. While she was glad for their success, she missed the steady supply of popular baskets.

"You did a friend a favor. It was a good thing," Henry said. "Wilma has a real friend in you, Mary. This is great marketing. The restaurant is in a high-traffic area, with customers who can afford the items. And just in case the patrons didn't get a good enough look on the way in, they'll see the baskets again on the way out."

"Okay, I'm happy for them. Now I'm working on being happy for me."

Henry chuckled and looked at his watch. "Abby once told me there's always something to be happy about. Think of her now. She's probably having a great time, right in the middle of a mystery. And I'm happy it's not mine."

CHAPTER ✿ TWO

Gusty wind pelted Abby's little hybrid car with rain and torn leaves. She whispered a prayer and leaned closer to the windshield. The turnoff was close and she didn't want to miss it. Suddenly, her headlights picked up a bounce of color, a bouquet of balloons tied to a nearly invisible street sign.

Sending a thank-you heavenward, she turned onto the narrow road. On both sides, spruce, Madrone and poplar shielded her from the brunt of the storm. Over a short rise, warm lights blazed from a two-story cottage.

She parked next to a big pickup truck that set her curiosity on fire. Airbrushed onto the doors and side-panels were murals of towering firs, native shrubs and sumptuous gardens. Below the scenes, neat gold lettering identified the truck's owner as Sven Dyer, landscaper.

Abby took a moment to recollect all her sister had told her about Sparrow Island's latest transplant. He'd made a great beginning by visiting every store in Green Harbor, introducing himself and handing out business cards. Mary liked him right away and was intrigued with the possibility that their businesses could be mutually beneficial.

Pleased she'd finally get to meet the landscaper, Abby turned off the headlights. Right away, the tatter-tapping rain sounded louder. She reached into the backseat for her raincoat and umbrella and came up empty. Her heart sank.

When time permitted, Saturday was a catchup and cleanup day. This afternoon she'd worked on her car and had removed the bulky items when she vacuumed. Now she realized she'd forgotten to return them to the backseat.

Phooey. Getting her ensemble wet wasn't an option. Neither was waiting out the storm. She'd have to improvise. She reached under the seat for her avian emergency kit—the one thing she'd never leave behind. Only heaven knew when a sick or injured bird would need her help.

The kit included a box of large lawn and leaf bags. The disposable lengths of plastic often made the task of transporting the birds easier and neater while protecting the poor creatures from further contamination.

Certain Mary would not approve of wearing the bags as disposable raingear, Abby shrugged. After all the time and effort they'd spent getting her ready, she didn't want to muss a single hair. Taking a pocketknife from the glove compartment, she went to work.

Moments later, she stepped out of the car, made her way to the front porch and rang the bell. The dark red door opened and a young woman dressed in green sequins gave her a suspicious once-over.

The skittish door-minder brandished a poke-your-eye-out cigarette holder with a thin peppermint stick taped to the end. "Who, uh, are you?"

Belatedly realizing her black plastic shroud might be intimidating, Abby hastily identified herself and added, "I'm sorry if I scared you. I admit my raingear's a little unusual."

"Come in. Come in. I'm Candace's cousin, Brandi Phelps, doorkeeper and"—she patted the tag clipped to the neckline of her dress—"for tonight only, torch singer extraordinaire."

"Pleased to meet you." Abby stepped into the foyer and elbowed the door closed.

Brandi's laughter made Abby want to laugh too. A couple of inches taller than Abby's five feet three inches, Brandi looked at home in the cocktail dress clinging to her lithe figure. Long, honey-blonde hair tamed in a 1940s Lauren Bacall style added the perfect air of allure to her nightclub ensemble.

"Here, let me take your dish." The large diamond on Brandi's ring caught the light and refracted into little rainbows before the ring twisted sideways.

"Be careful. It's hot." Abby passed off the heavily padded tray of twice-baked potatoes. Now, with both hands free, she carefully lifted the plastic protecting her ostrich plume and heavily gelled curls.

"Wow! I never would've guessed what you were hiding under there." A gleam lit Brandi's brown eyes. "How ingenious."

With a flick of her penknife, Abby slit the bag and hung it on the coat tree. "I forgot to put my raingear back in the car. So I had to improvise. At least this black beauty is lightweight and didn't crush my dress."

"I'll have to remember that trick. It might come in handy some day." Candace's younger cousin waved her long cigarette holder at a basket of party role tags. "After you get yours on, go mingle. I'll just put your dish in the kitchen. We'll be getting started soon."

A cheery fire burned in the living room hearth and drew the eclectic mix of guests to its warmth. Abby paused at the entrance to admire the décor and the costumes while fixing her tag to her dress. Bradford Collins, Candace's longtime boyfriend, joined her there.

They exchanged greetings and after a tease about her rain-gear, they examined each other's party attire. The pinstriped vest over his white shirt and narrow bowtie accentuated Bradford's broad shoulders. At six feet, his dark hair uncharacteristically slicked back and a fake scar on his cheek, the prominent Seattle attorney looked rather intimidating. The only softness in his even features was the playfulness of his gray eyes.

"You make a great bouncer," Abby said. "The scar's an excellent touch. It makes you look dangerous."

Chuckling, he said, "It's a fun change from the courtroom. At first, I didn't think a role-playing party was a good idea. Now, I'm glad Candace didn't let me talk her out of it. The way everyone has jumped into character is amazing. Your costume is dynamite. You get my vote for most authentic."

Startled, Abby blushed. "Thank you. I'll be sure to tell Mary. She masterminded the design and deserves the credit."

"Speaking of masterminds . . ." Bradford angled to a corner stand, snagged a flute of bubbly and handed it to Abby. "I think you'll enjoy this. It's courtesy of another mastermind, Keith Gordon, our black market gin-ger-ale runner for the evening."

Abby tasted the zesty soft drink. "*M-mmm*. Nothing but the best from Keith."

A man came toward them, his fedora cocked low and to the left. As he headed for the drinks tray, she tried to see his face, but only managed to read his tag. She recognized the exaggerated style of the gangster's pinstriped zoot suit. The long draped coat had wide lapels and the high-waisted baggy trousers narrowed at the cuffs.

He turned and Abby's chin dropped as she gaped at the owner of Al Minsky's garage. The chorus girl prancing up to him was his wife, Laverne.

"Saw your raingear, Abby. What an idea."

The front door opened again. A burst of cool wind swirled through the living room. "Hey everyone, we're starting to get breaks in the rain," announced Nathaniel Dawkins, owner of The Complete Boater. "If you ask me, by tomorrow morning the squall will have blown through."

Pleased nods greeted Nathaniel's prediction.

"Wonderful!" Candace hurried out of the kitchen. With her long strawberry-blonde hair caught up in a black hairnet and a severe apron cinched at the waist, she made a picture-perfect waitress. "Good evening, Banker Dawkins. What did you bring us?"

"A pot of stocks and bonds." He handed over a towel-wrapped dish. "That is, an edible version from the Springhouse."

Candace took the insulated package and hurried back to the kitchen. Abby gave Nathaniel high points for buying his potluck dish at the restaurant. He was a single fellow in love with the sea and his business. Domestic arts were not his forte and he didn't pretend otherwise.

She glanced down at the stiff, white fabric covers attached to the top of his highly polished black shoes. "Gracious sakes! Will you look at those spats."

He gave his top hat a rakish tilt and tucked his show-off walking stick under his elbow. "Did you know spats is short for *spatterdashes*? They were originally designed to keep mud off one's shoes."

Abby lifted her glass in salute. Not only had Nathaniel

acquired all the right attire for a wealthy young man of that era, he'd done a bit of research. Complimenting him in the lingo of the day, she said, "Spiffy."

His eyes and his grin widened. "Thanks, doll. You're the bee's knees."

She laughed and tossed more of the 1920s slang right back. "And you're the cat's meow."

Nodding approvingly, he retorted, "Ducky, doll. Where'd you find the giggle water? I'm a little dry."

For a moment, she thought about the nametags, then directed him to the drinks table. The dollar sign prominently embroidered on the handkerchief sticking out of the breast pocket of his three-piece suit seemed sufficient identification for a banker.

Candace came out of the kitchen again and fluffed her apron. Aglow with excitement, she addressed her guests. "I believe most of you know one another. If not, please introduce yourselves. Once we sit down at the dinner table, we'll take on our mystery personas and leave our Sparrow Island identities behind."

"This is so much fun," gushed Donna Morgan, like a teenager attending her first prom. The bubbly, forty-something owner of Bayside Souvenirs gave Abby an affectionate squeeze. "Your costume is fabulous, so much more fashionable than that thing you were wearing when you arrived."

Abby smiled sheepishly. Apparently, everyone had seen her improvised raincoat. Oh well. It had done the trick. Mary's craft project had survived the storm.

Playing the part of an upper crust socialite, Donna wore a soft, sleeveless dress with a tightly beaded top and a dropped-waist chiffon skirt with a dreamy, uneven hemline. Flowers made of rhinestones and tiny glass beads climbed the side of her elegant felt cloche.

"So is yours. And I love the hat. Cat's pajamas as they say. Have you seen Sven Dyer? I'd like to meet him before we start."

Donna looked around and pointed to a knot of people on the far side of the room. "Over there talking with Nathaniel. Those two are getting to be good buddies."

As Abby maneuvered around the couch, she overheard Laverne tell Brandi, "You should get a ring guard. I have them on all my rings 'cause they get loose when the weather's cold and my fingers shrink." The chorus girl leaned forward and confided, "Too bad my thighs don't shrink too. I'd be asking Al to move to Alaska."

Abby bit her lip. Leave it to Laverne to bring things down to earth.

"I'll look into it. Thanks for the idea." Brandi carried a mostly-empty tray of canapés to the kitchen.

Near the corner of the room, a tanned thirty-something man with whitish-blond hair and a strong jaw laughed with Nathaniel. The banker waved her over.

"Abby, have you met my friend, Sven Dyer, Sparrow Island's new landscaper?"

She extended her hand in greeting. "I'm Abby Stanton. Glad to finally meet you."

Sven bowed with a flourish that flapped the tails of his antique tuxedo. The music clef pinned to his yellowing satin lapel proclaimed him Big Band Leader. Revealing even square teeth he said. "Ah, Mary Reynolds's sister."

Returning his smile, Abby nodded. "She speaks highly of you."

"Will you two excuse me?" Nathaniel asked. "Before we jump into our roles with both feet, I need a word with Al."

Sven grinned knowingly. "Your truck?"

"What else?" Laughing, the banker headed across the room. He raised a backward hand. "Later, buddy."

Abby turned to Sven. "Mary says you have big plans for our little island."

"I believe a good number of people need what I do. Fact is, so does The Nature Conservatory."

Intrigued, Abby assessed his attitude as confident rather than cocky or arrogant. "You don't say?"

A deep chuckle softened his chiseled features and brought a sparkle to his keen blue eyes. "I spoke with Hugo today. If things turn out the way I hope, we'll be seeing one another quite often over the next few months."

"Really? He hasn't mentioned changing the landscaping." Abby recalled Hugo's complaints about the fallen leaves in the museum's circular drive. Although the red, orange and gold colors were stunning, the wet leaves could be very slippery. "Tell me you weren't discussing the big leaf maple in front of the museum."

Sven gave a wary shrug. "I can't. We did talk about it."

"Oh! You're not . . ."

"No, we're not. It's a prime specimen. Touching it with any-thing but loving care would be a crime. Besides, it's hosting a bunch of birds."

Feeling somewhat silly for jumping to the wrong conclu-sion, she heaved a sigh of relief. With a new understanding of why her sister was so impressed with him, Abby said, "Okay. Now that we have that cleared up, what are your designs for the conservatory's property?"

"Hugo and I discussed the northeast corner and the con-struction of several wildlife-watching shelters."

"Ladies and gentlemen," Candace announced. "Please come to the table."

Sven gestured toward the dining room, but Abby wasn't finished with their conversation. "What about the native grasses in that area? They're an important part of the ecology."

"I believe we can do the shelters and leave the grasses untouched. In fact, I've started the drawings."

Abby preceded the landscaper into the dining room. As she noted the excitement of the other guests, she chided herself for talking about work. They were supposed to be getting to know each other's party personas.

Taking a deep breath, she promised herself that for the rest of the evening, she would think of Sven as the big band leader, not the landscaper in charge of a project near and dear to her heart.

As the guests jockeyed to find their assigned seats Sven checked a place card on the beautifully set table. "Looks like you're here, Abby."

"Oh, Sven," Laverne called from the far side. "You're by me."

"Thank you," Abby told her escort. She tipped her head toward the living room to indicate their discussion. "Perhaps we could continue our conversation about the landscaping at The Nature Museum another time?"

"I'll look forward to it."

"Great. I'm always interested in any changes that provide better access for the public without disturbing the natural balance."

He grinned. "You sound like Hugo."

She grinned back. "Thank you for the compliment."

After the guests were seated, Candace remained standing. "The game begins now. Please stay in your roles. The meal's divided into three segments—salad, main course and dessert. At the end of the salad course, we'll change seats. The idea is to have different companions on either side. Then, we'll take a little break between the main course and dessert. Dessert will be self-serve and set on the dining table. You've all brought so much delicious food. I'll leave it to you to help yourselves when you're ready."

Candace consulted a green and white order pad covered with notes. "We're all here because of Uncle Elmer Gotrocks. He was a kindly crook who died of natural causes. His sudden passing affected each of us—some good, some bad. As a result, one of our characters will be murdered tonight."

Candace's pale brown eyes shone with anticipation. "Along with your invitations, you were given three important items. I'll begin with the heart of the mystery, the sealed envelopes. Eight of them contained a blank piece of paper. The other two designated the victim and the murderer. Only those two people know who they are.

"After the dastardly deed, the victim will assume the role of the inspector sent to investigate the crime. A word of caution—the inspector cannot reveal anything about his or her former persona.

"You also received the background information on your character. You may share it at your discretion. It includes an embarrassing or a possibly incriminating secret about one other person." She laughed softly and gazed around the table. "Of course, that means someone knows something embarrassing or incriminating about you.

"Which leads to the last item. All of us have a motive. None of us has an alibi. Before the night is over, the inspector will make an arrest. The way to clear your name is to ferret out enough secrets to lead the inspector to the guilty party."

As murmurs ran around the table, Abby admired the psychology built into the game. To have any chance of solving the mystery, every guest had to mingle and role-play.

Candace retrieved two serving bowls from the sideboard and sent them around the table in opposite directions.

Abby smoothed a linen napkin across her fringed lap before taking some salad from the bowl the socialite held. As Abby passed the first course to the person on her left, she did a double take.

Looking like he'd been off-loading cases of bootlegged hooch from a ship's hold, Keith Gordon dragged a grime-stained hand through his rumpled hair, then swiped at the smear of grease on his chin.

Abby gawked. Even though she knew his grease and grime were only makeup, she couldn't help it. The owner of The Dorset, Sparrow Island's upper crust hotel, was always meticulous in his attire. To him, *disheveled* meant a wrinkled handkerchief in his breast pocket. Never would she have expected to see him in a stained T-shirt a size too small. Biting her tongue, she tried to cling to her composure.

He smiled at her, revealing blackened front teeth as he helped himself to the salad and passed it on.

"Horse feathers and applesauce," she cried.

"Don't get all bluenose on me, baby," he responded, his Scottish burr lilting below the words. "Just 'cause I ain't no swell, don't mean I don't got prospects, ya know? Someday, I'll own this town."

"I don't doubt it for a minute." Fighting to control her laugher and stay in character, Abby picked up her flute of ginger ale. "How's business?"

"Everything's jake. You know, okay. I wanna hear about your dancing. Something tells me when you get those glad rags going, you're one hotsy-totsy hoofer."

Abby was pretty sure he'd just told her that if her fringed flapper dress was an indication of her dancing ability, then she must be good. She hoped he'd be content with that delusion. She wasn't giving demonstrations of her character's specialty—Charleston marathons. Although bird walks and hiking kept her in good shape, Abby couldn't imagine doing the high-stepping dance for hours on end.

Keith leaned close. She picked up the scent of his cologne, a rich blend of woods and spice sold only in high-end specialty stores. Thank heaven, underneath the rough exterior he was still the same debonair man she knew.

"Every hoofer has a favorite dance," he insisted. "What do you think of the fox-trot?"

A sizzle of excitement ran through her. Fox-trot was the key to her clue. "Irene and Vernon Castle were the first champions. Unfortunately, he died in 1918. It certainly is a graceful dance."

"Yes it is." The gin-ger-ale runner touched a fingertip to the tablecloth and traced the numbers 1-9-1-8.

Abby gave him a confirming nod. She was the go-between for her boyfriend, Bradford the bouncer, and the gin-ger-ale runner. Along with the word *castle*, 1918 was the address of the bouncer's secret new business venture—a speakeasy of his own.

Scant seconds later a question from the guest on his left claimed the gin-ger-ale runner's attention. Immediately, Abby had second thoughts. She'd learned nothing from him. From now on, she'd have to be more circumspect.

On her right, socialite Donna Morgan said, "I couldn't help overhearing. You didn't tell him your favorite dance. What is it?"

"There are so many," Abby stalled, determined to get more information than she gave out. "Have you heard of the shimmy?"

"Oh yeah, the shaking dance. Is that your favorite?"

"Not so much the dance," Abby answered. "It's the controversy around it that's intriguing."

"How so?" Donna inquired, obviously searching for clues.

"Some claim Gilda Gray invented it because she couldn't hold still when she sang."

"Yes, I've heard that," Donna mused.

"Others claim Mae West invented it when she sang in Hammerstein's *Sometime*. About the same time, Ziegfeld was doing his Follies and Bea Palmer claimed the dance."

"You don't say."

Realizing she and Donna were doing a dance of their own and going nowhere, Abby asked, "How did a socialite come to know Uncle Gotrocks?"

To Abby's amazement, Donna heaved a dramatic sigh and touched her forehead with the back of her hand. In a whisper so small, Abby could barely hear it, she said, "I miss him terribly. Some called him a crook, but I knew him as a kind man."

Abby smiled sympathetically and waited, hoping the socialite would reveal a juicy tidbit.

Donna gave a sly look, glanced briefly at Bradford the Bouncer and said, "Did you know he and the torch singer used to be a hot item? He promised to make her a star, then dropped her like a hot potato. I hear he's feeding the same pack of lies to someone new."

Hoping to conceal her surprise, Abby toyed with the remnants of her salad. She hadn't suspected the charming bouncer of such duplicity.

Suddenly, the ring of cutlery on crystal sent everyone scurrying for a different chair and new dinner companions. Falling deeper into the role and getting more comfortable by the minute, Abby hoped the torch singer would be one of her new tablemates.

She looked around for the young woman in the slinky green dress and spotted her in the living room refilling her flute of bubbly. As Brandi reached for the glass, she flinched. Her expression soured as she rummaged the drinks tray and picked up her ring.

"That's it," she exclaimed. Turning to the mantel, she put the ring beside a picture frame. "I'm not juggling you any more tonight. Just stay there."

Beside Abby, Chorus Girl Laverne shrugged. "I told her she needed a ring guard."

As they took their seats, the chorus girl leaned close and whispered, "I know you're the bouncer's new girlfriend, so I thought I ought to warn you. Be careful. You can't trust a man who doesn't like dogs."

"I . . . didn't know that about him. Are you sure?"

"Absolutely! He inherited Uncle Gotrocks' six Chihuahuas. That cretin was going to take them to the pound and have them put down. My sweetie—he's the gangster, you know— rescued them. So now, he has twelve of those cute little dogs."

"Oh my." Abby wondered how her character could be so clueless about her boyfriend. Even more startling was a gangster with twelve Chihuahuas. Dobermans or German shepherds would be more apropos. "How fortunate for the dogs they found such a champion."

The chorus girl kept a straight face as she confided, "Yeah, my guy was plenty steamed over it. So was I."

On the other side of Abby, Candace the waitress spoke up. "Uncle Gotrocks loved all dogs. Why, he came into the restaurant one day and saw me crying. My little terrier got hit by a car. I didn't have any money to pay the vet and little Scotty was suffering so. Uncle Gotrocks took us in his limousine straight to his vet."

The waitress's eyes grew wide. "And he paid for everything. Scotty healed up just like new."

"That's so like Uncle Gotrocks. He was such a fine man." The chorus girl nodded forcefully.

The waitress leaned around Abby as though she wasn't there. "He was. Which is more than I can say for the bouncer. He had the audacity to tell me I had to reimburse Uncle Gotrocks' estate for the vet bills."

"The nerve!" the chorus girl exclaimed. "What business of his is it anyway?"

Feeling like the net in a ping-pong match, Abby held her peace. She'd learned more by being silent than by asking questions. Her "boyfriend" sounded like the most likely one to do something dastardly. Smiling to herself, she vowed not to go out with him again.

After the main course had been eaten and the dishes cleared, the party moved to the living room. Before anyone could get comfortable, the lights went out.

Sounds of a scuffle filled the darkness.

There was a thud.

Then silence.

Someone lit a match and touched it to a candle. In the flickering glow, Abby saw her boyfriend, the bouncer, dead on the floor.

She put her fingers to her mouth. The scene looked real until she saw Bradford's fake scar twitching as he tried to contain his laughter.

CHAPTER ❦ THREE

A BBY'S "BOYFRIEND" WAS dead. She looked around the room. One of the others had killed him. Who? She wondered. All she knew was that it wasn't her.

Bradford placed the crimson scarf on the floor to mark the spot where the bouncer died. Without so much as a glance at anyone, he left the room.

The rest of the party guests milled around.

"I need a drink." Gangster Al went to the cocktail tray near Abby and refilled his flute of ginger ale.

"Pour one for me too." Big Band Leader Sven held out his glass. "Can't say I'm sorry to see the bouncer get his."

Abby noticed the gangster cast a sideways glance at the gin-ger-ale runner before turning his attention back to the big band leader. "I'll bet you're not. The gin-ger-ale runner told me the bouncer got you fired from your last gig."

"That's history. Besides, I know the gin-ger-ale runner planned to torch the bouncer's new speakeasy before it opened.

The bouncer was cutting him out of the trade. Said he was starting up his own runners. Guess the bouncer had big plans to take over the city's nightlife."

The gangster nodded. "Good riddance. I know I'm talking for all the speakeasy owners in the city. None of 'em were lookin' for more competition."

Abby sidled closer. How many people knew about the bouncer's new speakeasy? According to her character's background info, he'd told her on the QT. Apparently, it wasn't much of a secret after all.

"I suppose you didn't want him horning in on your territory either," the big band leader murmured to the gangster.

"Bouncer? Fat chance. He was a fly. Now, Gotrocks . . . *He* was competition. A good man. Good to his dogs."

When the conversation turned to Chihuahuas, Abby moved on to torch singer Brandi standing at the fireplace. "I understand you used to date the bouncer."

"I didn't just date that loser, I nearly married him. I never would've looked at him twice, but he was Uncle Gotrocks' nephew. I thought—hoped—he'd be cut from the same cloth. Boy, was I wrong. We're both lucky he's out of our lives."

Abby realized there was a great deal her character didn't know about her boyfriend. Then again, theirs was a whirlwind romance.

Socialite Donna and chorus girl Laverne joined them. "Whatever the torch singer's telling you is poppycock," socialite Donna said caustically. "She's just jealous. She wanted to marry the bouncer, but he left her standing at the altar."

"Sounds like a good reason to stab him to me," said the chorus girl.

"*Hmph*," scoffed the socialite. She wagged a finger at Flapper Abby. "Just wait until the inspector gets here. Then you'll see. When I'm done talking with him, he'll ask the torch singer about her knife collection. Remember, the bouncer was stabbed."

Torch singer Brandi lifted her nose into the air. "If one of my knives is missing, you took it. Don't think you can set me up, you, you . . . shoplifter."

The chorus girl's eye's widened. "How dare you say such a thing about the socialite."

"Because it's true. I saw her steal the dress she's wearing." The torch singer waved her cigarette holder in the air, nearly dislodging the candy stick. "Bold as brass, she put her coat on over it and strolled out of the store just like she owned the place."

Stricken, chorus girl Laverne looked at socialite Donna. "You didn't."

"Of course not. Consider the source." The socialite gestured toward the dining room. "Look. The inspector's arrived. Let's go talk to him. He'll want to know about the torch singer's knives." She started away, then glanced over her shoulder. "And about her *almost* marriage."

"You do that," the torch singer said, her hand on her hip in open defiance. "I'm going to have a cozy little chat with your banker."

The group broke up, leaving flapper Abby and waitress Candace staring at each other in amazement. Abby recovered first. "My goodness. I didn't realize my boyfriend left such a wake of ill feeling."

"You have no idea." Waitress Candace shook her head and looked down. "I went to Uncle Gotrocks' viewing. I was crying so hard that by the time I managed to get myself under control, nearly everyone had left the funeral home. I overheard the socialite and the bouncer arguing."

"Why on earth would they be arguing? I wouldn't think they were acquainted, let alone have two words to say to each other."

"From the sound of it, they went back a ways." The waitress patted her black hairnet. "If I tell you my secret, will you tell me yours?"

Abby thought for a moment. "Okay. The bouncer—my deceased boyfriend—told me he was opening a new speakeasy."

"Well, that doesn't help much." Candace's lips quivered. It appeared she was trying rather successfully to stifle her laughter.

Abby shrugged helplessly, setting her fringe flying. "Maybe not, but a deal's a deal."

"Right." Waitress Candace glanced toward the kitchen. "The socialite wanted money, but the bouncer wasn't going for it."

"She wanted money from my sweet bouncer? Do you know why?" Flapper Abby asked with as much naiveté as she could muster.

"No." Waitress Candace pressed her fingers to her mouth to hold back her merriment. "It sounded like she thought the bouncer owed her a bundle."

"*Hmm.* Why would the socialite loan my bouncer money? It makes as little sense as her shoplifting her dress."

"Beats me. All I know, is the bouncer couldn't be trusted. He had some kind of deal with the banker and stiffed him too."

Flapper Abby gulped. Would the banker be a problem? Did she dare tell the waitress the rest of her secret? She had to. A deal was a deal. "Well, I—"

"Excuse me. I need to bus the dessert table."

As waitress Candace hurried off, Abby felt a moment of chagrin. She needed to tell the waitress about the bouncer's money.

Resolved to look for an appropriate opportunity, Abby glanced at the dining room and nearly laughed aloud. Inspector Bradford wore a Keystone Cop helmet with a badge pinned to the front. The chorus girl and the socialite were giving him an earful.

Banker Nathaniel joined her with an offering of a fresh flute of bubbly. "Tell me, doll, what're you going to do now?"

Determined not to reveal anything without getting a tidbit in return, she batted her eyelashes. "Whatever could you mean?"

"Gonna play innocent, eh?" The banker shook his head. "Won't work. I know all about the bouncer's money sitting in your account."

Abby stifled a groan. She should have guessed, but decided to brazen it out. "It's my money."

"No. It's *my* money. The bouncer worked for me. Doing odd jobs—if you know what I mean."

Abby did know. Bouncer had told her he did collections on the side. Until her conversation with the waitress, she hadn't realized the banker was the bouncer's partner. The more she learned about her poor dead boyfriend, the happier she was that they were no longer an item.

As groups formed, dissolved and took turns sharing their theories with the inspector, time flew. Abby ate a piece of key lime pie and mulled over what she'd learned.

Undoubtedly, she headed everyone's list. The flapper had the bouncer's money, a prime motive. Although she knew she wasn't the murderer, her arrest was looking inevitable.

The torch singer, on the other hand, had motive and means. She'd been jilted by Uncle Gotrocks' nephew. Perhaps she'd found another use for her extensive knife collection.

The next most likely suspect was the gin-ger-ale runner. The bouncer's takeover plans would put the runner out of business.

Farther down on her list were the banker and the socialite. Both appeared to have good reasons to be upset with the bouncer, but killing him didn't make sense. They couldn't get money from a corpse. Abby finished her pie and looked around.

The waitress and the chorus girl weren't likely candidates. Neither was the big band leader. The two women were softies, and the maestro had already gotten another gig.

All of this brought her down to the gangster. According to the movies, the big bosses seldom did their own dirty work. Yet she was out of options. Even though he'd brushed off the bouncer, calling him a fly and not a threat, there still might be something there.

Taking another piece of key lime pie, she went over to the fireplace and offered the dessert to gangster Al.

"If you're trying to sweeten me up, sugar, it won't work." He waggled his eyebrows at her. "I've already got you pegged for this caper."

"You'd be wrong. But take the pie anyway."

He laughed, picked up the fork then took the plate.

"There's just one thing," Abby said. "I didn't kill the bouncer. I loved him, even though he was two-timing me with the socialite."

Gangster Al started to laugh and nearly choked on his pie. "If that's why you killed him, girlie, you made a big mistake. Him and the socialite were cousins and not the kissing kind. The bouncer couldn't stand her snooty ways."

Ka-ching. The last piece of the puzzle fell into place. And just in time. Here came Inspector Bradford with a set of hand-cuffs. The rest of the suspects followed close behind. "Flapper Abby. I—"

"—must wait one moment while I explain. I didn't kill the bouncer. I didn't have to. I already had what the murderer wanted. The bouncer put all the money he inherited from his Uncle Gotrocks in my account. Ask the banker."

All eyes turned to banker Nathaniel who nodded sheepishly.

"If you didn't kill the bouncer, who did?" demanded Inspector Bradford with a conspiratorial smile.

Abby stood as tall as she could and announced, "The socialite did it!"

SUNDAY MORNING, Abby found Mary at the sliding glass doors in the living room. A few pale streamers of gray lingered in the sky, clouds too exhausted to keep pace with the energetic storm front that had moved through during the night.

"I got your note," Mary said. "I didn't hear you come in. Were you very late?"

"I got home from the party around eleven. There were messages from my volunteer bird rescuers on the answering machine. They'd been out in force and brought in twenty-three storm victims. I changed clothes and met them at The Nature Museum. Most of our patients will be fit to fly in a day or two." Abby yawned. "I got back home around two thirty."

Mary frowned. "You just can't stay away, even on your night off, can you?"

With a shrug, Abby admitted, "The volunteers didn't really need me, but I'm glad I went. It was a bad storm and they brought in a pair of flickers whose chance of survival looked grim. With the TLC we gave them, I think they'll be okay in a few days."

"It seems you're on call twenty-four/seven. I'm glad you had the foresight to activate your helpers. Did you have a good time at the party?"

Upstairs, Abby's grandfather clock bonged the nine o'clock hour. "Let's go into the kitchen. I'll make coffee. I need a cup before I tell you about dinner and a mystery."

"That sounds more than fair. I could use a cup myself."

Finnegan's toenails clicked on the hardwood floor as he followed them into the kitchen. Abby went straight to the coffeemaker and turned it on. When she'd arrived home, she'd been too energized to sleep. Knowing that wouldn't be the case after she got a few hours slumber, she'd taken care of all the small chores she'd normally do in the morning.

On Mary's lap, Blossom cast an imperial eye over her surroundings before leaving her perch for a queenly stroll across the floor. It was almost impossible for Abby to imagine that the fluffy white Persian had ever been bedraggled and ill fed, but that's how Mary had found her at the back door of the shop a few years ago.

Raising her arms in a long stretch, Mary said, "I love mornings like this."

"Me too. Everything's clean and sharp, like God gave the world a bath." The night storm had scrubbed the air and scoured the dust from the fir trees standing a sentry line along the edge of the property to the beach.

Abby poured two cups of coffee, met Mary at the dining table and set them down.

"Okay. Now, tell me about the party," Mary said. "Was it as much fun as Candace hoped?"

"It was a hoot. An absolute hoot. We did a kind of musical chairs during dinner. Everyone got to expand on their characters, build alliances and learn each other's secrets."

"*Hmm*, you mean motives. I want to know everyone's roles, what they wore and how you eliminated them."

Describing the guests, their characters and clothing gave Abby a chance to practice her recall. She worked her way through the list, also explaining their fictional relationships. "After the murder, everyone had reason to suspect everyone else."

"Who was the victim?"

"Bradford. In the party script he was a bouncer and my boyfriend."

"Really," Mary drawled, leaning forward on the padded arm of her wheelchair. "How did he die?"

"Stabbed," Abby said solemnly. "When the lights came on after the nefarious deed, several people screamed. For an instant, the blood flowing from his 'wound' appeared real. It was just a crimson scarf."

"Did he have to lie still for the rest of the night?" Mary sipped her coffee. "It sounds like being the victim could be a very boring role."

"Quite the contrary. After everyone had a good look, Bradford left the room and then returned as the inspector sent to investigate the crime. The scarf took his place as the corpse." Remembering Donna Morgan's antics, Abby laughed.

"Go on," Mary urged. "Something tickled your fringy fancy."

"Donna's performance of a socialite slumming for the evening was worthy of an Oscar. First, she gave the inspector an earful about the torch singer. Then when suspicion turned her way, she told him she had nothing to say about anything. He should call her lawyer, her butler, her driver. Meanwhile, she'd offer an opinion on practically everything.

"She had the whole group pointing fingers at me—the innocent flapper who just happened to be the bouncer's new girlfriend. As the socialite, she was the bouncer's cousin. When their Uncle Gotrocks died, the bouncer was supposed to share the inheritance with her. He didn't. She was broke and turned to shoplifting for party rags. When she realized he'd never give her a dime, she killed him."

Mary's eyes narrowed briefly. "I'm guessing she didn't count on the unflappable flapper's sharp analytical powers." She rolled her cup between her palms and looked wistful.

"I want to thank you again for the great job you did on my costume. I wasn't sure I could carry off the role, but the dress helped me stay in character and I loved it," Abby admitted. "At times I rather enjoyed being a bit of a ditz."

"You? A ditz? Never. It must've been the costume. Or," Mary gave a teasing wink, "maybe your headband was too tight."

Relishing her sister's loyalty, Abby grinned. "I wasn't the only one who went a little overboard on my role. You should've seen Al Minsky when Inspector Bradford interrogated Laverne. Good grief, you'd have thought Al really was a gangster defending his moll."

Abby laughed at the memory of the car mechanic doing a Jimmy Cagney swagger and vowing to keep the "coppers" away from his chorus girl. "Bless his heart, I suppose Al doesn't know how *not* to protect his wife."

"Sounds like great fun," Mary said with a pleased smile.

"I can't wait to see you and Henry in action at the next 'dinner and a mystery' party. Talk about tough competition."

Mary's smile broadened. "Yeah. You pitted against Henry and me. That'd be wild."

CHAPTER ❦ FOUR

T HE DOORBELL RANG, startling Abby. Who would visit before church on a Sunday morning?

Mary smoothed her hair.

Understanding dawned and Abby slid out of her chair. "I'll get it."

"Henry said he'd be by to go to church with us."

"Really?" Abby teased. "I'm so surprised."

"Oh, you." Mary shooed her from the room with a backward wave.

Abby liked Henry personally and professionally. He possessed a rare combination of sensitivity and directness along with a healthy measure of tolerance. While sleuthing the mysteries that came her way, she'd found him a very helpful friend, although she tried not to impose. There were certain lines he couldn't cross without compromising his law enforcement duties.

She opened the door. Even in civilian attire—khaki trousers, Prussian blue shirt open at the collar and a muted brown and blue cardigan—Henry retained an air of authority. "Word has it," he said, "a man can get a good cup of coffee here."

"And breakfast, too, if you're hungry." She stepped back.

He followed Abby toward the kitchen. "I don't want to be a burden."

"You're not," she tossed over her shoulder. "We haven't eaten." Taking an apron out of the drawer, she said, "Okay, folks. What'll it be—oatmeal or French toast?"

Looking a little distracted, Henry poured coffee. "Oatmeal's good for me."

"Me too," Mary chimed in. "We had French toast yesterday."

Abby put on the apron and tried to ignore a vague sense of something amiss. Maybe Henry and Mary just needed a few quiet moments. Since she couldn't leave, Abby focused on preparing the meal. It was the closest thing to privacy she could give them. If anyone could ferret out the reason for the puzzled crease in Henry's forehead, it was Mary.

Nevertheless, Abby felt his curious gaze boring into her back. She shot a sideways glance at the dining table and found a big surprise. Instead of taking his customary seat next to Mary, Henry sat at the opposite end of the table watching Abby's every move.

"How was the party last night?" he asked.

Abby was much more interested in finding out what had gone on in Friday Harbor the night before. *What had happened between her sister and Henry?* "The party was . . . fine. Fun. Fanciful."

"Who were the guests?"

Arranging the place settings on the floral mats, Abby caught her sister's mystified gaze. *Ah, so it isn't my imagination and the problem has nothing to do with Mary. She, too, suspects something's up.*

Abby continued chatting about the party while she finished making and serving breakfast. Once she'd taken her place and they'd said the morning prayer of thanksgiving, she was ready to turn the tables on the deputy sheriff.

But before she got the chance, he asked, "Do I have this right? The only one you hadn't met before was Brandi Phelps?"

Abby shook her head. "No, there was the landscaper, Sven Dyer. I met him for the first time last night. Mary had told me about him, so he didn't feel as much of a stranger as Brandi." Abby reached for a piece of toast. "I knew Candace had family on the mainland, but this was the first time I'd met one of her relatives."

"Have you met Brandi before?" Henry asked Mary.

"Not that I recall," she answered slowly. "Candace talks about her cousin occasionally and I knew she was coming for a visit."

"What—" Abby started.

"—about Sven? How do you know him, Mary?"

"He came in the store one day, saying he plans to open a landscaping business here." Mary put down her spoon. "At the time he was visiting all the business owners in Green Harbor, introducing himself and getting acquainted. Now he drops by once a week. He knows plants, Henry."

"Okay. Time out." Abby's curiosity had reached the bursting point. "Why the third degree over breakfast?"

Henry sat back. "I'm sorry. Bombarding you with questions is a poor way to return your hospitality."

"What's going on?" Mary's satin-toned coaxing won a rare look of helplessness from him.

"I'm not sure," he answered after a moment.

"It's breakfast and a mystery," Abby said, trying to lighten Henry's growing discomfort.

Mary smiled, but Henry did not. "Apparently, you're right on target, Abby."

Wondering what the mystery could be, she folded her hands on the edge of the table. "Tell us, please."

"I stopped by the station on my way here." Henry finished off his coffee and set down the cup. "Just as I was leaving, a call came in." He looked directly at Abby. "From Candace."

"Is she all right?" Mary and Abby asked together.

Beside his mistress, Finnegan rose to his feet. "What happened?" Mary asked. "She and Brandi are all right, aren't they?"

"The women are fine," Henry said, his deep voice calm. "Candace wanted information."

"About who?" Mary asked.

"About what?" Abby asked at the same time.

"The procedure for reporting something missing or . . . stolen," Henry said softly.

Mary gasped.

Abby settled back in the chair. "Something happened at the party last night?"

Henry gave a one-shouldered shrug. "Possibly."

"I see." Abby sighed. If there'd been a theft, she could very well be a suspect. And yet—if Candace had filed a report, Henry couldn't be discussing this with them at all.

"Candace wanted to know how an investigation's conducted. I explained the sheriff's office would take over if she filed a formal complaint. Thing is, I could hear Brandi giving directions in the background. So I couldn't tell which one of them didn't like the idea of the investigation being out of their hands."

Abby thought for a moment. "Brandi and I just met last night, so I'm not sure how she'd react. However, Candace is the least controlling person in our circle of friends."

Mary nodded matter-of-factly. "We all know how passionate she is about the environment and health foods. If you ask her, she's thrilled to share the wealth of her knowledge on those subjects. But I can honestly say she's never been pushy about it."

Abby tapped her fingers on her chin. "Did Candace say what was missing?"

"Brandi's engagement ring," Henry answered. "Did you see her wearing it last night?"

"Yes. It's lovely, although much too loose. In fact, I overheard Laverne telling her to get a ring guard."

"Wouldn't her wedding ring have kept it from falling off?" Mary asked.

"I noticed that she wears her wedding ring closest to the heart, then the engagement ring." Abby lifted her hands in mock surrender.

"Let's be clear, Abby. You're saying the ring could have slipped off Brandi Phelps's finger and gotten lost in the house. Right?" Henry asked.

Abby shook her head. "Sorry to complicate your life, Henry. The ring did slip off her finger last night, but she put it on the mantel."

"You saw her do it?" Henry asked in a very official-sounding tone.

"Yes, I did. We all did."

"So . . . it could have been stolen," Mary said.

Silence settled in as the previous night's mystery party poked a sinister finger at the bright morning.

CHAPTER ❦ FIVE

Aᴄᴛᴇʀ ᴛʜᴇ ᴄʜᴏɪʀ's ʟᴀsᴛ song, Abby leaned down and told Mary, "You and Henry go on ahead. I'll be out in a few."

Anticipation sparkled in Mary's blue eyes. "Take your time."

Her sister's delight in Henry's company gave Abby a reason to smile as she waited for Rev. James Hale, the pastor of Little Flock Church, to make his way to the nave.

Normally she didn't give unsolicited advice, but after Rev. Hale's blunder during the announcements, she decided to make an exception. From her position in the last pew, she'd seen the upset rippling through the members of the congregation when Rev. James trampled the holy ground of tradition.

Abby shuddered. She hoped one of the well-wishers who usually stopped him on the way out of the church to shake his hand or pat him on the back would clue him in. Alas, he rounded the last pew in record time.

Gratefully reaching out, he clasped her extended hand in both of his. "It's so good to see you, Abby."

"And you, Rev. James. Your message today was excellent, but the announcement afterwards was . . . perplexing."

His bewildered expression left her no choice but to continue. "If I understood your announcement correctly, and I believe I did, you said we should get rid of the old traditions and adopt new ones. Is that what you meant?"

He uttered a shocked gasp. "Good heavens, no! Did I really say that?"

"In a nutshell, yes."

The color drained from his face. "Oh, mercy me." Rev. James returned to the nearest pew and sat as if the starch had gone out of his legs. "I've had so much on my mind this last week. Patricia made taking care of a two-year-old look easy. Since she's been gone, I've gained a new appreciation for everything she does."

"Where is she?"

"Down in Los Angeles with her parents. Her mother's condition took a turn for the worse. We decided it would be best for all concerned if Toby stayed here."

"How's her mother doing?"

"Not well. That's the problem. Patricia wants to take her mother to a new doctor, but her father doesn't. He and her mother are stubbornly loyal to the one they've been going to for the last thirty years. Even though he freely admits he has no idea why she's getting worse instead of better, they won't consider a second opinion."

"Ohhh," Abby said. "I think I understand what happened today."

"Me too. My personal life spilled over into the announcement," James said dismally. "When I was telling the congregation they should give up their old traditions, I was rehashing the conversation with my father-in-law."

Rev. James groaned and rubbed his cheeks with his palms. "No wonder everyone looked at me strangely and couldn't run out of church fast enough. What I meant to say was for our people to *keep* their old traditions and *add* a new one. I have to fix this . . . somehow."

"I know where you can start." Abby gestured toward the door. "Your secretary's probably still in the parking lot."

Suddenly energized, Rev. James rose. "Thanks Abby. You're brilliant. Will you excuse me please? I need to catch her before she leaves."

Knowing there was no better way to correct the misunderstanding than telling Janet Heinz, Abby stepped aside. Her talkative best friend lived for the chance to pass on every interesting tidbit of information that came her way. "Be my guest."

Following the pastor, Abby stepped out of the double doors of the church. Tall and narrow with white clapboards and a traditional steeple reaching for the puffy clouds now dotting the blue sky, the wooden building was a historic structure. A fixture in time, it promised permanence and continuity, while serving as a witness to worship and the cycle of life.

She let her gaze roam the arched windows and the old stained glass. No wonder people resisted change. There were so few constants in a fast-moving world—particularly for those not fortunate enough to live on Sparrow Island.

Near the rhododendron hedge marking the church's property line, Frank Holloway, the hardware store owner, had Henry engaged in what looked like a deep conversation. The most telling clue was that Mary wasn't with them. Leaving the men to their discussion, Abby headed for Mary's van.

Henry was on call, so he'd driven his own car to the service. If she and Mary left before he did, he'd catch up with them at the Stanton Farm where Sunday dinner was another rarely broken tradition.

As she walked across the lot, Abby spotted her sister and almost didn't recognize the couple with her. Compared to their alter egos at the party, Al and Laverne Minsky in street dress were shadow of their former, glamorous selves.

Look who's talking! Abby heaved a self-deprecating sigh. Without her gold satin, miles of silky fringe, spit curls and feather headdress, she wasn't a glamour queen either.

Laverne kicked up a heel and mimed the Charleston's hand movements. "Hey, Abby."

Realizing she wasn't the only one feeling a little nostalgic for the flashy finery and make-believe roles, Abby returned the greeting. Her cha-cha step was a little slow, but she didn't begrudge a minute of lost sleep, though it was taking a toll on her energy today.

While Al and Mary discussed when Mary's van would be ready for an oil change, Laverne told Abby, "Al and I had so much fun last night. We're thinking of hosting a mystery party of our own. We'll probably have it in January or early February when it's cold and dreary."

"Count me in," Abby said.

With a nod to Abby, Al slid his arm around his wife and gently turned her toward their car. "Say good-bye to the nice ladies, doll. We don't want to be late for our reservations."

Pleased that the forty-something couple was still so mutually smitten, Abby waved farewell. As the Minskys strolled off, Bobby McDonald called, "Abby! Mary! Wait up!"

A precocious child with hazel eyes, a freckled nose and an abundance of curiosity, the neighbor's young son was a frequent visitor to the Reynold's home and a constant source of surprise and delight. Ducking his head, his dark brown hair flying, he pumped his arms as he ran, his feet seeming to skim the ground.

"Ah, to be able to run like he does." Mary sighed wistfully.

"Ditto." Abby palmed her sister's shoulder. "But we both have to get real. Nobody runs like a ten-year-old boy—except another ten-year-old boy."

Mary laughed softly. "How right you are."

The boy-sized package of raw energy skidded to a halt in front of them. His gaze fixed longingly on the big golden dog by Mary's chair, he breathed, "Hi, Finnegan."

Because the dog wore the service cape showing he was on duty, he didn't move a muscle. He eyed the boy but stood attentively at Mary's side.

Bobby quickly crossed his arms over his chest.

Pleased with his restraint, Abby said, "Hey, kiddo, what's up?"

"I, ah . . ." He balled his fists, thrust them into his trouser pockets and dragged his gaze from Finnegan. "Are you gonna be at The Nature Museum on Tuesday?"

Abby mentally sorted through her obligations for the next couple of days. "I believe so. Why?"

"Oh good. I was really hoping you'd be there. 'Cause I'm doing a school project about turkeys for Thanksgiving and you know so much about the land and birds and wildlife. You know how it was when the Pilgrims landed."

Out of the corner of her eye, Abby saw her sister cover her mouth to stifle her laughter. "Well, Bobby, I wasn't exactly there when the Mayflower docked—"

"Gosh, I didn't mean it like that. I was just hoping you'd maybe answer some questions for me."

She one-fingered a stray strand of hair over his ear. "If I have the answers, they're yours. Okay?"

"Cool. See you then. Bye, Mary." With one last, longing

look at the dog, he said softly, "Bye, Finnegan," then dashed toward the family car.

Blue eyes wide with feigned innocence, Mary asked, "What *was* it like when the Mayflower docked?"

"Be careful," Abby warned. "Remember, you are my *older* sister."

"I'LL GET IT." Just back from Sunday dinner with their parents and Henry, Abby hurried through the laundry room and into the kitchen. She snatched up the phone. Too late. All she heard was a dial tone.

"Who was it?" The sound of the garage door closing followed Mary and Finnegan into the house.

"I have no idea."

"If it was important, they'll call back." Mary took the kettle to the sink and started preparing tea.

Abby saw the rapidly blinking light on the answering machine. "I think they already did. We have a message." She pressed the play button.

"Abby, this is Candace," said the voice through the small speaker. "Could you come over? We have a genuine mystery on our hands and need your help to solve it." There was a pause, then, "Please." And another pause. "Right away."

Mary set the kettle aside and rolled over to the telephone table. "Goodness gracious. Candace sounds thoroughly rattled. Almost as if she's desperate."

"I've been thinking about her call to the sheriff's substation. It's strange she'd ask the procedure for reporting a theft, then not file one," Abby mused. "Maybe what she's really looking for is another pair of hands and eyes to help her and Brandi search for the ring."

"Could be," Mary said thoughtfully. "If she and Brandi

were certain the ring had been taken, they wouldn't have any qualms about asking Henry to investigate." She looked up at her sister. "I know you've had a very long night and a full day. Between church, dinner at Mom and Dad's and your late-night, early-morning rescue mission, you must be tired. Maybe you should call Candace and tell her you'll see her tomorrow."

The idea had its appeal. However, Candace almost never asked for help. It must be important. "What are friends for if you can't call on them in times of trouble?" Abby retrieved her purse and her car keys. "I'm not sure I have a lot left to offer, but I'll do my best."

Fifteen minutes later, she stepped onto Candace's heavily shaded walkway. Funny, a couple of trees seemed tilted. Abby rubbed her tired eyes. At the far end of the side yard a compost pile sported layers of orange and red leaves. Someone had been busy. A wooden ladder lay on its side tucked neatly beside the mound.

Before she could ring the bell, the door opened. Candace and Bradford filled the entry. "Thank you for coming." Candace wove her fingers together and seemed to draw strength from Bradford's hand on her shoulder.

"It sounded urgent." Abby gave what she hoped was a reassuring smile. As an attorney, Bradford had a reputation for thoroughness. Confident he'd already conducted a meticulous search, she wasn't sure what more she could offer besides a sympathetic ear. Hoping for a flash of intuition, she said, "Of course I came."

The couple stepped aside, inviting her to enter. Ahead, the foyer and living room appeared much the same as the night before—minus the tray holding the elegant flutes for the ginger ale.

"We need fresh ideas," Candace confessed, as she closed the

front door. "Bradford and I have looked everywhere, Abby. Brandi's ring has to be in the house. Somewhere."

"Where is she?" Abby was surprised the young woman hadn't come out to welcome another pair of searching eyes and hands or just to say hello.

"She went into town," Bradford said evenly, his lips a thin line. He apparently thought Brandi ought to be helping.

"Brandi's beside herself," Candace volunteered sadly. "She was with us all morning and most of this afternoon while we searched. Now, she's fretting about how to tell her husband. I believe she went to the park to walk around and think. The ring was pricey. Wayne worked a lot of side jobs to pay for it."

"A diamond that size would be quite expensive," said Bradford. "I've seen them in the display windows when I'm walking to and from work every day. It would be terrible to have to admit to losing it when her husband worked so hard to give it to her."

Abby agreed. Regardless of the numbers on the price tag, the true cost was the sacrifice made to acquire the ring in the first place. She found herself liking Bradford more every time they met.

Although she'd never seen his home, she knew there was more to the man than a hefty bank account and a strong sense of self-assurance.

"I presume you've already searched everywhere." Abby put her purse by the door.

"Thoroughly. Three times." Candace threw her palms up and shrugged.

"So, how can I help?"

With a glance at Bradford the young florist said, "I was hoping you could come up with another idea of what might have happened. I refuse to consider words like 'steal' and 'theft.'"

The softly spoken statement sent an icy shiver through Abby. She cast an inadvertent glance at the fireplace mantel. The spot where Brandi had placed her ring the previous night was naked.

"I'm not accusing anyone," Candace continued quickly. "I've just run out of ideas and places to look."

"How well do you know the people who were at the party last night?" Bradford asked Abby.

"With the exception of Brandi and Sven Dyer, I know all of them better than I know you," she answered. "Last night was the first time I met either of them."

"Sven is a very straightforward man. I can't imagine that he took the ring," Candace said. "Then, I can't imagine any of my guests taking it."

"Ah, therein lies the rub." Bradford crossed to the fireplace and stared down. Flames crackled over a glowing log. "Despite the sour note at the end, the evening went much better than I expected. Candace and I had never given a party together and it was high time we did."

The young woman's tender smile betrayed the depth of her feelings for the Seattle attorney. "You made it special."

He gave a muffled laugh. "You're so generous."

Abby's fatigue tugged at her. She needed facts. "When did you notice the ring was missing?"

"Not until after our guests left last night."

"We were gathering up the empty ginger ale bottles and flutes," Candace said slowly. "I reminded Brandi to get her ring. She went to the mantel. The ring wasn't there."

"Any chance it wound up in the trash?" Abby asked.

"None," Bradford and Candace said together.

"We dumped it onto a tarp and sorted through it piece by piece," Candace said.

"I'm presuming you've looked all over the floor and in every corner," Abby mused.

"Yes," Candace said. "But we can look again."

"If it got knocked off the mantel, it could have bounced or been kicked anywhere. Have you looked inside of things? The cushions? In the bookcase?"

"You're brilliant, Abby," Candace said. "I'll check the couch."

Going down on one knee, Bradford took a piece of wood out of the burnished brass cradle on the hearth. "I suppose looking in here wouldn't hurt."

While he examined the firewood, Abby spotted a large plant partially hidden behind an end table near the fireplace. She scooted over to it and carefully inspected the dieffen-bachia's leaves. Hoping to see a sparkle, she picked through the sphagnum moss around the base.

Candace took the cushions off the couch and stacked them on the coffee table. A long scratch on the back of her hand drew Abby's attention. "That looks painful. How did you get it?"

"On the screen when I cleaned out the fireplace."

Bradford put a protective arm around Candace's shoulders. "When I came over from The Bird Nest this morning, she was outside sifting the ashes. Standing in the cold, half-frozen and bleeding, she gave me a good scare. Still, she wouldn't go inside until we checked every cinder. I can tell you with certainty the ring wasn't there."

Abby swallowed thickly. She'd touched a nerve and come face-to-face with the attorney's strong feelings for Candace. Steering the conversation to a new topic, Abby said, "Back to the party. What did you think of Donna Morgan?"

"The socialite who murdered me when I was the bouncer? That sounds crazy, doesn't it?" Bradford's eyebrows twitched. "I'll have to be careful how I tell my friends about it back in

Seattle. To answer your question, Donna's a bit of a puzzle. She's not comfortable asking straight questions, yet she's adept at misdirection. She managed to keep everyone confused longer than I thought possible."

"Everyone but Abby," Candace said. "She's Sparrow Island's sleuth."

"I wouldn't go so far—"

"Candace is right about your deductive powers." Bradford returned the logs to the brass cradle. "You have a rare talent for putting seemingly unrelated things together and building a new picture. As the victim, then as the inspector, I enjoyed watching you investigate, Abby. If you ever want to change careers, there's a place for you in law enforcement."

Flattered, she laughed softly. "Thank you for the compliment, but I'm where I belong." She dusted the loose potting soil from her fingers. "You see, as a child, I fell in love with birds. I've never wanted to do anything other than study and learn about them. It must be my passion or I wouldn't have gone out rescuing them after the party last night."

Abby glanced up at Bradford. "You'll understand if I'm not the sharpest tack in the box right now."

Abby went to work on the magazine rack. She hoped if she rearranged the contents, the ring would fall out. She picked the publications out one by one. They dealt with organic food preparation, gardening and nature. One featured an enticing article about making an organic seed mix for a winter bird feeder. Resolutely, she put it back with the others. "It's a good thing you didn't have the party outside. A shiny bauble the size of Brandi's ring would have attracted the attention of several species of birds. Crows, gulls and jays are notorious for swooping up unguarded treasures."

"None of those birds were here last night. In fact, nothing

else is missing. We've been all through the house. The only odd thing we found is a black garbage bag." Candace slid her uninjured hand down the side of the couch. "Too bad it had a big hole in it or I could have reused it."

Abby shrugged. "It was probably my makeshift raincoat. I looked for it before I left. When I couldn't find it, I figured someone had discarded it."

"You know, even though we'd never find the ring, I wish someone had seen a bird take it. Then, we'd know what happened to it. I could live with theft by bird." Candace put the cushions back on the couch.

"For your sake I wish it was so too," Bradford said. "But it's time to face facts—the ring isn't here."

"There simply has to be another explanation. I just can't believe any of my friends could be a thief." Tears glistened in Candace's pale brown eyes as she folded in on herself.

Bradford caught her shoulders and gently drew her to his chest. "There may be one and we're missing it. I do know things are not always what they seem."

Abby hoped he was right, although the situation seemed rather clear-cut to her. If the ring wasn't in the house, someone took it out of the house. The only questions were who, why and when.

As Bradford comforted Candace, Abby checked along the edge of the carpet to give them a bit of privacy.

The attorney's tenderness with the free-spirited earth child transcended the cultural disparity between them. Clearly, they trusted one another.

Struck by an idea, Abby exclaimed, "You know... Bradford's right. We were all in costume and playing roles— most of them a little nefarious. It's entirely possible someone got a little carried away and pocketed the ring, intending to use it in their party role. The opportunity obviously didn't arise and they forgot about it."

Candace immediately perked up. "Or maybe it was like you said earlier, a misdirection thing. Someone could have dropped it into someone else's pocket for the same reason. The person who ended up with it might not even know they have it."

Liking an alternative that didn't include theft, Abby immediately felt more optimistic. A little checking should clear up the mystery in no time.

Bradford exhaled a deep sigh. "A prank is the most reasonable explanation anyone has come up with since this debacle started." He placed a kiss on the top of Candace's strawberry-blonde crown.

She looked up. "You always keep a level head. Thank you."

"You're very welcome." He checked his watch. "I'd like to stay, but I need to catch the ferry. Tomorrow's a very important day for my client."

Candace stepped out of the circle of his arms. "That's right. You have to be in court early."

He picked up a cashmere blazer from the back of a dining room chair and grew solemn. "I've already checked out of The Bird Nest and packed my car, so we have a few minutes. Look, if Abby's theory doesn't hold up and the ring's still missing, file a police report and cooperate with the investigation. Let them search anywhere they like."

Already a little frayed around the edges, the young florist protested, "They'll have to do one? But we looked everywhere."

"Considering the value of the ring, it's the best course of action. Furthermore, Brandi and Wayne's insurance company will insist on it."

Abby swept the beam of a flashlight beneath the couch. Not even a stray M&M or dust bunny had survived the previous searches. "Henry's the best. He'll cross all the *t*'s and dot all the *i*'s."

"And one last thing, if either of you need legal counsel—"

Abby popped to her feet.

Candace lost all color, paling so quickly even her freckles faded. In a voice barely above a whisper she asked, "Do you think it'll come to that?"

"It's highly doubtful, sweetheart. But just in case it does," Bradford touched the tip of her nose with his fingertip, "you have one of Seattle's top attorneys in your corner."

"You're the best, my knight in shining armor."

Abby retreated to the kitchen for a drink of water while the couple said their good-byes.

Minutes later Bradford joined her at the sink and held out a business card. "I hate leaving with this unresolved. It's a messy business and it has Candace tied in knots. If there's anything, and I mean anything . . ."

Abby tried to take the card. Bradford held on. She looked up, letting her confusion show.

"I mean absolutely anything, Abby. Please call me."

She didn't know this man very well, but was quickly gaining more respect for him. "Candace—"

"You and I both know Miz Independence is far too trusting at times. Please Abby, I'm counting on you. If you think she needs me, call."

Abby nodded and took the card. Watching him leave, she wondered just how bad things could get if the ring didn't turn up soon.

CHAPTER ✤ SIX

Monday morning, finnegan growled low in his throat as wind shook the van and another November storm pelted the islands with rain. Undaunted by the fitful blasts playing tag in the treetops, Mary turned into the little alley behind Island Blooms and parked as close as possible to the back entry of her store.

The heavy metal door opened and her heart skipped a beat. No one was supposed to be here. Besides Abby, who'd gone to work at The Nature Museum, Candace was the only other person with a key to the shop. But she wasn't scheduled to work today. She'd reserved it to spend time with Brandi.

Mary looked around the parking lot. Except for her van, the spaces were empty. She squinted through the fogged side window, trying to make out the identity of the figure motioning in the doorway. *Candace? What's she doing here?*

"Something's up," Mary told Finnegan as she released him from the security harness. Freed from the restraint that was actually a safety belt designed for dogs, he went to work helping her out of the van.

Moments later, Finnegan bit into the leather strap attached to the door handle and dragged the van's door closed, while Mary wheeled to the door Candace held open.

Today, the wispy woman wore her long strawberry blonde hair in a loose bun on the crown of her head in a style reminiscent of the Gibson Girl. Along with a gauzy midi skirt in paisley earth tones, she wore a loose-fitting ivory blouse under a dark velvet vest with matching wool socks and a pair of Birkenstocks. On anyone else, the outfit would have conjured images of a refugee from another era. On Candace, it looked terrific. All that was missing was a smile.

"Finnegan's amazing," she murmured, handing Mary one of the thick towels they kept for him at the shop.

While drying his soft coat, Mary said, "I thought you were taking some time off to spend with your cousin while she's visiting."

"I was. I mean, I am," Candace stammered. "It's a long story."

Hoping to hear it, Mary kept quiet and stroked Finnegan with the towel. Her waiting strategy didn't work. Before the silence stretched into awkwardness, she let the now dry Finnegan take the lead and maneuvered her chair through the back room and into the shop proper.

On the workbench behind the main counter sat an elaborate arrangement of greenery and autumn flowers. "This is beautiful."

"Thank you." Candace fiddled with a spray of maidenhair fern. In a trick of the light, the shadows under her eyes seemed to deepen. "Working with the flowers and chatting with the customers helps take my mind off my problems."

What customers? Mary wondered. The store wouldn't officially open for another twenty minutes. "This is The Dorset's order. You must have come in very early."

"Yes. And I want to thank you for teaching me the art of flower arranging. It's so soothing, like painting with nature," Candace said with the first hint of a smile.

"With God's creations," Mary agreed softly.

If Candace heard, she gave no indication and as always Mary didn't press. She preferred to share her faith through example, but didn't stifle heartfelt comments.

Candace wrote out the ticket for the autumn arrangement. "Keith will send the Dorset's van to pick up the flowers in a little while."

"Bless his heart," Mary said gratefully. "I'm glad we're just down the street." Kindnesses like his definitely made her life easier. As much as she liked to think of herself as independent, she recognized her limitations. She could deliver some arrangements, but in this weather, attempting one this size, would have been foolhardy. In all likelihood, it would have ended up smashed on the ground.

She looked up and found Candace working on the next order. Eight years ago, they'd started as employer/employee. Now, despite the differences in their ages and lifestyles, they were good friends. Laying a hand on the young woman's arm, she coaxed, "Talk to me. What's wrong?"

After a heavy sigh, Candace said, "I listened to Brandi cry half the night and spent the other half wondering what she was crying about."

"Her lost ring?" Mary asked tentatively.

"Maybe. In part. But it just sounded like . . . I don't know, like so much more."

"Did you get a chance to ask her about it this morning?"

Candace leaned a hip against the worktable. "That's just it. I did."

"Can you share?" Mary didn't want her dear friend to breach a confidence.

"Brandi was shocked when I told her I heard her crying. She didn't remember it at all. In fact, she looked positively . . . rested. I'm guessing she was crying in her sleep. I don't even know if that's possible."

"It is." Mary remembered crying in her sleep. It was shortly after her husband Jacob died and she'd often woken to a damp pillow. "I'm not sure it helps or solves anything. Most problems don't just go away. Eventually we have to face them and do something."

"I know." Candace reached across the table for a cluster of deep orange chrysanthemums. "I loaned her my car so she could drive around the island or go window shopping. She loves to browse. As for me, I'd rather be at work. It's beautiful and relaxing here, the right place to find my center. Maybe then I can figure out what's bothering her."

"While you're mulling things over, you might want to consider if there's been a recent upheaval in Brandi's life. Something other than her ring. Perhaps she's facing another kind of loss or maybe she's afraid of something." Mary held up a hand to keep Candace from speaking. "I'm just giving you suggestions, places to start."

"I did that at about two in the morning." Candace slipped a willowy frond into the vase. "I couldn't come up with anything. Brandi has a good job and a husband who adores her. They live in a nice townhouse in downtown Seattle. If one of them was . . . unhappy in the marriage, I know she'd tell me.

But there hasn't even been a hint in that direction. The only thing she's mentioned is the ring."

"And you? What conclusion have you come to?"

Candace shook her head. "I haven't come to any. The only thing I know for sure is that the ring is just . . . temporarily lost. It has to be somewhere in the house. In fact, I'm moving the furniture and taking up the carpets tonight."

"I can see you have a fun time planned," Mary said lightly, admiring Candace's faith in the honesty of her friends. Abby had confided the details of the fireplace search. Now, moving all the furniture seemed an even bigger task and Mary doubted Bradford knew about it. If he did, he'd insist on being there to help.

Deciding to ask the prayer chain to include Candace and her cousin on their list, Mary angled her chair around. "Well, unless you want to change your mind about working today . . ."

"No, I really want to be here. If it's okay?"

"As you wish." Candace obviously had everything under control here. At her hand signal, Finnegan headed for the back door. "You can reach me on my cell phone if you need me, okay?"

Candace turned. "Will do. Thanks for understanding. I guess the shop has become my refuge in a number of ways."

Nodding, Mary waited for Finnegan to push open the back door. Outside, the storm had temporarily exhausted its fury. A faint blue stripe of sky split the mottled gray clouds. Out on the water, whitecaps rode the steely waves, a promise the squall wasn't over yet.

Deciding to take advantage of the unexpected free day,

Mary drove over to In Stitches and admired again the ideal location of Ana Dominguez's well-stocked craft store. It sat across Kingfisher Avenue from The Tackle Shop, a hangout for those bored souls whose wives were Ana's loyal customers.

With a growing sense of excitement, Mary entered the store. It was literally bursting at the seams with sewing supplies. Yet, somehow, Ana had managed to carve out a corner for the Busy Bee Quilting Society and had filled it with comfortable chairs, frames and tables. Despite her goal, Mary lingered first in the forests of fabric where a person could get lost in creative ideas.

Barely escaping without a purchase, she wheeled past a wall that displayed handmade articles crafted of natural materials gathered from the island. It was a tremendous tourist draw. The locals loved the unusual showcase too, taking it as proof of the island's uniqueness.

Looking around the shop, Mary decided this was a crafter's idea of heaven. It certainly was hers. Over the years, she'd purchased everything from macramé jute to glass beads, knitting needles to patterns and stitch counters.

Today she was in need of yarn. Perhaps *need* wasn't exactly the right word, she admitted silently and turned in to the aisle packed with a rainbow of color. She wanted several skeins of something especially soft. Christmas wasn't far away and after she finished her commitment to the Sweaters for Kids project, she wanted to knit a sweater for Abby. Making it a surprise was the challenge. Mary picked up a silky skein of variegated yarn . . . perhaps during the slow periods at Island Blooms.

Her thoughts returned to Candace, but before she could do some mental digging into the situation, Wilma Washburn touched her shoulder and demanded, "Don't you agree, Mary?"

Caught unawares, she almost uttered an amiable yes. Then she caught Beverly Hodges's defiant gaze and Ana's desperate expression. "I, uh, am not sure what you're talking about."

"Each craft requires special skills," Ana said carefully before turning to Wilma. "The weaving is part of your heritage. For generations, your ancestors relied on the baskets. They were part of their daily life, part of their survival. My own ancestors in Mexico, we were much the same way. Before there were pots and pans, there were baskets."

"Thank you for making my point." Triumph lifted Wilma's chin.

"Without quilts, there wouldn't *be* people. They'd have frozen to death," Beverly retorted. "Quilts and blankets are kin to clothing—they're all made with thread, fabric and pattern. How many of our ancestors made other essentials of living— from baskets to a meal—with a quilt or blanket wrapped around them for warmth?"

Mary suddenly felt she was in the middle of a debate about which came first—the chicken or the egg. In this case, it was about which craft was the most important. "Ladies, ladies. The truth is, as a society we need both."

"Mary, she is right!" Ana brightened, her hands clasped at her waist. She was doing her best to placate and mediate between her customers without alienating either by taking sides.

As her understanding of the size of the controversy grew, so did Mary's sympathy for Ana. Feuding customers were a bane to any shopkeeper.

"You tell us, Mary." Beverly put her fists on her hips. "Which requires more skill and creativity—basket weaving or quilting?"

Mary blinked. This was certainly becoming a day filled with

indecision and conflict. First, Candace and Brandi. Now, Wilma and Beverly. Ana's anxious brown eyes were on Mary and she wished she could come up with a satisfactory answer. In truth, there wasn't one.

"I'm primarily a knitter. At times, I've sold your baskets at Island Blooms, Wilma. And during special events, I've sold quilts made by the Busy Bee Quilters. As a knitter, I appreciate the hours of work both endeavors take. But there's no way I can say one requires more skill or creativity than the other." Mary hoped her diplomacy might satisfy them.

"Well, there's another way to solve this question," Beverly said slowly.

Disappointed, Mary pressed her lips together. Not every question had an answer. Some, like beauty, were in the eye of the beholder and some were more work to answer than they were worth.

"Ah, I see where you're going," Wilma said cagily.

"What do you intend to do?" Ana asked warily.

"We'll have a contest," Beverly said.

"I don't see how—"

"With you, Mary," Wilma explained. "We'll teach you about our crafts, then you decide."

Mary held up her hands in protest. "Oh no. I don't want to be in the middle of this. Besides, I don't have the time to—"

"We understand you're a busy woman," Beverly said, nodding at Wilma. "So are we."

"Right. I'm only here to pick up some things for the museum," said Wilma. The conservatory's receptionist and go-to gal for getting things done checked the time. "Hugo will be watching for me to return with the supplies he ordered."

The shopkeeper placed a large sack on the counter. The

plastic bag with the In Stitches logo and location crinkled. "I'll put this on his account," Ana said.

"Don't rush her. We have to get things settled with our judge, here." Beverly focused her concentration on Mary. "A couple of hours each is all we're asking. We won't even charge you for the lessons." A big grin spread across the quilter's generous features.

"Well, I—"

"Good. It's settled." Wilma collected the package. "We'll be in touch to coordinate schedules. I must get back to the museum."

Beverly picked up an even larger bag resting against the display case. "Great. I'll walk you to the parking area, Wilma."

Mary gaped at Ana.

"Thank you," the shopkeeper said with sincerity.

Mary swallowed hard and remembered her upbringing. She couldn't say anything nice about being steamrolled into a lose-lose situation, so she didn't say anything at all.

CHAPTER ❦ SEVEN

Monday afternoon, Abby whistled a cheery tune as she drove to The Green Grocer. The bright sunshine breaking through the clouds added to the sense of exhilaration she'd shared with the birds she'd released at The Nature Museum.

Fourteen of the original twenty-three were now back in the wild. They'd flitted and twittered, exulting in the return of their freedom. She exulted in the quick return of their good health.

Savoring the sun breaks and hoping they'd last for a while, she parked in front of The Green Grocer. She and Mary were nearly out of eggs and very low on orange juice and a number of other staples. Considering they'd opened the last box of green tea several days ago, it was definitely time to replenish the larder.

The aroma of freshly baked bread teased her nose the minute she entered the grocery store on Kingfisher Avenue. She paused to take an appreciative sniff.

"Hello," called Archie Goodfellow from the checkout counter. The rotund proprietor wore his trademark royal green butcher apron with a cute caricature of himself stenciled above the words The Green Grocer. "You're just in time for some of Kari's fresh multigrain bread."

With a conspiratorial wink, he tilted his head and inhaled. "I can smell it coming out of the oven now."

Enjoying the hardworking grocer's enticement, Abby dropped her purse into a cart. "I'll just follow my nose."

He rubbed the mound of his stomach and murmured, "I sure hope heaven smells this good."

On the way to the crowded bakery section, Abby detoured to the nearly deserted butcher's corner. To her surprise, she found Brandi Phelps in front of the meat counter staring at the filet mignon. The young woman's lips moved, but no sound came out.

"Hello?" Abby waited, but there was no response.

Brandi's expression changed from shades of sorrow to hope and back again. Suddenly, she looked up. Surprise chased away the sadness in her eyes. She removed the tiny headphones attached to the iPod on her arm.

Just then, Brandi's pocket buzzed, startling them both. She reached in and withdrew a phone. "Excuse me." She flipped it open from the side, revealing a tiny keyboard and a screen. With a frown at the screen, she nodded and closed the phone. "I'll text her back later."

"It amazes me they can fit a phone, a camera and a mini keyboard into such a compact package," Abby said.

"Yeah, it's neat. It was a gift from my husband, Wayne." Brandi put the phone into her pocket. "I'm sorry. When you walked up I had on my earbuds and couldn't hear you."

"I just wanted to say hello. You looked a million miles away."

"I guess I was." Uncertainty rippled across the young woman's face for several heartbeats before recognition arrived. "Abby! I didn't recognize you. It must be the clothes. I'll always picture you in the flapper costume."

"Oh! I rather like that idea," Abby said. In her customary earth tones, she tended to blend into the background. Not so for Brandi. Whether she wore a slinky sequined dress or lime colored fleece and trim Levis, her good looks and honey-blonde hair were instantly recognizable.

"It's ironic," Abby continued with a little laugh. "Unless they were at the party, most of my friends wouldn't recognize me in feathers and fringe." She gestured to the chilled glass case. "Can I help you find something? The Green Grocer prides itself on its organic products, including meat."

"No, thanks." Brandi immediately stepped away. "I was enjoying a moment of temptation. Candace doesn't eat meat, so I'm abstaining as well."

"How very thoughtful of you. Is the dietary change difficult?"

"Not terribly. She's taught me how to cook some excellent tofu dishes, but when I get back to the mainland, watch out. Wayne's taking me to our favorite restaurant so I can have a giant hamburger." She glanced at the meat case. "Or maybe a steak."

"There's no reason you can't order either one at the Springhouse or Winifred's," Abby suggested.

"No. Candace has gone out of her way for me so many times. Changing my diet while I'm visiting is a small thing to do for my favorite cousin." The ghost of a wistful smile touched Brandi's lips as she thumbed her wedding ring, turning it on her finger as though searching for its companion.

Too brightly, she added, "Candace is a great listener and gives terrific advice. I'm afraid I just about wore her ear off before my wedding. She was my maid of honor and I don't know what I'd have done without her encouragement and support during all those months of preparation."

"She's a real blessing to Mary too." Abby debated the etiquette of asking about the engagement ring. The day before, Candace had seized on the idea that the missing ring was part of a prank and had resolutely announced her intention to phone all the party guests.

Abby had returned home hopeful the matter would be resolved. Maybe it had. Just because Brandi wasn't wearing the ring, didn't mean the calls weren't fruitful. Until she obtained a ring guard or had the band resized, she might have wanted to keep the costly bauble in a safe place.

Curiosity spiking, Abby looked around for other customers. Satisfied she and Brandi were alone, she asked, "How many calls did Candace have to make before she found out what happened to the ring?"

"Humph! The ring's still gone." Brandi lifted her left hand and spread her fingers. "Candace made two calls, then dissolved into tears. She says it feels like she's accusing her friends."

"What's she going to do now?"

Brandi rubbed her palms together. "Make the rest of the calls, I guess." She met Abby's gaze. "I wish she'd taken care of it yesterday. Dragging it out is hard on her . . . and me. All this dithering is making her sick and me crazy."

"I see." Abby's heart sank. Part of her had feared this would happen. Making those calls ran counter to Candace's determination to see the good in people. No matter how delicately the question was phrased, asking it would be awkward at best.

"It's so frustrating." Brandi lowered her hand and rubbed the empty spot on her finger again.

Abby agreed wholeheartedly. If not for the fact the ring was still missing, given the unlikely suspects, the whole episode was a bizarre impossibility. "I'm sorry, Brandi. I know this must be difficult for you."

She sighed and nodded. "I guess I'll keep searching even though I'm afraid the ring is gone for good. I shouldn't have been so foolish."

"Accidents—"

"You don't understand." Tears glistened in Brandi's eyes. "It was my fault."

"Why would you say that?"

"Accidents are far more likely to happen to careless people. I shouldn't have taken off the ring." Shaking her head, she stared at the floor. "I should have put it in a safe place like my jewelry bag or my suitcase. It's my own fault. I should have known better."

Looking up in horror, her gaze met Abby's. "I'm sorry. I don't want you to think I'm accusing anyone."

But she was. Understandably so. In truth, the ring's disappearance was an accusation against everyone who attended the party. "It's an awkward situation," said Abby.

"I hate this. I just want it to go away."

"So do we all." Glancing around Abby was relieved to see they were still alone and unlikely to have been overheard. Awkward was only one pothole on what looked like a bumpy road ahead.

"We've looked everywhere," Brandi lamented softly. "But Candace wants us to keep searching. She's sure it's in the house. Somewhere."

"I take it you don't agree."

"No, I don't. I don't want to file a police report either. She's so positive we're going to find it ..." With a gesture of helplessness and a look of undisguised misery, Brandi implored Abby's understanding. "I'm caught in the middle. I don't want to further distress Candace, but I can't file an insurance claim without a police report." Her gaze fell to the floor. "I don't know what to do now."

Abby took a deep breath. Worst case, the ring was truly lost and Brandi would have to involve the insurance company. "What does your husband advise?"

"I haven't told Wayne yet." Brandi closed her eyes for several seconds. "He's an efficiency expert and very detail oriented. He'll go ballistic when I tell him."

For Abby, some things began to make sense. A detail-driven man might not understand how his wife could treat a valuable diamond ring in so cavalier a manner. "Do keep looking," Abby encouraged. "It's bound to turn up."

Brandi's knuckles whitened on the handle of her grocery cart. "I'm afraid my time on Sparrow Island is limited. When Candace and I planned my visit, it was just for a weekend. Then I learned I had to use up my vacation days. Wayne couldn't take time off. So Candace suggested I come early. I got here last Wednesday. I told Wayne I'd be back this coming Sunday, before Thanksgiving."

"So we have less than a week to find the ring."

"Once I leave Sparrow Island, all my options run out. I'll have to tell Wayne the truth."

Shivers ran down Abby's spine. Brandi would have to involve Henry before she left. Once she did, everyone at the party would become a target of mistrust.

MONDAY EVENING, Mary opened the sliding glass door leading to the patio. Filled with energy from his post-dinner romp in the crisp air, Finnegan bounded inside. After giving Abby a quick nuzzle, he wiggled next to the wheelchair and put his head in Mary's lap.

Although technically off duty, and free to roam the house at will, he stayed close as if to tell her he was available, in case she wanted or needed him. Giving him a good scratch, she cooed, "You're such a good boy. If diamonds had a scent, I bet you could sniff them out."

On a half laugh, Abby said, "Wouldn't that be great? We could put Finnegan on the case of the missing ring and he'd solve it in no time."

Stroking his ears, Mary looked at her sister and wondered how to lighten her spirits. The perplexing business of the missing ring was bad enough. Telling her about the squabble between Wilma and Beverly might be a double whammy. But . . . shared burdens were lighter and Abby might find this one amusing.

"Come on, there's something I want to show you." Mary led the way to the craft room, pivoting her chair through the doorway, pausing only long enough to flip on the lights.

"This morning I landed smack-dab in the middle of my own controversy. I've got Wilma Washburn on one side and Beverly Hodges on the other."

"Good grief, whatever for?"

"They're embroiled in a dispute over which of their crafts requires more skill and creativity—basket weaving or quilting."

Abby made a sound that could have been a chuckle or a moan.

Hiding her satisfaction, Mary continued with mock indignation, "It's not funny. This is serious stuff."

Her cheeks turning red, Abby covered her mouth with her hand.

"I'm in big trouble here," Mary complained. "I'm stuck being the mediator and judge."

Abby's eyes sparkled as she rubbed the laughter from her cheeks. "How did this happen?"

After explaining the whirlwind events at In Stitches, Mary concluded, "Ana was in big trouble. Anything she said would just get her in deeper."

"And that explains everything . . . how?"

Mary pushed one of several piles of library books across the craft table toward her sister. "As the shop owner, Ana relies on good relations with her customers for continued business. Even in the craft trade, competition is a—" she glanced at Finnegan—"bunny-eat-bunny world."

"Bunny-eat-bunny?" Abby asked incredulously.

Mary looked at Finnegan again. She'd never refer to a dog-eat-dog world in his presence. "Think about it. There are craft and fabric stores on the other islands, particularly Orcas and San Juan. Then there's the mainland—"

"You're right." Abby rolled her desk chair closer. "It's a long way to go for craft supplies, though."

"And there's the Internet."

"Somehow that doesn't sound very enticing. I've never known a quilter who didn't want to physically feel the yardage and check the fabric for consistency before buying it."

Intrigued by the unexpected observation, Mary pinned her sister with a questioning look. "Have you been holding out on me? Where did you learn about quilting? How many quilters do you hang out with?"

Abby answered the questions in order. "No. All I know about quilting and sewing came from you, Mom and Francine, my best friend at Cornell. All of you have to touch everything two or three times before you're satisfied."

"Oh, you. You like to rattle my chain, don't you?"

"Haven't I always?" Abby reached out and gave Mary's arm

an affectionate squeeze. "I know this isn't funny to the people involved. And I understand that your empathy for Ana put you between the old rock and hard place. If I can help, name it. I'll do it."

Mary tapped another of the four stacks of books. "Let's sort these. Basket weaving here." She indicated a spot on the table. "Quilting over there."

"Too bad we don't have a stack for missing rings. I don't want to scare you sister dear, but I must warn you. If Henry becomes involved, this could get very awkward."

"It would be a pickle," Mary agreed. "My employee, my sister and my beau wrapped up in a criminal investigation." She shuddered at the thought. "Who would have taken the ring, Abby? And why? Surely, they had to realize Brandi would have no choice but to call in Henry and his troops."

"Honestly, I'm a little afraid of this mystery," Abby said softly. "Everyone associated with the party could be hurt. The detrimental fallout could even reach Island Blooms. If there's a criminal investigation, reputations could be permanently sullied."

Mary met her sister's gaze. "I hate to be the bearer of more bad news, but we can't forget the editor of *The Birdcall*. If William Jansen gets wind of the missing ring, you can count on the story making the front page news."

"Pray it doesn't happen. In the meantime, there's nothing we can do tonight." Abby picked a book off the stack. "Tomorrow is another matter."

Flipping open the cover of a basketry how-to, she added, "Thanks for keeping me out of this dustup."

"Who would have ever thought we'd be working on controversies involving each other's employees?" Mary sighed and started sorting her stack of books. "There's an awful lot to learn about quilting and basket weaving."

"You won't get an argument from me," Abby said lightly. "When it comes to those arts, I'm at my best in a gallery admiring what's on display and pretending I have a clue."

Mary didn't bother keeping a straight face. Despite a lack of interest in the creative arts, Abby made an effort to have a passing acquaintance with them. Given a free moment in a gallery though, she'd slip around the corner and find the prints done by master avian artists, particularly Robert Bateman and John James Audubon.

"I know just enough quilting and weaving to get me into trouble," Mary admitted, daunted by the two dozen volumes on the craft table. "If you have any suggestions on how to attack this project, I'm wide open. The women want the judging before Thanksgiving. If I don't find a way to maximize my time, New Years will come and go and I'll still be reading these books."

Abby put down her book and traced the tightly woven design on the front cover. "I do have an idea. Several weeks ago, Wilma came up with a proposal for the Thanksgiving season at The Nature Museum. Hugo loved her suggestion and put her in charge. She's bringing in the best art of the Native American Basket Weavers from all over the Northwest. It's a big event for The Nature Museum and starts this coming weekend."

"If Wilma's part of it, it might be a little ticklish for me," Mary thought aloud. "I don't want to give even a perception of unfair advantage."

"I don't see a problem. The Association is working hard to popularize their traditional crafts. They don't want them to die out. To get the public more involved and draw in new acolytes, they're also giving demonstrations and hands-on lessons." Anticipation lit Abby's eyes. "Interested?"

In an *aha* moment, Mary realized the reason behind Wilma's sudden zealotry. It wasn't just pride in her art, but in the artists who were coming to Sparrow Island for the event. "Neither rain, nor sleet, nor hail, nor the rest of it could keep me away. I'm the judge. I have to learn about basket weaving. I couldn't do better than learning from those who still practice the generational craft."

"It's too bad Ana can't come," Abby said with a suggestive taunt. "She's got the Busy Bee Quilters right there in the store, so she'll be getting an earful on the value of quilting every day."

The realization hit like a thunderbolt. "Abby, you're a genius! If the Busy Bees see the basket-weaving demonstration, I'm sure it will be a giant step in the right direction."

"Think you can convince them to come?"

Recalling the entrenched attitudes at In Stitches this morning, Mary wasn't sure. "It's a tall order. Some of the Busy Bees aren't open to new ideas. But, if I find the right approach, it might work."

"Maybe Ana could get someone to fill in for her, so she can attend too." With a grin full of mischief, Abby added, "Of course, the Busy Bees couldn't let her go alone."

"You can be such a rascal, and I'm so glad!"

CHAPTER ❧ EIGHT

TUESDAY MORNING, WITH a specific agenda in mind, Abby headed for town. When the steeple of Little Flock came into view, she turned toward it. Nine in the morning wasn't too early for Rev. James or his young son to be up and about. She rang the rectory bell. Her friend Janet Heinz, with Toby perched on her hip, answered the summons.

"Abby! Come in, so I can put this little guy down. He's not very big, but he's solid and heavy." Janet set the toddler on his feet and watched him make a beeline for a stack of colorful blocks.

Whispering so the child couldn't hear over the noise of the wood blocks banging on a toy xylophone, Abby asked, "How's Patricia's mother?"

"Oh, Patricia plans to come home tomorrow."

"Wonderful! Did Rev. James convince them to see a new doctor?"

"He didn't have to. Their doctor brought in a friend to consult. It turns out Patricia's mother is what's called a 'paradoxical reactor.' That means a medication has the exact opposite result than the one normally anticipated. The pain medication her mother was taking actually made the pain worse. They've changed her treatment plan."

"Paradoxical reactor," Abby murmured. "How unusual."

"It isn't common, but it happens often enough that the medical profession gave it a name," Janet explained.

"It's great the way God answers prayer. Often in ways we never expect."

"How right you are."

Abby glanced at Toby. "I dropped by to see if the family needs anything."

Janet waved her hands as though warding off a swarm of bees. "Please, no. The kitchen is full. I can't get another cheese stick into the refrigerator." She put a hand on her hip. "I don't know why. I only told a few people about Patricia being gone and now the cupboard is overflowing."

Abby couldn't help grinning. Even without intending to, Janet had a way of making herself heard across the island. "I presume Rev. James is working?"

"He's calling and visiting members of the congregation. He's amending the announcement he made Sunday about throwing out old traditions." Janet watched Toby knock down a lopsided tower of blocks. "There's nothing we need, Abby. Thanks for stopping by. I'm having a great time with Toby here. It'll be hard to give him back to his mom."

Abby hugged Janet. "You just want to get some practice in for when you become a grandma, don't you?"

Janet returned the hug with a loving squeeze around Abby's shoulders. "That's me. The grandma wannabe."

ABBY SPENT THE REST of Tuesday morning observing the birds still caged at the laboratory. Although their progress was slow, they were all getting better. Buoyed by her visit to the rectory, she had more reasons for celebration.

Between the basket-weaving demonstration and the special Thanksgiving exhibits she and Hugo had planned for the museum, she'd been working long hours and extra days. The situation wasn't likely to change. Many of the events took place on weekends and evenings so working people could attend. The flip-flopped hours gave her more flexibility during the day.

Satisfied with the progress of the northern flicker pair, she moved on to her next project. In the main hall of The Nature Museum, adjacent to the Wonderful World of Wings, she constructed the background for the wild turkey display. It kept her busy, yet thoughts of Brandi's missing ring continued to roam the corridors of her mind.

Several hours later, while driving into town for lunch, she reviewed the guest list from Saturday's party. She began with Al and Laverne Minsky. They weren't keen on jewelry—gold wedding bands, inexpensive watches and small earrings seemed to be mainstays of their collection.

"Wait a minute," Abby mumbled to herself as she parked in the first available spot near the café on Shoreline Drive. Laverne had mentioned a ring guard and that her rings got loose when the weather turned cold.

How strange. Abby couldn't recall ever seeing more than a gold wedding ring on Laverne's fingers. Then again, unless shaped like a bird, jewelry of any kind ranked very low on Abby's radar.

She glanced across the street at Seibert's Jewelry. Logic suggested no one would wear a ring guard for a costume piece. Pearls and gemstones were another matter. She considered marching over to the upscale store to have a chat with Gordon Seibert. It would be interesting to learn which of the party guests had a taste for fine frippery.

Maybe later and maybe not at all. She didn't want to explain her reasons for asking. Resigned, she headed for the Springhouse Café, although her thoughts kept traveling down the guest list.

Of all the women present, Donna Morgan had the most flamboyant personality. She wore flashy rings. She'd notice them on someone else.

Candace wasn't a possibility, Abby decided, opening the front door of the restaurant. Or was she? If she wanted to steal the ring, creating a scenario that included eight other suspects made more sense than being the only one. And if Candace had taken the ring—

"Ridiculous," Abby murmured, approaching the café podium. She scanned the restaurant looking for the absent hostess and spotted Ida Tolliver leading Sven Dyer to a table in the corner.

Opportunity seemed to be knocking.

Under his left arm, Sven carried a manila folder. Abby hesitated. He might be behind on a project and bringing work with him so he could catch up during lunch. On the other hand, it might be there to keep him company. There was only one way to find out. She walked up to him and said, "Hello, Sven. Mind if I join you?"

Startled blue eyes regarded her before he smiled and rose to his feet. "Hullo, Abby. Good to see you." He held the chair for her. "A lunch companion would be nice."

Bolstered by his amiability, she sat. At the party, he'd come across as an open and friendly man. He was easy to talk with. "What are you working on?"

Sven moved the worn manila folder to the side of the table. "A proposal for Summit Stables. They're thinking of putting in a retaining wall and some new trails."

"I imagine riders and their horses will love having new territory to explore."

Ida arrived with ice water and menus. The busy noon hour allowed no time for the waitress to indulge in small talk. Because Sven and Abby knew what they wanted, Ida took their orders and menus when she left and returned almost immediately with a pair of coffees.

"Actually, I have Mary to thank for passing my name along to Summit Stables." Sven lifted the steaming cup and took a sip. "I'd forgotten how fast word travels in a small town."

"Sparrow Island can use a good landscaper." Abby added a couple of ice cubes from her water glass to her coffee. "Introducing yourself around Green Harbor was a creative way to spark interest and drum up business."

He lowered his cup, a smile parting his lips. "Thanks, but I was also referring to you. People call you the Bird Lady or the town sleuth. Most say you're both."

"I dabble in mysteries," she said guardedly.

"I heard you do more than dabble."

"From who?"

"Nathaniel Dawkins for one." Sven leaned forward and lowered his voice. "Mind if I ask what you're investigating today?"

She wouldn't get a better opening. Quickly she glanced around. In their secluded corner, it wasn't likely they'd be overheard. "I was wondering if you'd seen anything unusual during the party Saturday night."

"Other than ten adults dressed up and acting like characters out of a 1920s melodrama?"

Abby laughed. "You've pegged us well."

"I had fun." He sipped his coffee. "It looked like everyone else did too. Am I wrong?"

"We all had a great time." Thinking she needed to be more direct, she wrapped her hands around her cup and took the plunge. "Until the party ended and a certain item went missing."

Folding his arms on the table, Sven leaned closer. "Candace called me. It was awkward as all get out, but I don't hold it against her. Frankly, Brandi either took a foolish risk or the stones weren't real."

Surprise pushed Abby's eyebrows up so high, she wasn't sure she could blink. She hadn't even considered the possibility of the diamonds not being real.

"But for my money—" Sven abruptly stopped and sat back, his expression warning her to keep silent.

Carrying their lunches, Ida breezed to the table. She managed a little chitchat while serving their hearty sandwiches and steaming soup. She placed a basket of piping hot herb and cheese scones beside Sven. "The butter's in the basket."

"Thanks." When she left, he turned to Abby. "Ida's a class A waitress. Never forgets a face or an order."

"Or a friend. I like her very much. She's good-hearted and hardworking." Abby's gaze followed Sven's as he watched the twenty-four-year-old move on to another table. If his interest was more than casual curiosity, she'd find out soon enough. As he said, Green Harbor was a small town.

After a silent prayer over the meal, Abby smoothed her napkin onto her lap and picked up her spoon.

Quietly, Sven asked, "What do you think happened to the missing ring?"

Abby sidestepped his question in order to explore his earlier comment. "Was there something about the stones that made you think they weren't real?"

"Let's face it, the ring was a stunner. It looked real to me, but it takes an expert to know." He slathered butter on a steaming scone. "I'm not an expert. However, when a man contemplates buying an engagement ring for his ladylove, he develops a working relationship with the four Cs."

Torn between which thread to follow, Abby opted for the personal. She could come back to the four Cs later. "You bought an engagement ring for your ladylove?"

Sven gave her an appraising look. "You don't miss much, do you?"

"I try not to, but I'm constantly amazed by all the things I don't know. Where is your ladylove now?"

A growing bleakness in his taut features suggested a deep hurt. For a moment, Abby didn't think he'd answer, then he said, "We went our separate ways. She proved not to be my love or a lady."

"I'm so sorry."

"Yeah. Well, live and learn."

Abby toyed with her sandwich. Hoping to get the conversation back on track, she asked, "Tell me about the four Cs, okay?"

"Sure." He visibly relaxed. "Gemologists use color, clarity, cut and carat weight to establish the worth of a stone."

She sipped her coffee. "I do know carat is the weight and a diamond with perfect clarity is very rare. I think cut means emerald, pear or marquise."

Sven shook his head. "You're thinking about the shape. That's not the same as cut. When gemologists refer to cut, they mean the proportions, not the style or shape. It's the depth, width, and uniformity of a stone's facets that control its brilliance."

"So, it's not just one thing that makes a diamond sparkle?"

A flicker of a smile acknowledged her naiveté. "Some synthetic diamonds have more sparkle than real ones. These days, it's nearly impossible to tell the difference between a natural gemstone,"—he pointed his spoon at her—"not all of which are valuable, and an engineered one." He took a spoonful of the thick broccoli cheddar soup.

"Making synthetic diamonds isn't easy," Sven continued. "Most methods require extremely high temperatures. Each produces a slightly different product."

"Like cubic zirconia," Abby offered, impressed by the depth of his knowledge.

"Those were some of the early efforts at manufacturing diamonds. A cubic zirconia, or CZ, weighs almost twice as much as a real diamond of the same size."

She put down her spoon. "Twice as much is a big difference."

"Not as big a difference as having a ring one minute and not having it the next." He gave a matter-of-fact nod. "For what it's worth, I don't think you took it."

Abby sat bolt upright. It never occurred to her Sven might

have his own list of possible culprits or that she'd be on it. "Thank you. I think."

"I'm aware as the new guy in town I instantly become a person of interest—probably the first on everyone's list." He pushed away his dishes and centered his nearly empty coffee cup. "Now, I may be an interesting guy," he said lightly, "but not because of the ring. Last time I saw it was when Brandi put it on the mantel."

Questions clamored for answers. How had he acquired the depth and breadth of his diamond knowledge? It seemed more than what was necessary to buy an engagement ring, but there wasn't time to ask. He'd finished eating and would head back to work soon.

Instead, she took advantage of his openness and straightforward manner. "Because you are the newcomer, you may have seen things at the party in a different light than the rest of us. Did you notice anything unusual? Or anyone doing something . . . odd?"

She couldn't say "out of character" because he'd just met the majority of the group Saturday night. He wouldn't have had an opportunity to learn their habits.

Ida came around with the coffeepot and Sven nodded.

After she'd given both of them a refill and departed, he grumbled, "Define odd."

"Unusual. Unexpected. Unexplained."

His lips thinned as he stared at his full coffee cup.

"What did you see?"

"You don't know what you're asking me to do."

"I'm asking you to help nine of the ten people at the party. Most are business owners, like you. I want to get this resolved before it becomes a police matter." She leaned forward. "And before all of us become front page news."

He sat statue still for a full minute. "About an hour before the party ended, I saw Nathaniel by the back door."

Certain there had to be more, Abby prodded, "And?"

"He was cleaning mud off his shoes. His suit jacket was damp." Sven met Abby's gaze. "So were the cuffs of his trousers. His spats were gone."

The news set her back in her chair. She didn't recall Nathaniel's damp clothing or seeing any mud on his shoes. Why had he gone outside? Why hadn't she noticed?

Because I was having a very good time and not paying attention to anything other than the party's murder mystery. I had to clear the flapper's name.

Sven's cell phone rang. He reached for it, then hesitated.

She appreciated his manners. "Go ahead. I don't mind."

"Thanks." He answered and spoke softly for a moment before taking out a pen and jotting notes on the outside of the manila folder. He seemed more at ease as his focus shifted from her to his business call.

While he answered his client's questions, she finished her soup and sandwich and took the tab for both lunches. It was the least she could do.

She'd learned a lot from Sven and understood his reluctance to say anything that cast the light of suspicion on Nathaniel. At the party, they seemed to be building a friendship.

As she left the café, she puzzled over why Nathaniel had gone outside. What could he have been doing to get damp clothing and muddy feet?

CHAPTER ✿ NINE

I'LL GET FINNEGAN." BOBBY popped off his seat belt and turned to the back of the van. Catching himself in mid-movement, he looked hopefully at Mary. "If it's okay?"

"It's fine." She ruffled his hair. "Watch for cars pulling up beside us before you get out."

Parked in the middle of three well-marked handicapped spaces at The Nature Museum, she doubted anyone would whip into the vacant slots on either side. However, where a curious, lightning-fast boy was concerned, building a habit of safety was an ongoing task.

Moments later Mary rolled her chair away from the van. Finnegan walked proudly between her and Bobby, the three of them taking over the wide sidewalk leading to the main entrance. Flowerbeds filled with late-blooming pansies and aromatic landscape bark flanked the walkway. Although not likely to last past the first good snow, the vivid purple and yellow blooms were a bright spot of color against the sandy tones of the two-story stucco and stone building.

"Those flowers sure are pretty," Bobby said. "Mom says they remind her of me, because one of their names is Johnny-jump-up. I don't know why. They're not jumping." He gave an unconcerned shrug. "I think they look like faces."

"So do a lot of people." Mary loved the way his mind worked. "See how the flowers nod forward?"

He stopped, squatted and looked close. "Yeah?"

"The French decided they looked like faces in thought. That's how the pansy got its name, from the French word *pensée* which means *thought*."

A sharp gust of cold wind nipped at their ears and sent pie-plate sized leaves skittering across the asphalt.

"Brrr." Bobby rose and shot an accusing glance at the big leaf maple dominating the island in the center of the circular drive. Pulling up the collar of his jacket and scrunching his chin into its warmth, he said, "It always feels really cold when the trees lose their leaves."

"I do believe you're right." Mary pulled her muffler a little closer. "I wonder why that's so."

"'Cause you can see the bare branches shivering," he said matter-of-factly. Pointing to a tall Sitka spruce, limbs full and ponderous in the fitful breeze, he continued, "The firs are different. They don't care about the cold 'cause their needles are like hard green coats that keep them warm."

She'd never quite thought of the evergreens in that way. Trust a ten-year-old to give things a different slant.

He hurried ahead to The Nature Museum entrance and held the door open for her and Finnegan. They scooted inside to the entry area between the small gift shop and the reception desk.

"Hello Mary, Bobby." Wilma Washburn stood behind the

reception desk. "Is there anything in particular you'd like to see?"

Bobby spoke up. "Uh, actually, Mrs. Washburn, I came to see Abby, I mean, Dr. Stanton."

"You're in luck." Wilma smiled warmly and gestured toward the east wing. "She's with Mr. Baron over at the animal hibernation exhibit."

"Great!" Bobby turned in that direction, his eagerness to get started making it difficult for him to stand still. "I see her. Mary, can I?"

"Go ahead." She waved at her sister who waved back, acknowledging the transfer of responsibility for the boy.

"School project, I imagine." Wilma looked questioningly at Mary.

"Yes. Something about turkeys, which ought to be right up Abby's alley. This is Tuesday, Sandy's day for after-school tutoring. Otherwise she'd have brought him."

Wilma's knowing grin grew broader. "Anything else?"

"What do you mean?"

"Surely you came to tell me I'm right. Basket weaving is indeed the finer, more difficult craft."

"No, in fact, I—"

"You can't be seriously thinking there's any real contest—can you? Just take a look around." She nudged the small basket on her desk toward Mary. "How can you look at this and have any questions in your mind?"

Mary wished she could make a graceful escape, but retreat wasn't an option. Folding her arms, she met Wilma's challenging gaze. "Are you trying to influence the judge?"

Mouth open, eyebrows raised, Wilma stood speechless for a moment. Then she erupted, "Of course, I am. How else will you learn the truth? Here." She practically dropped the basket in Mary's lap. "This was made by a Tsimshian woman from old Metlakatla in British Columbia. Have you ever seen such expert weaving or such beauty?"

Intrigued by the intricacy, Mary took the work. "Okay. Tell me about this piece. About the Tsimshians."

Wilma's features softened. "Their name means 'People Inside the Skeena River.' Once they were many and known for their noble clans, fearsome warriors and beautiful weaving."

The careful design of the little basket in Mary's hands spoke an ancient language she recognized. Wife, mother, sister, daughter, these were women's roles and she knew them all. In the worn pages of her Bible, she'd seen how throughout time different societies and cultures had defined the value of women. Yet no matter how they were treated, what status they were accorded or achieved, women remained a mystery, feminine creatures born with soft hearts and a compelling need for beauty.

Whether it was colorful carpets spread over the sand in a Bedouin's tent, a frilly curtain on the window of a crumbling dirt soddy on the plains, or a blazing yellow dandelion in a jelly jar, the need for beauty asserted itself.

Pulling herself back to the present, Mary listened to Wilma describe the style and pattern. "Most Metlakatla," she said, "prefer using yellow cedar bark because the stitches are smoother. This one is done using close-twined red cedar bark and canary grass."

"Goodness," Mary breathed, wondering about the woman whose fingers knew how to twine the bark and hold the grass in just the right way. "It must take years of practice to make something this exquisite." Suddenly aware of the basket's delicacy, she handed it back. "Twining you say."

With a nod, Wilma turned the basket bottom up and pointed at the center. "Twining begins with a foundation of rigid elements. The subtle elegance of this basket came from changing the number of wefts."

"Like weaving," Mary said, awed by the complexities.

"It's called basket *weaving* for a reason."

"Sorry, I was thinking of fabrics. You know, the loom, the warp and the weft."

Wilma shrugged and nodded, a sort of understanding forgiveness. "When these baskets are finished, some have over one hundred thousand individual stitches." She pointed to the design on the top. "This is called false embroidery. Getting it this neat and fine is difficult."

Mary marveled at all the steps and the variety of individual stitches. As a knitter, she followed a pattern and counted stitches, but her materials were soft, pliable, easy to use and came from the store. She had trouble visualizing the need to set her projects aside for a week or two while she went out to gather more raw materials. "Why do you call it *false* embroidery?" It looked like the real thing to her—done with some sort of grass instead of embroidery floss.

"It's a technique for wrapping grasses or roots around the wefts to create a pattern on the outside of the weave."

"So in addition to the basket itself, all the decorations are done by . . . twining the materials on the wefts," Mary said slowly. Embarrassment washed over her as she thought about the baskets she'd sold at Island Blooms. She'd simply admired the finished products and offered them for sale.

"Twining and lattice-twining are similar but different methods," Wilma continued as though she hadn't noticed the flush staining Mary's cheeks. "There is also coiling, which requires a sewing technique, and plaiting." Wilma settled onto the chair behind the reception desk. "How much time do you have? I could go on for hours."

"There's more?"

Wilma laughed softly. "Oh yes. Baskets were designed for specific tasks. Some, like burden baskets, were custom woven to evenly distribute the load and conform to the wearer's back."

Feeling she was giving an order to an eighteen-wheeler on a freeway, Mary raised a hand. "Stop! I'm on overload."

Clearly enjoying the situation, Wilma folded her arms across her chest. "Remember, baskets are older than pots and pans. They are basic and essential tools of living. Before people made fabrics, they made baskets."

Mary held up both hands. "I'm crying uncle here."

But Wilma obviously had one more point to score. "Look at your jacket."

"I know. It's quilted."

"In an old basket-style stitch." Wilma's smile conveyed confidence. "Are you convinced now? Can you admit the basket makers have the most skill and create the most beauty?"

Mary shook her head. "I will admit you've given me a lot to think about. Here's something for you. Why don't you and the Native American Basket Weavers come to a session of the Busy Bee quilters tonight?"

"Why would we want to?" Wilma asked.

"It strikes me that each group has a great deal to teach—and learn from—the other. I'm inviting the quilters to the basket weaving demonstration here at The Nature Museum."

"I don't see—"

"That's the point. You don't see," Mary pressed. "You and Beverly charged me to learn about your respective crafts. I didn't like being pulled into the middle, but now that I'm here, I'm going to follow through."

"Good. You'll be better qualified to make a decision." The set of Wilma's jaw indicated she didn't consider any decision correct unless the basket weavers came out on top.

For a moment, Mary was tempted to pray for patience, then thought better of it. She already had a proving ground on which to practice. "It seems to me you and Beverly need to learn about each other's crafts. You've asked me to make a comparison between two very different skill sets with common elements. How will you know if my impressions are correct if you don't know anything about quilting?"

"You may have a point," Wilma conceded reluctantly.

May? Mary raised a questioning eyebrow and waited with more patience than she thought she possessed.

"Okay, Mary, you win. It's short notice, but I'll make a few calls to my fellow basket weavers. And I promise to be at In Stitches tonight for the Busy Bee Quilters' meeting." Wilma flicked a curious glance at Mary's jacket. "It might be interesting to see what goes into making a quilt."

Before she could give in to her version of a victory dance—pumping her fist in the air—and ruining the hard-won detente, Mary wheeled sedately into the museum.

"DID YOU KNOW Benjamin Franklin wanted the turkey to be the national bird?" Bobby asked as he carefully shook seed into the bird feeder.

Abby let her gaze roam around the laboratory. Empty cages meant success. Today, the Northern flickers were slow to the seed, but faster than yesterday. "I think I remember reading that," she answered slowly, "but I don't recall why. Do you know?"

"He said bald eagles were characters of bad morals...
I think."

"Could he have said they had 'bad moral character'?" She
fought a smile.

"That was it." Bobby nodded rapidly. "Mr. Franklin didn't
think eagles earned an honest living, so they shouldn't be the
bird of America. The turkey should 'cause it defends its young
and doesn't bother anyone."

"Benjamin Franklin was a man of great learning with probably as much curiosity as you have, Bobby."

"Really?"

Abby nodded. She truly enjoyed this boy and was grateful
to have him in her life.

"How does a bird earn a dishonest living, Abby?"

The grin escaped and she turned her head away. "I believe
Franklin was referring to the way eagles scavenge their meals
when the opportunity arises."

"You mean they steal it?"

"Yes, and they feed on carrion."

"Already dead animals somebody else killed?"

Not wanting him to make a reactive judgment against birds
of prey, she explained, "Many raptors, including falcons,
hawks and some owls have to feed on carrion when live game
is scarce or unavailable. They're meat eaters and not equipped
to live on anything else."

"I guess that's the way God made them."

"Did you know turkeys or their domesticated descendents
can be found just about anywhere in the world?"

Bobby shook his head in wonderment. "The whole world?"

"Yep. Scientists call such animals generalists. That means
they don't require special foods or habitat."

"Pretty cool."

"Of course turkeys like some neighborhoods better than others," she teased. "The ones that have TV."

He gave her a skeptical look. "Not really."

"No, not really." She touched him lightly in the ribs with her elbow to show it was a joke. "Even though wild turkeys are wary and agile fliers, they like places with some cover. Bushes not too crowded and less than three feet tall give them places to hide and food to eat while they spy on the predators that want a drumstick or two."

"Oh, Abby," he chided. "What else do you know about them?"

She was glad he'd given her an inadvertent heads-up at church last Sunday. She'd had a chance to refresh her memory. He was already stretching her. "We know they were in England during the reign of Henry VIII. It's rather surprising they survived as well as they did in that damp climate."

"Yeah and if people were hunting them too . . ."

"This was back in the 1500s, when people preferred to eat beets, cabbage and eels."

"Eels?" A look of horror passed over Bobby's face. "People ate eels?"

"They still do."

"*Ohh*. But not on Sparrow Island."

"I don't think they'll be on the menu at your house any time soon."

"Good. Let's not talk about them any more. Let's talk about turkeys. How do we know England had turkeys then?"

"Because Shakespeare wrote about them. He put turkey jokes in his plays."

"I wonder if Mom knows he did. She reads Shakespeare to

Dad and me sometimes. It's kinda interesting after you figure out what he's saying." He gave an uncertain shrug then brightened. "How come we don't have any turkeys on Sparrow Island?"

"We do. Not very many, but I've seen a few." Abby raised an eyebrow. "You do realize wild turkeys look nothing like the bird you see on the table for Thanksgiving and Christmas dinner, don't you?"

Bobby nodded. "I've been coloring pictures of 'em for years. Everybody at school does. They're hanging all over the walls. Some are green, some are blue and some are even pink. I saw one colored like a rainbow." He peered through squinted eyelids. "Tell me some more."

"Well, adult wild turkeys have small featherless heads. They have red throats, long reddish-orange legs and a dark brown body. The males have red wattles on the throat and neck. That's the loose fold of skin under their beaks."

"That's kind of what I thought," Bobby said. "They have fan tails too."

"They're usually long and darkly colored."

"I thought all male birds were brighter, you know, their feathers, than female birds."

"It's true with wild turkeys. The toms—the males—are substantially bigger than the hens. The toms have rear spurs on their legs, but the hens don't."

"What else is different between the toms and the hens?"

"Hens are dull brown and grayish. The toms are flashier. They have areas of red, green, copper, bronze and gold iridescence in their feathers. All the adult toms have beards about nine inches long."

Bobby straightened. "Really? That's pretty long. The hens don't have beards, right?"

"Some do, but they're usually shorter and thinner." Abby smiled. "Not to worry. A tom would never mistake a hen with a beard for another tom. Both toms and hens roost in trees at night."

"Wow. They're really cool birds." He heaved a wistful sigh. "This is really bad news."

"Bad news? Why?"

"Thanksgiving has been really bothering me for a couple of days."

"Can you tell me why? Maybe I can help."

The spattering of freckles over his nose scrunched and the long lashes of his hazel eyes swept his cheeks. He tugged folded papers out of his back pocket and held them tightly. "You know, with turkeys being noble birds and all, I'm thinking it isn't right to ... well ... eat them." He spoke the last two words in a despondent hush.

Eyeing the papers, Abby suspected whatever information they contained had influenced his thinking. "I thought you liked turkey."

"I like *turkeys*, so I'm not going to eat them. It just wouldn't be right."

"Why have you had this change of heart?"

"Maybe this'll explain it." He unfolded the papers and gave them to her.

Abby read a poorly metered poem titled "Ode to a Turkey." In it, an intelligent turkey strove to remain small and thin in order to avoid being the main course at Thanksgiving dinner. The bird succeeded and became a well fed personal pet. When it was too late, he learned he was still on the menu. Christmas was coming.

She suppressed a smile because Bobby took the oratory seriously. This wasn't the first time something he'd read had influenced his thinking or behavior. She'd have to be careful with her response.

"You know turkeys can't write." She returned the papers.

"But if they could, maybe they would have written this." He refolded them and tucked the wad into his pocket. "I just can't take the chance."

"I see," she said slowly.

"How can you be a bird lover and still eat turkey for Thanksgiving dinner, Abby? It doesn't seem the bird has anything to be thankful for."

Taken by surprise, she didn't know what to say. She wanted to think about it for a while and then get back to him. But curious boys weren't known for their patience and Bobby was definitely a curious boy. "I guess it looks that way."

"It sure does. And I don't see how I can love birds and eat turkey too."

The implication was clear.

CHAPTER ❧ TEN

AFTER BOBBY LEFT TUESDAY afternoon, Abby finished cleaning the empty birdcages and pondered the boy's quandary. She had to take his predicament seriously. Now that he'd raised the issue, her Thanksgiving dinner might be in jeopardy too.

Why had it never bothered her to eat turkey? Or chicken for that matter? She recalled having pheasant several times, as well as goose and duck.

How does *a respectable ornithologist eat fowl?*

She laughed softly. *Using a knife and fork of course.*

With no solutions to Bobby's dietary dilemma coming to mind, she gathered her tools and headed for the museum's storeroom. On the way, she saw Sven and Hugo in the reception area shaking hands. Then her boss ushered the landscaper in the direction of the offices.

Briefly, she considered joining them before deciding against it. When Hugo was ready to discuss his plans for the conservatory's landscaping, he'd let her know. Of that, she had no doubt. Past actions on his part amply demonstrated how much he valued her opinion.

Instead, she went to her office to analyze her growing sense of unease. Why would a landscaper know so much about diamonds? Sven's explanation made sense—sort of. But she couldn't recall any of her friends doing the kind of research he had for an engagement ring. They went to a reputable jewelry store and bought what they liked.

More puzzling was Mary and Hugo. They'd accepted Sven at face value. Abby wondered if she was missing something or if they were. To her, Sven seemed a little too good to be true.

Hoping to silence her unease, she logged onto the Internet and typed his name into the search engine. The pages of results heightened her disquiet.

The first article was blatant sensationalism. The second and third were better, but the fundamentals were the same. By the time she finished the sixth article, she realized the truth was as sad as it was disturbing.

Sven's words echoed in her thoughts. *You don't know what you're asking me to do.* Now, she knew what he really meant.

A year ago, he'd been asked to tell what he knew about someone he cared for in front of a judge and jury. And what he revealed helped put the defendant in prison. The ladylove who wasn't either one had a nasty habit of preying on the unsuspecting.

Entering someone's home as a caregiver, she'd earned the person's trust before asking to borrow a piece of jewelry for a special occasion. Although the items were promptly returned, the genuine stones had been replaced with synthetics.

In Sven's favor, when he learned of the crimes, he went to the police. On the other hand, he'd lied to Abby. He hadn't gained his extraordinary knowledge about gemstones while pursuing an engagement ring. He'd gotten a crash course during the investigation.

Despite his cooperation and testimony, some court watchers insisted he'd been involved in the substitution scheme.

Abby blew out a breath and sat back. Maybe finding the ring was only part of the battle. They'd have to take it to Seibert's to make sure the stone was genuine.

If it wasn't—

In the circle of partygoers, Sven was the only one who might know how to pull off the switch.

Feeling a need to move on with her investigation, she turned off her computer.

After fetching her jacket and purse, she left The Nature Museum and headed for Al's Garage. He'd be open for another hour and a half, plenty of time for him to put new tires on her car. Keeping her vehicle in tip-top condition provided its own rewards. Hopefully, a conversation with Al would provide rewards of another kind.

She needed answers before the clock ticking in the back of her mind ran out of time. Once Brandi filed a formal report, law enforcement would consider everyone who attended the party "a person of interest." There would be interviews and fact-gathering sessions, each question and answer indelibly recorded and destined for a permanent place in the police files.

Abby shuddered.

Driving down Primrose Lane, past Stanton Farm, she tooted the horn at Sam Arbogast as he trundled down the path to the chicken coop. He waved a rake in her direction, giving her a momentary sense of peace. He'd been her parent's faithful friend, as well as their employee for the last eleven years. As an adopted member of the family, Sam was someone she could always count on.

Thank You, Lord, for Sam's steadfast devotion to Mom and Dad. Thank You for sending such a willing worker—one who also cherishes the love they lavish on him.

When she said "Amen," peace settled around her heart. Giving voice to her gratitude, even regarding the smallest things, always made her feel better about everything else.

Her thoughts returned to Al Minsky and she found herself looking forward to her impromptu visit. The garage owner was an honest man with simple tastes and a love for his family and business, and she'd always known him to be straightforward.

In the back of her mind, she could almost see Henry wagging a warning finger and reminding her that in private, people were often much different from the image they presented in public.

The imperfection of human beings wasn't a sudden revelation. She liked the fact most tended to keep their faults private. It meant they recognized goodness, truth and virtue and wanted, at the very least, to be seen as practicing those qualities.

She turned down Municipal Street and headed for the garage. On the surface, its position as the only automotive shop on the island looked like an ideal situation. Al had a relatively steady, "captive" clientele, particularly during the off-tourist months.

On the flip side, growth was difficult. His customer base tended to be limited to the island residents. People didn't come from the mainland or the other islands for an oil change or a tune-up. Now, with his son in college in California and his daughter a college-bound senior at Green Harbor Public School, finances might be tight in the Minsky home.

Abby didn't think college tuition would be a sufficient reason for upstanding citizens to resort to theft. Yet she couldn't discount the possibility. Stranger things happened every day. For proof, all a person had to do was turn on the national news.

If she had her druthers, the whole episode would end with Brandi or Candace shouting, "Hey! Look, everybody! I found a diamond ring in my pocket!"

She sighed. She'd settle for a quiet, "Guess what?"

Except she hadn't heard so much as a whisper.

She turned into the shop's driveway and parked in front of one of the open bays. While she waited for Al, she reflected on another growing threat. The missing ring wasn't the best-kept secret on Sparrow Island.

It wouldn't be long before it "got legs" as editor William Jansen liked to say. If the island grapevine laid this morsel on his desk, he'd dine on it for weeks. As a responsible journalist, he wouldn't have a choice.

Al came out to her car. He wore his familiar mechanic's uniform with his name embroidered in red on a white patch. "Hello, Abby. What can I do for you?" The laugh lines around his light blue eyes deepened with his smile.

"I need new tires. Am I at the right bay?" she asked with an impish grin.

"You are if you want to beat the rush." He bent sideways to look at the tires of her little hybrid. Straightening, he said, "I can fix you right up."

Tucking her purse under her left arm, she climbed out of the car.

He wiped his hands on an oil-stained red work rag, then pushed it into the bib of his striped gray coveralls. "Are you planning ahead for any particular reason?"

"Around here, winter has a habit of sneaking in when we're not looking. I can't afford not to be prepared. I never know when I'll need to take off on a bird or animal rescue mission."

Al cocked his head and regarded her with respect. "I've never known you not to go out and search for storm victims. But you be careful out there. Bad weather isn't just a hazard to birds and animals. It's a hazard to those trying to help them. I'm guessing you went out after the party. Did you find a lot of injured critters?"

"Not as many as I'd feared. I've already released most of them—sparrows, kinglets and wrens."

"I guess the little ones take the brunt of the storms."

"It depends. This time, a pair of Northern flickers got the worst of it. However, below-freezing temperatures, wind and hail are hard on all wildlife. I'm never sure what I'll find, so I'll take the best all-weather tires you have. I may need them on the back roads."

"Good thinking. I'll have you fixed up in a jiffy. When you leave here, you'll be ready for any rough weather that comes our way."

"Being winterized isn't the whole reason I came to see you, Al. I need to ask you a few questions." She handed off her keys just as a sharp gust blew up Harbor Seal Road from the marina, carrying a stinging cold and a salty tang.

"Best you wait inside." He glanced at the gray sky and headed for the building. "Feels like the storm you're preparing for just might be blowing in."

With a grateful nod, she pulled her jacket tighter and followed him into the cozy customer area.

"Be right back." He went out the glass door to the work bay. Moments later, he drove her car onto a lift.

Confident he'd do right by her, she found a comfortable

chair near the pellet stove and relaxed in its radiant warmth. The waiting/sales room had a familiar odor. She took several cautious sniffs and pronounced it a mix of rubber, degreaser and years of experience.

Funny how the garage had changed hands a couple of times since her childhood, yet the peculiar fragrance was as constant and dependable as the tide.

The scent permeating the walls and floors inspired a sense of belonging, confidence and trust, almost as if she was part of the little family-run business. Abby the person was more important than the dollars her trade brought into the till. Watching the owner returning through the door, she finally could put a name on the good feeling: It was Al.

"This is my first hybrid car," she told him as he poured two cups of coffee from a freshly brewed pot. "To be honest with you, I don't recall what the owner's manual said I needed to do." Gratefully, she wrapped her cold fingers around the steaming mug he offered. "Thanks."

"Knowing what to do is my job. It's what I'm here for. Let me say right up front, I appreciate the business." He gave her an amused sideways look. "You sure did give me the business the other night."

"What? Oh! When we tied for best costume?"

"Yep. Was that a blast or what?"

Despite the questions she was there to ask, she chuckled and said, "It was fun. You were a mighty convincing high-rolling gangster in your zoot suit." Gesturing at her earth-toned trousers and jacket, then his coveralls, she continued, "Now we're back to the real world."

"Yeah. Can't remember the last time I got such a kick out of getting duded up as I did Saturday night."

"That makes two of us."

He turned solemn and gave a brief, tight headshake. "I'm thinking maybe I played my gangster role too well."

"Why?"

"Cuz Candace called me yesterday."

"She did?" Abby sipped the coffee and found it as good as what she and Mary brewed at home.

Al nodded. "She sounded so . . . not like Candace. It was hard not to take offense when she asked if I'd put her cousin's ring in my pocket or anyone else's as a joke." He frowned and pulled back. "Like I'd do something like that."

Inwardly, Abby groaned. "I'm sure Candace didn't mean to offend."

"I sorta figured that." Al ran his grease-stained fingers through his short, brown hair and stopped when he reached the spot where it thinned. "I've known Candace since she came to Sparrow Island eight years ago. She was driving a '72 Volkswagen bug with flowers painted around the rust spots on the fender."

Abby smiled. Candace would have fit in so well with the flower children of the late 1960s and early 1970s.

"She barely got off the ferry when the number three valve called it quits. The car sat in my back lot for months while we waited for the parts to come in. Meantime, she went to work for Mary and found a place to live."

He looked at the ceiling, his gaze glassy with remembrance. "I rebuilt her engine and put in an oil cooler so it wouldn't blow up again." He peeked through the glass door at the help in the work bays. "That's the reason it went out in the first place, ya know. The carburetor sits over number three and it got too hot."

"As I recall, she had the only VW bug on the island."

"She did."

Suspecting Candace hadn't handled the inquiry about the ring very well, Abby deliberately encouraged Al's ramble. Hopefully the reminiscences would remind him what good friends he, Laverne and Candace were.

"I didn't make a dime on those repairs." He set his coffee cup aside. "Made a friend instead. A few years ago, Candace did some talking to my son, the kind he needed but wouldn't listen to from his folks. Next thing Laverne and I knew, Ronnie was filling out scholarship and grant applications."

Al's eyes twinkled over his grin. "Candace also put him in touch with a friend of hers. It's how he wound up in California."

Abby met his grin with one of her own. "It's wonderful the way things work out, isn't it?"

"Yep. Laverne and I got married young. We had Ronnie and Eileen before we were twenty, then we moved here. There were some lean times when we lived on peanut butter and crackers, but we've been rich folks since the day we arrived."

Abby set her cup aside. "In friends?"

Al nodded. "What else? Clothes wear out, and heck, I don't know one brand from another." He raised his work-worn hands. "Jewelry? Ya gotta be kidding. Lucky for me, Laverne's tickled pink with a bauble from Bayside Souvenirs.

"Besides, the only serious conversation I've had with the owner of Seibert's Jewelry was about a short in his taillight. Bottom line is, my wife and I don't care how much money people have or how they spend it as long as they pay their bills here at the garage."

"I hear you," Abby said. "Integrity's priceless. What I'd like to know is if you noticed anything unusual at the party Saturday night. Anything at all."

She knew she'd just given him an invitation to bend her ear for another hour or two, but if that's what it took to ferret out a clue, she didn't mind. Henry often said if there were five eyewitnesses to a collision, there'd be five versions of what happened. Perhaps Al saw something he didn't know was important.

"I did notice the great poster of cars from the 1920s Candace had in the bathroom." He shrugged sheepishly. "I don't know, Abby. Ask me what vehicle somebody drove and what kind of shape it's in, and I'll tell you tons of stuff. You can pretty much tell a person's character by the way he or she treats their car."

Intrigued, she asked, "How so?"

"In my opinion, a person who doesn't show respect for their home or car doesn't have much self-respect. Consequently, they have even less for the folks around them."

His homespun philosophy made sense although life was full of exceptions. "I hadn't made that connection, but I can see the wisdom behind it."

"Well, I've been doing a lot of thinking since Candace called. She's gotta be out of her mind with worry."

Curious where Al's thought patterns and bits of wisdom would lead them, Abby asked, "How so?"

"Her house. Her cousin. Her party. From the sound of her voice—her problem. I'd been meaning to get down to the flower shop and talk with her." Al came around the corner.

"She's gotta find the ring, Abby. If someone took it, you gotta find out who. If a person steals, he lies. If he's a lying thief, there's no telling what else he or she'll do. We can't have somebody like that running around Sparrow Island and pretending to be our friend."

"I couldn't agree with you more."

"You'll solve this mystery, Abby. I believe you can. I have

faith in you and the Lord. Laverne and I have been praying for Candace and her cousin since we got the call. I think you might be the answer to our prayers."

Speechless, Abby stared at the mechanic.

Cold air rushed into the office when a young man in coveralls opened the glass doors to the work bays. "Hey, boss. Got a minute?"

"I think we've covered all my questions," Abby said quickly, "but do me one favor, please."

"Sure thing."

"Go through the pockets and cuffs of everything you and Laverne wore Saturday night. It's possible the ring rolled off the mantel when no one was looking. It could have landed in a trouser cuff, a pocket or got caught in the lace on a dress." Abby had been over every inch of her flapper costume.

"We've done it and we'll do it again." Al crossed the waiting room, then turned to her. "Just 'cause you asked us to." He opened the door. "By the way, we checked the car too. Like we were putting it up for sale. No ring there either. You know Abby, if it got caught in somebody's clothes, they could've tracked it outside without even knowing it. In that case, it's history and we're hosed."

Abby flinched and prayed he was wrong.

CHAPTER ❦ ELEVEN

THE STORM THAT THREATENED all Tuesday afternoon became reality after dinner. Mary looked up hopefully as Ana Dominguez made her way toward the group gathered at the quilting tables. The proprietor of In Stitches automatically paused now and then to straighten a colorful bolt of fabric or fluff the cascading material. Surrounded by soft fleece in warm autumn and bright Christmas colors, she looked especially dejected.

Shaking her head, she walked up to Mary and said, "It's too bad Wilma didn't come. We have a special guest. One who has written four quilting books. She agreed to visit with us because we're on her way to Canada. She's the featured artist at the quilt show in Victoria this weekend. Her works are hanging in the La Conner Quilt Museum on our mainland. And they are *muy bueno.*"

Mary felt doubly bad. She'd counted on Wilma's promise to attend the quilting bee and raised Ana's expectations with the news. Together they'd dared hope Wilma could convince some of the other Native American basket weavers to join her.

Rather than dwell on her discontent, Mary turned her attention to the prestigious guest teacher.

A burst of rain thrummed on the roof. Realization struck Mary and she could have kicked herself for not considering the turbulent weather. Wilma *was* dependable. She did mean what she said, including her oft-repeated aversion to driving in the rain at night.

Just as Mary wished she'd had the forethought to call and offer her friend a ride, Wilma hurried in and settled onto the seat beside her. Mary leaned close and whispered, "Glad you could make it."

Wilma flashed an exasperated glance and adjusted her damp clothing. "Well, I'm late, wet and alone, but I'm here, so this better be good. What's the topic?"

Mary handed over the extra flyer she'd saved. A lengthy paragraph on the back listed the guest instructor's awards. When Ana explained the importance of those accolades in the quilting world, she'd inadvertently reminded Mary that gaining recognition in one's field was only half the battle. Unless the audience shared the passion for the craft, they wouldn't understand the importance of the accomplishments.

Making a mental note to explain the awards to Wilma at a more opportune time, Mary turned her attention to the front of the room.

The instructor demonstrated how to do appliqué work using a stabilizer fabric and immediately moved on to the finished product.

"I like to think of appliqué as frosting on a cake," she said, her gaze roaming the audience. "What's most important is the quilt.

"Quilting has a history we can trace back through the Middle Ages to Ancient Egypt. It may be even older, but few remnants have survived the hardships of time."

With the help from a teenager in the front of the room, the instructor lifted a large case onto the quilting table.

"*Harrumph.*" Wilma folded her arms. "What's Rebecca Cody doing here?"

"Her grandmother's one of the Busy Bees. Rebecca brings her to the meetings. I understand she's learning to quilt too."

"Why? I thought she wanted to learn basket weaving." Wilma tapped the flyer against her knee.

Mary realized the cause of Wilma's upset. The teenager worked part time at The Nature Museum alongside Wilma. No doubt, the older woman thought she had a willing candidate to learn basket weaving. Now, it looked like Rebecca had moved into the enemy camp.

"My guess is Rebecca still wants to learn whatever you can teach her. She's sixteen. Her mind is a sponge." A soft chuckle escaped Mary. "The girl wants to learn and do everything."

Wilma harrumphed again, a much mellower sound than last time. "Well, it's good to see she shows honor to her grandmother."

"I think so too."

With the flyer in her hand, Wilma gestured at the instructor. "This paper says she's supposed to talk about appliquéing."

Mary shrugged helplessly. "I don't know how these meetings are run. This is my first time too."

Wilma sat back, apparently ready to wait and see. Mary did the same. Then, the instructor said, "Because appliquéing is a form of embellishment, I thought you'd be interested in some history of quilts as decorator items."

"Are you referring to wall art, landscape quilts or clothing?" Beverly asked.

"Actually, all the fabric arts are interwoven." The instructor smiled sheepishly at the group. "No pun intended.

"Although technically, tapestries are not quilts, you can draw a line from those beautiful works of the Middle Ages to the most fanciful of today's pictorial quilts." She held up a plain white rectangle of several fabric thicknesses quilted together. "This is not one of them."

Subdued laughter rippled around the room. "Who knows? Maybe the design is sewn with invisible thread," quipped one of the quilters.

"It is a representative sample of the quilting brought to Europe in the twelfth century, most probably by men return-ing from the Crusades. They'd discovered their opponents, the Turks, wore layers of this under their armor. The padding offered warmth as well as protection during battle." She handed off the sample for the attendees to examine.

"Well, I'll be," whispered Wilma.

As though speaking just to her, the instructor continued, "The Turks and the Ottomans were not the first quilters. In its basic form, the art of stitching through padding sandwiched between layers of fabric is much older. One of the earliest examples dates back to 3400 BC. The work didn't survive, but an exquisite ivory carving from that era, the Egyptian First Dynasty, shows the pharaoh wearing a quilted mantle." She passed a picture of it to Rebecca who studied it for a moment before sending it down the first row.

"Quilted items were worn for warmth, protection and con-venience. Many think quilts began as bed coverings. In fact, the word *quilt* is derived from the Latin *culcita*, which means a padded and tied mattress. Yet antiquity gives us decorative uses as well. A quilted carpet was found in a Siberian cave tomb. Quilted linen slippers made an appearance on the Silk Road between AD 600 and 900, and quilted petticoats were all the rage in France in the seventeenth century.

"Climate often determined how quilts were used. In Europe, quilted draperies and bed hangings kept out the cold and damp and added unexpected beauty. Henry VIII commissioned a quilt of green silk with gold thread and a central medallion of roses and pomegranates."

She removed a small blue and white coverlet. "In the 1700–1800s, well-made bed quilts became quite valuable and were handed down from one generation to the next. This is a small replica of the one George Washington's mother bequeathed to him in her will."

Mary was enthralled. Things couldn't have worked out better. And the timing was so short, there was no way the instructor could have prepared the historical perspective just because Wilma was coming tonight. Perfect.

"Quilts preserve memories. They depict family trees and history." The instructor shook out a quilt that brought a gasp from the entire group. An enormous oak reigned over a green valley and blue sky. In its bountiful branches, embroidered names and dates marked the growth of a family.

"Sometimes, the most important aspect of quilting is not the sewing," the instructor said softly. "It's the relationships it fosters. Crafts done in the company of others provide community, conversation and camaraderie. The quilting bee wasn't exclusive to early America. Throughout history, whenever women gather to work together, they gain friendships along with experience."

Mary took her time examining each of the pieces as they came her way. The hours, skill and patience required to make them both humbled and inspired her. Beside her, Wilma said nothing, though her fingers often traced the designs.

After the meeting, she and Wilma took advantage of the instructor's offer and looked through a large book containing photographs of her work. Both women were stunned by the quantity and variety. Some quilts were embellished with lace, ribbons and felt designs. Others boasted elegant patterns of brilliant colors but were made for utilitarian purposes.

Afterwards, Wilma fingered a hand-stitched, crib-sized baby quilt displayed at the back of the store. "I like this one."

"Ah, it appeals to the grandma in you," Beverly said from behind them. "The founder of the Busy Bee Quilting Society, Betsy Lyle, made that for her grandson years ago. He donated it to the Society when he moved off the island."

"I can't imagine parting with something this special," Wilma whispered, tracing the figure of Noah at the helm of an ark full of cuddly animals. "Didn't he see the love in here?"

Mary remembered that the Lord gives wisdom and from His mouth comes knowledge and understanding. Tonight may not have swayed Wilma completely, but it had definitely softened her.

WEDNESDAY MORNING, Abby and Hugo worked inside one of the Thanksgiving displays, arranging and securing the final additions to the exhibit. She'd used the opportunity to bring him up to date on her investigation of the missing ring.

"I'd like your opinion," she said. "Am I too close to the situation to see it clearly?"

"I don't think so." He straightened an errant feather in the plumage of a wild turkey. The display wiggled and he frowned. "Logic says the ring is gone."

"I didn't want to hear that," Abby sighed.

Hugo stuck out his hand and waggled his fingers. She slapped the small hammer into his palm and went to work securing the bushes in back with the cordless screwdriver. Between the two of them, they'd finished in record time.

Too bad she couldn't say the same about finding the missing ring.

"Yesterday afternoon," he said, "I ran into Candace over at Holloway's Hardware. The way she talked, I doubt there's anywhere she hasn't looked."

Abby stiffened and Hugo sat back on his heels.

"Precisely." He stroked his mustache. "I consider myself a man of discretion, but I may not be the only one outside the party she's spoken with. If she continues this course, sooner or later, William Jansen will get wind of it."

Abby felt herself deflate like a pricked balloon. "This is going from bad to worse."

"I believe so. You must discover what happened to the missing ring," Hugo said softly. "Quickly and quietly."

"Easier said than done." She gathered her tools and scooted out of the exhibit. "So far, I've only spoken with Al and Sven." She looked directly at Hugo. "Al doesn't set off any warning bells. Sven has rung the whole carillon. He knows an awful lot about gemstones—real and synthetic.

"And I can't discount what he told me about Nathaniel." Abby looked away. "I can't fathom any reason for him to have muddied his shoes."

"Then you don't have the whole picture."

Managing his exit from the display with more dignity than she thought possible, Hugo followed her out of the structure.

"I'd hoped it wouldn't come to this," he said solemnly while putting the tools in their proper drawers. "There's something I must tell you."

Abby rested on the stepladder and waited.

A few tense moments passed, then he closed the lid and sat on the toolbox. "In my explorations of local history and lore, I learned of a con man who once roamed Vancouver, Victoria and several of the big cities along the West Coast."

Her hopes rising, she leaned forward, counting on Hugo to know the nitty-gritty details. A bona fide shyster might be the answer she sought. "Who is he?"

Hugo rubbed his elbow and looked over both shoulders.

Sensing his unease, she lowered her voice to a whisper and repeated. "Who is he?"

"'Digger' Dawks was his name. He was a real legend in his own time."

"Was?" Hoping her disappointment wasn't too evident, she murmured, "You're talking about a historical figure?"

"Not exactly. Digger was active in this area until about thirty years ago."

"Was he caught?"

"Once. While out on bail, he disappeared. His wife and son had to sell their home to pay the bail bondsman."

"How awful. Did Digger go back to his old ways?"

"No one knows where he went or what happened to him. Some said he died. Others thought he'd moved to the East Coast. There was even some speculation he'd gotten religion, as they say. But I doubt it."

"Why? Don't you think a con man can repent?"

"I'm sure some do." Hugo rubbed his palms together uneasily. "I doubt it was the case here."

This time she checked for eavesdroppers. Satisfied the wing was deserted, she said, "What are you trying to tell me, Hugo? This person has ties to Sparrow Island?"

"I know you to be a woman of great discretion, Abby. Nevertheless, I feel a tremendous responsibility. You must keep this confidential."

His nonanswer said she was on the mark. A swindler was the equivalent of a thief. The methods might be different, but the results were the same. A thief with ties to the island was a factor she hadn't considered. Rather than try to rush Hugo into revealing the identity he guarded, she reminded him gently, "You know I'll honor your confidence."

"Yes, I do." Satisfied, Hugo ensured their privacy with another careful assessment of their surroundings. "Digger Dawks is Nathaniel Dawkins's father."

Abby felt her chin drop and her eyes widen. Of all the people at the party, she would have never guessed Nathaniel carried such a dark secret from his childhood.

Pulling herself together, she swallowed thickly. Asking if Hugo was sure about Nathaniel's connection with Digger Dawks would be an insult. The steely set of Hugo's blue eyes convinced her he wouldn't have shared this secret unless he thought it was critical.

"After his mother left the Northwest, Nathaniel stayed," Hugo said quietly. "He was a young fellow wanting to make his mark on the world. Mostly, he wanted out from under the shadow of his father's reputation, but he wasn't going to run from a place he loved."

Abby immediately sympathized. Even one kid caught in a dilemma like that was one too many.

"Our Nathaniel is a caring individual. He didn't have it in him to totally divest himself of his father's surname. Yet, considering Digger might still be active in his . . . chosen profession, Nathaniel had to do something. So he legally changed his last name from Dawks to Dawkins."

"Then he came here," Abby surmised. "And opened The Complete Boater."

Hugo nodded. "The islands weren't quite so popular in those days. Few people were investing in our little town. I wasn't here yet so you would know better than I the criteria Islanders used to judge a man."

"By his actions," she said. "But now, if people learn about the missing ring and who his father was . . ."

"That's part of my concern. There has to be a reasonable explanation for Nathaniel's muddy shoes. Some folks may think the apple doesn't fall far from the tree. If they learn what we've just discussed, they'll immediately assume he's the thief. I'd hate to have a good man's reputation sullied. The genie doesn't ever fit back into the bottle once it's let out."

"Sad but true." She checked her watch. Speaking with Nathaniel was imperative. The sooner she had an explanation for what Sven saw, the better. "I don't have anything pressing this afternoon—"

"Excellent. Take the rest of the day off. In fact, take as much time as you need to solve this mystery. But please be here for the demonstration by the Northwest Native American Basket Weavers."

"Absolutely. I wouldn't miss the opportunity to show off The Nature Museum, and we'll have a crowd. Meanwhile,

I'll check in with you often," Abby assured him. "Plus you have my cell number."

"Of course." Hugo straightened the cuffs of his shirt. "Keep me posted and I'll keep my ears open too."

"Great."

After retrieving her purse and jacket from her office, Abby drove into town to The Complete Boater.

She'd enjoyed Nathaniel's verbal sparring at the party. As the Banker, he'd regaled her and the other guests with his command of 1920s slang. In fact, the more she thought about him, the more she realized he'd been an ideal guest. Not only had he adopted the appropriate lingo, his attire had been impeccable for his role, right down to the natty spats.

Struck by an oddity, she paused at the door to his store. What did he do with his spats? She didn't recall seeing them mud-spattered. Had Sven told her more than he actually saw? Determined to find out, she pushed on the door.

It didn't budge.

Startled, she realized she'd been so absorbed in her thoughts she hadn't been paying attention to her surroundings. The Complete Boater's windows were dark. She jiggled the doorknob. Locked tight.

Disappointed, she tried to come up with a plausible reason for Nathaniel to close in the middle of a workday. Maybe he didn't need one. With winter rushing in, business slowed to a crawl. Maybe he'd taken a day off.

She checked the sign by the side of the door to see when he'd return. The only thing there was a CLOSED placard hanging crookedly in the window.

CHAPTER ❦ TWELVE

Abby took a step away from the door, then looked back at The Complete Boater. The locked doors and darkened building bothered her more than they should, and with Hugo's secret fresh on her mind, she knew why.

Nathaniel wasn't the first proprietor to close unexpectedly for a day. Storeowners were people, too, and experienced their fair share of emergencies. As a single man, he had fewer of those than his married-with-children counterparts. Then again, the reason didn't have to be earth shaking. It could be something as benign as needing a little time to oneself. Or as mundane as a dentist's appointment.

She thought of the occasions when she'd been so busy at Cornell, filing the paperwork for grants and studies, there'd been no time for a bird walk. Only the knowledge she could spend the entire weekend outside had kept her from slipping off for an hour or two.

Perhaps Nathaniel had a similar yen. Maybe he'd simply grown tired of the four walls and flat floor of his store and taken a spur-of-the-moment jaunt in his boat. Her father often said there was nothing like standing on the deck with the wind in his sails and the sea rolling beneath his feet.

As her feet carried her away from the locked door, she knew Hugo's revelations were the underlying cause of her uneasy suspicions. She needed to put a stop to those thoughts pronto. Tarring the son with the father's actions was the very thing Hugo sought to avoid.

From now on, she'd have to be extremely careful; examine her findings two or three times. These were her friends. She had to be absolutely sure of her conclusions. Swallowing against the queasiness in her stomach, she found a much deeper sympathy for Candace.

As though her feet were in charge and knew where to go, Abby crossed Primrose Lane. *Great*, she thought, *new avenues to explore are exactly what I need.*

She raised the collar of her warm coat against a chill wind. This time of year, numerous squalls raced through the islands. Out in the strait, the harbinger of another storm teased the water with fitful breezes. As though irritated with the superficial disturbance, the ocean responded by frosting the waves with whitecaps.

Abby tugged her coat closer and walked briskly to The Dorset. She loved everything about the old hotel, its history, elegance and ambiance. Originally, the home of a railroad tycoon, the four-story mansion had been converted into one of the most prestigious hotels in the San Juan Islands.

Its owner, Keith Gordon, had done an excellent job of preserving the building's antique charm while expanding the hotel's reputation.

Many guests were regular visitors. Others, usually locals from the mainland or the surrounding islands looked for

reasons to reserve the hotel library for meetings or small con-
ferences. The steady influx of guests meant The Dorset's
upscale day spa was often fully booked. The experienced staff
knew how to pamper guests and held nothing back, particularly when a wedding filled the elegant ballroom.

Entering through the polished brass doors, Abby drank in
the sight of the gleaming floors and lustrous cherry furnish-
ings. Dust must avoid the hotel. There was no other way to
explain its total absence every time she visited.

Drawn by the flames dancing in the large fireplace, she
passed the conversation area featuring a circular sofa tufted in
red velvet. After detouring around a youngish couple carrying
several brochures for whale-watching tours, she arrived at the
Persian carpet in front of the hearth.

Warmth curled around her legs. She sighed with pleasure
and unbuttoned her coat. Thanking the Lord for the unexpected blessing, she stretched her cold fingers out to the blaze
and decided to take a few minutes to indulge. When she was
good and toasty, she'd get busy and look for Keith Gordon.

Suddenly he stood beside her. Dressed in a dark business
suit, snow-white shirt and subdued burgundy and charcoal
striped tie, he exuded an Old World charm. "Good afternoon,
Abby." His friendly grin revealed sparkling teeth instead of the
blackened disguise he'd worn as the gin-ger-ale runner. "'Tis a
brisk day we're having."

Enjoying his Scottish brogue, she shook his offered hand
and marveled again at his easy manner. "Yes, it is, which is why
I was surprised to find The Complete Boater closed."

"It is?" Keith's brow knit. "Nathaniel talked about taking
his sloop out. If he did, it's a good time businesswise, but the
weather leaves a bit to be desired."

Abby shrugged. Right now, she had to take advantage of

Keith's free time. His openness renewed her confidence. The discussion ahead would be ticklish, but he was adept at handling uncomfortable situations. He did so with such aplomb everyone walked away feeling like a winner.

Hoping to find a more private spot, she glanced around the lobby. "Can you spare a few minutes to talk with me?"

"Aye." His soft tone imparted his understanding. He gestured toward a hallway beside the reception desk. "Let's go to my office. You can join me for a cup of hot tea."

"I'd love to." Her smile broadened. Keith was an astute man, as well as a perceptive business owner. He led her down the short hall.

Three of the walls of his office were hunter green with dark wood wainscoting. The fourth was an expanse of glass overlooking the hotel's inner courtyard. It didn't seem to matter what season or how moody the weather, the immaculately groomed area had flowers in bloom. Today, chrysanthemums in gold, russet and claret added seasonal color to the evergreen shrubs lining the brick walkways.

Ivy topiaries provided a Thanksgiving themed backdrop to the stands of corn sheaves, pumpkins and colorful gourds.

Seated in a comfortable wingback chair and sipping a hot cup of tea, Abby looked up at her host. "For what it's worth, I am impressed. You do an excellent job of making this a first-rate hotel."

Beaming brightly, he said, "Coming to work is a labor of love, not a job. The day it becomes drudgery . . . Ah, that'll be the day I'll put this grand dame on the market." He settled in his leather desk chair. "Now, what brings you to The Dorset in the middle of the day, Abby?"

She wondered if Candace had gotten around to calling

Keith. Even though the two of them were good friends, he could be intimidating. Rather than verbally fence with the hotelier, Abby decided to come right to the point. "Has Candace called you about Brandi's missing engagement ring?"

Keith nodded sadly. "It was with great distress she did so. The misery in her voice hurt me. She's such a sensitive lass. I'm telling you true, I took no offense to the implications she tried so hard not to make."

Abby winced. For one of the partygoers, the thorny ramifications included a possible felony charge. "This is a difficult situation."

"Since she called, I've given the party and the people who attended a great bit of thought." Keith raised his cup toward her as though making a toast. "I pretended I was you, Abby."

She laughed. "Why would you do that?"

"You have a knack for finding the truth. It's an enviable skill to have. I'm trying to sharpen mine."

"Really?" She sat up and regarded him. "Let me get this straight. You're trying to hone this skill in yourself?"

"Absolutely. As a hotelier, it's incumbent on me to protect my guests. I've made it my business to learn the various 'tells' of criminals who prey on unsuspecting vacationers. I also train my employees. Watching out for predators is something we do every day. The Dorset's reputation depends on how well we develop our skills."

"I didn't realize you were a sleuth." She tipped her head and raised her cup as a gesture for him to continue.

"I hadn't thought of myself as such. It's one thing to invite friends into our homes as Candace invited all of us to the party." He grinned suddenly. "I had a bonny good time."

Abby returned the grin. "So did I."

"Back to my explanation. Unlike a private residence—yours, mine or Candace's—a hotel is a special place. Here at The Dorset, we don't know who's coming through the front door. Are they old friends or an accomplished band of thieves? The best defense is to be canny and prepared. Learn how to watch people. Pick out the wolves in sheep's clothing."

This aspect of the hotel business gave Abby a new appreciation for Keith. "I suspect you're a very shrewd—and accurate—judge of people. You're able to size up a guest within a few minutes, aren't you?"

"Usually," he answered modestly. "Every now and then one fools me. But not often enough to cause a great deal of grief."

Mentally returning to the night of the party, she reviewed the image of Keith as a bootlegger, a gin-ger-ale runner. Despite his unsavory attire and artificially blackened front teeth, he'd mingled adeptly with the other guests.

She doubted that, dressed as he had been, he'd garner the same reception in a real-life scenario. "What did you observe about Candace's guests? Anything in particular?"

"Other than I'm not the next Sherlock Holmes?"

"Neither am I." Abby laughed softly. "But earlier, you spoke about 'tells'. . ."

"Tells are nonverbal behaviors. Clues to what's going on inside a person. Poker players study each other's tells constantly. Knowing a gambler rubs his chin when he's holding a pair is a significant advantage."

Abby's eyes widened. "I see . . ."

"Nonverbal cues exist everywhere. The clumsy person bumping into others might be self-conscious or just lack grace. More likely, though, in a public setting, he's a thief, lifting wallets and taking money out of purses."

"What tells did you notice at Candace's house on Saturday night?"

"None that fit the usual profile of a thief." Keith stood and walked to the window. A strong gust of wind swirled down into the atrium, ruffling the outer leaves of the corn stalks beside the benches. "I didn't sleep much last night," he admitted. "Frankly, I did a great deal of praying and more than my share of scheming."

Abby was pleased to hear another of the partygoers spent time praying on the distressing matter. But as far as the other, she asked, "Scheming? What do you mean?"

He barked out a self-deprecating laugh. "'Tis not something I'm proud of, but it crossed my mind to go see Gordon Seibert and have a duplicate ring made."

Abby gulped. "You didn't."

"Nay." He gave an embarrassed shrug. "Temptation comes in many forms. I felt so bad for Candace, I wanted to help the wee lass." He shook his head sadly. "Getting a replacement ring would be as dishonest as taking the original. Even if my conscience hadn't balked, which it did, I couldn't've described the ring if my life depended on it."

Nodding sympathetically, Abby said, "Even if you managed to get a replica, you would've had to lie and pretend you 'found' it."

"Aye. That would be just as wrong as actually taking it. The thing is, I wanted to fix the problem. But God and I know it's out of my hands." Keith moved to the leather chair behind the desk.

Abby trusted God had a reason for this mystery at this time. He'd put it squarely in her path. She knew He'd lead her where He wanted her to go.

"All of us gathered at the fireplace at one time or another," Keith continued. "I saw Brandi place the ring on the mantel, but I didn't notice it after that. We were all too intent on staying in character and trying to win the game.

"Now I wish I'd paid more attention." Keith leaned back in his chair. "Anything could have happened to it—including getting tossed out with the trash. I'm afraid our reputations might wind up there too."

"Candace and Bradford went through the trash. They didn't find anything."

"Too bad."

"When did you last see the ring?"

"When Brandi put it on the mantel. Rather obviously, as I recall. Only Candace, and maybe Bradford, really know Brandi. Until Saturday night, she was a stranger to the rest of us. Even now, I can't say that what I learned about her during the party is really her or the role she played."

"Excellent observation," Abby agreed as her thoughts ran off in another direction. Keith had easily switched roles from hotelier to bootlegger and back again. He'd used the subtle tells he'd studied to flesh out the gin-ger-ale runner. His facility suggested a mastery of misdirection.

Keith tented his fingers and rested his hands on the desk. "I wonder if I'm too much of a skeptic or if Brandi was too trusting."

Abby set her teacup aside. "I ran into her at The Green Grocer. She struck me as an open, sincere person. Apparently, she felt at home at Candace's. And why shouldn't she? They're cousins."

"You're right. Sometimes people are too naïve for their own good." Keith sounded frustrated and resigned. "At The Dorset we try to cultivate a feeling of hominess. We succeed much too well at times. Although we ask them not to, guests leave valuables in plain sight in their rooms.

"We offer in-room safes and inform our guests of the availability of the big safe." He gestured toward the black behemoth with gold lettering built into the back corner of his office. "And still they leave expensive jewelry, watches and wallets on their dressers or beds. It makes the staff nervous."

He straightened his tie. "I can't understand why Candace hasn't brought in Sergeant Cobb to investigate. Here at the hotel, we like to nip problems in the bud—before they've a chance to bloom into disaster."

Abby recalled Henry voicing the same opinion. Although she agreed there was merit to the idea, she wasn't convinced it would hasten a solution. Instead, she became more certain she needed to continue her investigation and rely on God's timing.

CHAPTER 🌸 THIRTEEN

WEDNESDAY EVENING MARY watched her sister close her eyes and inhale.

"*Mmm,*" Abby purred, exhaling. "I love the way your store smells. It's like being in the midst of hundreds of bouquets or a heavenly garden."

"Glad you stopped by to smell the flowers," Mary teased, although she couldn't help noticing the faint smudges of fatigue under her sister's eyes.

"Can I help you close up for the night?" Abby asked. "It's a small price to pay for such magnificent perfume."

"I'm just about done, but check these out." Mary pointed to the new display of terrariums she'd spent the afternoon assembling.

Abby bent to examine one with small pilgrim and turkey figurines. "These are really cute, but this one looks a little odd." She leaned closer. "I'd say the hunter is doing his best to ignore the turkey."

"You'd be right. It's the Bobby McDonald influence. But thanks for noticing. They were fun to make."

Abby straightened and adjusted her purse strap over her shoulder. "Since we have Bible study tonight why don't we let the Springhouse Café fix dinner?"

"Good idea." Mary closed the cash register drawer and secured the bank bag. "I need to make a drop-off at the night deposit first. It may take a while. Finnegan hasn't quite gotten the knack of keypads and drop drawers yet."

At the mention of his name, the service dog came to attention.

"Would you like me to do it and meet you at the restaurant?" Abby volunteered.

"Hey, yes, I would. It's getting late and you doing the deposit will save some time." Appreciative of the countless ways her sister stepped in, Mary handed over the bank bag. "I'll get us a table at the Springhouse." She knuckled the favored spot behind the dog's ear. "I have food for you in the van. How about you eat while we do Bible study?"

His small woof of agreement made both women smile.

Ten minutes later, they met at the table Mary had secured in Green Harbor's busiest dining spot. "It's a good thing you came ahead," Abby said as she slipped into her chair.

"And it's a good thing you did the deposit or I'd still be enroute," Mary agreed. "A big wave of patrons arrived just after I did. For some reason everyone wants to eat out tonight."

A large group squeezed by. Automatically, she reached down to put a calming hand on Finnegan's head and to make sure no one stepped on him. As usual, the reassurance was only psychological. He lay with his back against the big left wheel of her chair, his legs tucked close to his body.

Nevertheless, she felt she'd done something for him and he seemed to enjoy her concern.

"How's Candace doing?" Abby asked.

Mary groaned. It physically hurt to see her dear friend and stalwart employee in such a quandary. Before answering, she drew a quieting breath and opened her menu. "Most of the time Candace is her normal, serene self. But every now and then she's . . . I don't know, angry, hurt, exasperated." Mary lowered the menu so she could see over it. "All at the same time."

"Total frustration," Abby said. "I can relate."

"Even though they've searched everywhere, she wants to believe the ring is still in the house. She can be stubborn, and in this case doggedly so."

"What you're describing doesn't sound typical of Candace. You know her much better than I do. Why do you think she's behaving this way?"

"I'd say it has to do with conviction. One of Candace's most endearing qualities is her loyalty to her friends. She just can't believe anything bad about any of them. I suspect that when she gets to the point of even considering someone took the ring, she'll get a heated case of the heebie-jeebies."

The waitress chose that moment to take their drink order. Because they knew what they wanted, they ordered their food too.

Mary turned her attention back to Abby. "Are you having any luck with your investigation?"

"Yes and no." Abby toyed with her place setting. "I've just started my rounds of the partygoers so it's much too early to form any conclusions."

Mary recognized her sister's contemplative look and measured tone of voice. "No guilty culprit is ready to jump up and take the blame, I gather?"

"Afraid not. But I'm learning more about our friends, about what makes them tick." Signaling with her eyes, Abby continued lightly, "Speaking of friends, a couple of yours are headed this way."

Mary braced her hands on the arms of her chair, pushed up and turned to look. Two members of the Busy Bee Quilting Society headed straight for their table.

Beverly Hodges in flowing trousers and Ana Dominguez in a brightly colored dress were a study in contrasts. Tall, willowy Beverly often wore 1940s hairdos like those in the old movies she loved. Never mind the styles went out of fashion twenty years before she was born.

Ana kept her long, black hair tamed in a pair of neat braids that nearly reached her waist. She preferred beribboned blouses and colorful skirts.

"You might ask them to join us," Abby suggested. "There aren't any empty tables."

Mary cocked her head giving her sister a "we'll see" message. Abby looked weary, in need of a quiet meal and a soothing change of pace. Another controversy might not be the best of dinner companions, and Mary wanted to test the waters there first.

After they'd all greeted one another Beverly told Mary, "Things were a bit chaotic last night after you and Wilma left. I'm amazed she actually came to a Busy Bee gathering. How did you manage to convince her?"

Mary was sure she saw a Divine hand opening a door of opportunity. She had to make the most of it. "Why don't the two of you join us for dinner? I have a few things to tell you while we eat." *And hopefully keep the conversation steered to lighthearted subjects.*

Abby scooted over. "Mary and I have already ordered, but just barely. There shouldn't be too much of a gap. Do you know what you want from the menu?"

As though on cue, the waitress appeared. Even before she handed out menus, Ana and Beverly both ordered the evening's special.

"That's one good thing about a small town with a limited number of restaurants." Beverly spread her napkin over her lap. "Not only do you run into friends, it's easy to memorize the menu."

"*Sí.* Much easier than memorizing Juan's work schedule. This month he's working the late shift at the clinic." Ana removed her coat and hung it over the back of her chair. "Fortunately for me, I have good friends to share the evening meal with when he's at work."

In the brief exchange of looks between the two women, Mary was very glad she and Abby had offered to share their table. Every now and then, she needed little reminders of how something that seemed small and insignificant to her could make a big difference in another person's life.

"Back to Wilma," Beverly prompted. "I never expected to see her at a Busy Bee meeting. Does it mean she's ready to concede?"

Laughing, Mary shook her head. "Not by a country mile." She watched Beverly and Ana as she recounted her discussions with the basket weaver. Their body language indicated they were more interested than they'd verbally admit. Mary found it very heartening.

She also discovered she didn't want to abdicate her spot between the weavers and the quilters. She'd rather take her role as judge and morph it into something along the lines of an information facilitator. Get the two sides talking and sharing. To keep moving in that direction, she had to keep each side curious about the other.

Abby seemed to clue in intuitively. She leaned forward and

said, "Wilma told me this morning the meeting surpassed her expectations. If I were you, I'd call it high praise. When it comes to creative arts, she's not easy to please."

Just then, the waitress demonstrated the efficiency of the Springhouse kitchen staff by delivering the four meals together.

After a silent prayer of thanks, Ana said, "I can't wait until the next Busy Bee meeting. My prize delivery came today."

"What prize is that?" Abby poured hot tea into her cup.

"One I've been waiting for for over a month. Finally, this afternoon I received a bolt of genuine Turkey red. I am so fortunate to get it."

"Turkey red. Sounds like something sold in the saloon of an old western movie," Mary said facetiously, knowing she was revealing a distinct lack of knowledge.

"Oh no." Beverly shook her head emphatically. "Turkey red cloth is special. Very desirable."

"Special to Thanksgiving?" Abby asked. "Or something else?"

Clearly at a loss for the right words, Ana rolled her warm, brown eyes in a manner that said all those present were understating the facts. "Special as in kind. No. One of a kind."

"You mean a particular shade of red?" The idea was almost too much for Mary. From fall's deep russets and merlots to the candy cane colors of Christmas, there were so many tones and hues of red, she didn't even try to match them from memory. Without a color swatch, she was lost.

"Many quilters think Turkey red is a specific color," Beverly said. "But it isn't. It's a special dye process that produces a rich, colorfast bluish-red."

"A hand-dyed fabric?" Mary knew anything hand-done would be quite expensive.

"*Si.* It got the name long ago, hundreds of years. The secret belonged to the people of Turkey. You know how it is with secrets. Everyone wants to know them. Same thing here. They want to know the process and the ingredients.

"But once this secret was out"—Ana waved her left hand dismissively—"the cloth manufacturers threw up their hands. The recipe took too long. It was too complicated."

"What made it complicated?" The way Abby leaned toward Ana made Mary smile. Her sister loved ferreting out the fine details of any complexity—an essential quality for becoming the island's sleuth.

"First the yarn or the cloth to be dyed is thoroughly cleaned by boiling it in alkali," Beverly explained. "Then they steep the material in rancid olive or castor oil, soda—"

She looked around. "The uh, let's just say the rest of the ingredients are not suitable dinner conversation. Everything is cooked in a large cauldron. The whole process takes about three weeks, sometimes more."

Mary could guess what a vat of steeping rancid oil smelled like. From the looks on Beverly and Ana's faces, the other ingredients probably smelled worse. "Okay, I get the picture. We have a stinky secret process."

"How does it make the fabric special?" Abby asked.

"The color doesn't run and it doesn't fade." Ana's forehead puckered as she searched for the right words. "In the old days, such a red was all but impossible. Old dyes made from madder root were more orange than red. But the bad thing— they would bleed every time they got wet. This red never does. It wears with the fabric."

She kept her gaze fixed on Abby. "You like to wear denim out in the woods. You have favorite old jeans you always reach for, no?"

Abby nodded an affirmative.

"Turkey red is like the denim blue. It takes much wear, but in time, the rubbing places turn white. Same thing with Turkey red. You wear it out."

Satisfied they'd all learned something new, the foursome ate in silence for several minutes while their food was still warm. Then Beverly asked, "Did you hear about the expensive ring that went missing after a party last weekend?"

Mary met Abby's gaze across the table. "What about it?"

"I heard nothing," Ana said. "Who lost a ring?"

Mary could have hugged Ana for saying "lost" instead of jumping to a different conclusion. "The ring belongs to Candace's houseguest and cousin. During a small get-together, the ring was misplaced and they're still looking for it."

"Why did she take it off in the first place?"

Leave it to Ana to ask the practical questions. Before Mary could respond, Abby spoke. "The ring was loose. Brandi removed it and it got misplaced. I'm sure she feels bad enough about it."

"I'll bet she does," Beverly asserted. "Rumor is the ring was stolen."

Abby caught and held Beverly's gaze. "Rumors are nothing but wildfires of gossip. Please don't fan the flames of this one by passing it along. Innocent people could get burned and their reputations charred."

"You're right," Beverly said solemnly, pushing her empty plate forward. "There's already enough talk and I don't want to be responsible for more."

Ana clasped Abby's forearm. "It is not good to have people looking at neighbors with suspicion. It makes them ugly and angry. We want to have a peaceful Thanksgiving and Christmas. We trust you will solve this mystery."

"I'm working on it." Somewhat mollified, Abby still looked

none too pleased at how readily the news was circulating through the town.

"If we can help . . ." Beverly offered. Ana eagerly nodded her agreement.

Mentally, Mary held her breath and stepped out in faith. "There is something you can do. A way you can help to ensure a pleasant Thanksgiving and Christmas."

"What is it?"

Holding Beverly's gaze and silently praying for her cooperation, Mary answered, "Bring the Busy Bee Quilting Society to The Nature Museum this Friday or Saturday. Members of the Native American Basket Weavers will be demonstrating their dyeing and weaving methods. It's a terrific opportunity right here in our own backyard. We can all learn about the weaving arts from master weavers."

"I don't know . . ." Beverly's protest faded.

Ana leaned forward. "They will be dyeing materials?"

Mary nodded. "The quilters might pick up some good tips, especially those who dye their own fabrics."

"This, I would like to see. And it would be good for me to watch how they do their weaving. I may try it in my wall hangings." Ana pulled a little notebook out of her purse and checked the dates. "*Si*. I can change Friday's schedule."

"What about you, Beverly?" Abby coaxed gently.

"Friday afternoon?" she asked, her gaze meeting Ana's.

"*Si*," Ana said stubbornly. "I want to go. How can you say one thing is better or more difficult than another thing if you do not know what goes into it?"

Thank You, Lord.

"Well . . . all right then. I'll come."

CHAPTER ✿ FOURTEEN

THURSDAY MORNING AFTER seeing Mary off to visit their mother, Abby returned to the living room, then stood by the sliding door to the deck. Outside, some of the trees bordering the yard were already bare. Their bony limbs pointed at the wintry sky. At their feet, the tired grass huddled under a windblown shawl of orange and yellow leaves.

Folding her arms and rubbing them, Abby imagined Mary's arrival at their parents' home. The air would be redolent with the scent of spiced tea and a homemade cinnamon treat. A cozy fire would be blazing in the hearth, the stage set for Mom and Mary to work in secret on their Christmas presents.

The two would have a marvelous time, knitting, chatting and laughing. Abby smiled and whispered, "Let love and faithfulness never leave you." She was happy for them, tickled that their shared passion brought them such joy, and delighted her own presence wasn't required.

Her passion soared on feathered wings. Even on her best knitting day, she seldom lasted an hour before she started feeling like a caged bird desperate for freedom. As far back as she could remember, whenever the Stanton women pulled out their yarn, she slipped out the back door and ran down to the barn, or the dreaming rock, or any of the other great bird-watching sites on the farm.

Wishing she had time today to indulge in her great love, she went through the dining room, straightened the table runner and headed for the garage. The sooner she solved the mystery of the missing ring, the sooner she could scoot over to Paradise Cove and watch the migrating cormorants settle in with their local cousins.

In Green Harbor, Abby found a parking place equidistant from her twin destinations. After a quick stop for mochas at the Internet Café, she headed for Bayside Souvenirs.

Despite clear, blue skies and warm sunshine, the air was still chilly and few tourists roamed the city's sidewalks. In the water, harbor seals called to each other while gulls argued overhead. A pair of Canada geese kibitzed as they waddled down the sidewalk ahead of her. Harvest decorations surrounded by asters, chrysanthemums and yellow pansies filled the concrete pots along the curb.

Thanksgiving is nearly upon us, Abby thought, then we'll turn our attention toward Advent and the Christmas season.

The jingle bells on the door announced her entrance to Bayside Souvenirs.

"Good morning, Abby." Vibrant in a pink fleece jacket with matching pants and a cheery red turtleneck, Donna Morgan hurried forward. Red, white and clear cut glass beads sparkled on the fine gold earrings dangling from her ears. A matching pendant reflected the light with eye-catching brilliance.

"I came by to chat." Abby went up to the sales counter and set down the mochas.

"You come bearing gifts." Donna's left eyebrow rose questioningly. "Or is it bribes?"

"I call it mocha from the Internet Café." Abby picked up the cup closest to her and took a sip. The rare indulgence was for a good cause. And the extra calories were an excellent excuse to spend more time on her next bird walk. "*Ahh.* There's nothing like a fine blend of coffee and chocolate."

Donna put her left arm behind her back, leaned to the side and gave a mock grimace while she groaned, "I'll talk. I'll talk. You found my weak spot. Just don't take the mocha away from me."

Abby grinned at the theatrics. "You should have pursued a career on the stage."

Primping her naturally curly blonde hair, Donna batted her eyelashes. "I'm afraid Barbra Streisand cornered the market on blonde actresses with bumps on their noses."

The bump on Donna's nose came from a childhood bicycle accident. The break had left a noticeable bump midway up the slope of her nose. "I suppose she did get there first," Abby said. "But it's Broadway's loss and Sparrow Island's gain. Your performance at the party was outstanding."

Donna sipped her hot mocha. "I did make a decent villain, didn't I?"

In her role as a socialite slumming for the evening, the proprietress of Bayside Souvenirs had not only "murdered" the bouncer, she'd confounded most of the guests by convincing everyone—except Abby—that she couldn't possibly have been the culprit.

Proving Donna committed the deadly deed and knocked off Bradford had been surprisingly difficult. Recalling chorus girl Laverne's indignation, Abby chuckled. "Al's wife was your most ardent fan."

"Bless her heart. I thought she was going to cry when Bradford told her I really was guilty." The big diamond ring on Donna's right hand sparkled as she swirled her cup to mix the contents.

"Whoa," Abby gasped. "Where'd you get the eye-blinding rock?" She recognized Donna's other two rings. Elegant and understated, they were gifts from her parents years earlier.

Donna held out her hand and waggled her fingers. She rotated her wrist one way, then the other. Refractions of light shot through the store. "Nice, eh?"

"Shiny. Big. And very you." The shopkeeper reminded Abby of a magpie and the bird's preference for things bright and glittery.

Donna nodded. "Some people call it gaudy. I call it fun. I love anything that sparkles, shines or has a bazillion colors." She reached behind her, pulled a high stool around, and sat. "I also love online auctions and shopping. You can get such great deals."

"Did you get your diamond ring online?" Abby asked lightly.

The shopkeeper laughed and waggled her splayed fingers again. "It does look like a big, honking diamond, doesn't it?"

Noticing the shopkeeper's nail polish matched her fleece, Abby nodded. "Is it?"

"Heaven's no. It's a cubic zirconia." Donna planted her

heels on the stool's bottom rung. "Pardon me, but I've learned to sit when I have the opportunity." She blew at her bangs. "My holiday inventory is turning over so fast, there's a lot of sorting to do in the back room. I plan on starting today."

Remembering her last excursion into the store's back room and Donna's less than stellar organizational skills, Abby deemed it an excellent idea.

The shopkeeper grew serious. "Since it's only the two of us here, let's talk about a different ring."

Glad she brought up the subject first, Abby agreed, "Yes, let's. What were your impressions of it?"

"A bit too old fashioned for my taste. I like modern bling."

"Bling?" Abby repeated.

"Yeah. Isn't it a cool word? It's even in the dictionary now, so as far as the kids are concerned, it's passé. I still like it. It started out meaning expensive and ostentatious jewelry. Supposedly bling is the sound light makes when it hits a diamond."

"Oh my!" At Cornell, Abby never had to think about keeping up with the young people's vernacular. She was around them so much she'd simply absorbed their lingo. Now it seemed she'd have to pay closer attention.

Donna's grin turned conspiratorial. "I hear you've been asking around about the ring. Must be my turn now."

So much for being coy. "I'm hoping somebody remembers something that'll point in a new direction. Anything, no matter how small, might help."

Donna looked down at the glass countertop, her brows knit with concentration. "Actually, I remember quite a bit. I recall wondering why Brandi's engagement ring was loose and her wedding ring seemed to fit. Usually, they're the same size."

Abby blinked. She hadn't made that connection earlier. The next time she spoke with Brandi, she'd raise the question. "Excellent point, Donna."

"I also wondered why she was so cavalier about it." Donna rubbed the antique ring on her left hand. "I always wanted a real diamond. My wedding ring was a simple gold band from a chain discount store." Her head rose sharply. "Not that I'm knocking it. It's what we could afford."

"It isn't the ring that makes the marriage," Abby soothed.

"Don't I know it." Donna rapped her fingernails on the counter. "Larry always talked about getting me a diamond for our anniversary, but never did. When he left me for his college student, he bought her a ring very similar to Brandi's. I guarantee if I was going to steal a ring, it wouldn't be one that reminded me of my philandering ex-husband and the woman who replaced me."

Heartbreak lingered in the divorcee's blue eyes along with a steely resolve and Abby ached for her. Nothing hurt like a loved one's duplicity. "I'm so sorry. A betrayal like that cuts deep."

Donna did a double take, then her stare softened and her shoulders relaxed. Perhaps the empathy Abby couldn't hide had convinced the shopkeeper of her sincerity. Or Donna had just needed someone to validate the anguish she'd endured.

"Ya know, Abby, I'm guessing things came pretty easy for Brandi. Otherwise, she would have guarded that ring with her life. But I don't really know her." Donna gave a shaky laugh. "We didn't talk much about our real selves during the party."

Abby remembered the range of attitudes of the students at Cornell. Those struggling to pay for the privilege of attending seldom missed a class or failed to turn in an assignment.

Donna's observation was excellent. Those who worked hard for their dreams protected them.

"Sounds silly, doesn't it?" Donna continued. "There we were, talking up a storm while pretending to be other people. I gotta tell you, though, I had a blast. Playing the socialite let me spend a few hours in a vastly different world.

"Don't get me wrong. I love Sparrow Island and my shop." A sweeping arc of her hand encompassed the whole store. There wasn't an empty space anywhere. If three hundred tourists dropped in this afternoon, each of them could leave with several mementos of their visit. "I may have fake diamonds on my fingers, but this place is my real gem. And despite what happened with my ex, I thank God every morning that I'm here and it's my baby."

The probability of Donna Morgan being the thief dwindled to razor thin. Like Keith Gordon and the Minskys, the only reason any of them were still on the suspect list was the fact they'd attended the party.

Abby could almost hear her father *harrumph*. He'd say that was like being blamed for losing the Super Bowl just because you had a ticket to the game.

Although she felt a little silly doing so, she decided to finish asking her mental list of questions. "Do you recall anything unusual or odd during the party? Anyone doing or saying something out of character?" Shaking her head, she amended, "That is, both characters—the one they were playing and themselves."

"Glad you clarified that." Donna put a finger to her chin. "There was something. At the time, I just figured . . . I don't know . . ."

"What was it?"

Donna's left hand made uncertain circles in the air. "It sounds silly. I know Brandi's staying with Candace, so she was probably helping with the hostess duties."

"What was she doing?"

"Taking out the trash. Since you're asking, it seemed to me she picked an odd time to do it. It was still raining hard when I saw her come in the back door."

Donna shrugged. "Anyway, Brandi couldn't have been out there long. Her hair wasn't mussed. Neither was her gorgeous green sequin dress."

"Was that before or after she took off her ring?"

"I don't recall." Donna's eyes narrowed uncertainly and she shrugged. "Before. I think, but I'm not sure. So I guess it doesn't mean anything."

Not if Brandi was still wearing the ring. "Probably not. Thanks though."

"Hey, I appreciate the mocha." Donna raised the cup. "And the excellent company. I really hope you figure out what happened before the holiday season gets into full swing."

Suddenly she frowned and slid off the stool. "If this mystery shows up on the front page of *The Birdcall*, it could be disastrous for the whole island."

Abby raised a questioning brow. "The whole island?"

"Yeah. Think about it. Nearly everybody who was at the party owns a business here or works downtown. Who wants to shop in a store run by a suspected thief?"

CHAPTER ✿ FIFTEEN

Aᴠ ᴛᴇʀ ᴅ ʀ ᴏ ᴘ ᴘ ɪ ɴ ɢ   ᴀ
second stitch on the same row, Mary put her knitting on her
lap and folded her hands on top of the soft yarn. *Get a hold of
yourself,* she silently admonished. Discontent had no place in
her mother's cozy living room.

A special blend of tea Ellen was experimenting with for the
holidays steamed in delicate porcelain cups and perfumed the
air with a spicy rose fragrance. In the hearth, red and yellow
flames danced to the soft strains of Rimsky–Korsakov's
"Scheherazade."

Hoping to reclaim a sense of peace, Mary watched her
mother. In a wingback chair angled partly toward the fire and
mostly toward Mary's wheelchair, Ellen worked on a heavy
white cotton sweater, a fisherman's cable-knit. She made one
for her husband every few years.

The tradition had begun when they first moved to Sparrow
Island and he ran a charter boat business. In addition to an air
of seafaring dash, it provided welcome warmth. Even now,

with all his outside chores at the farm, he usually reached first for one of those handmade cable-knit sweaters.

"What is it, dear?" Ellen asked. At the end of a row, she automatically fingered the stitches, checking her tension and gauge. "Are you having trouble with your pattern?"

"It's not the pattern, Mom. It's me. I'm having trouble staying focused."

Ellen stowed her knitting in the canvas bag at the side of her chair. "It's the silly quarrel between the weavers and quilters, isn't it?"

"Yeah." Mary put her project away and picked up her teacup. "I'm beginning to see that this is a huge task. It's crazy to think one person could judge all the pieces fairly."

"I quite agree. It's simply not practical to expect you or anyone to visit every home on Sparrow Island and look at all the quilts and baskets before the deadline."

"Mercy," Mary gasped and quickly gulped her tea before she spilled it. Fortunately, it had cooled enough to go down easily. "I never thought of doing such a thing, but you're right. Some people will expect it. They'll think one more example will turn the decision another way."

Mary was so shaken, her teacup rattled on the saucer, so she returned it to the table. "Well, the home visits are impossible. I'm overwhelmed as it is."

Ellen gave an inquiring look.

Suspecting her mother already had a good idea of all the undercurrents the dispute had put in motion, Mary took the opportunity to unburden. "Everyone seems to have a different slant on what's most important. Is it the history and traditions associated with the craft? Is it the artistry of the designs or the selection of the materials? Is it the practicality or the execution?"

Mary sat back and rolled her shoulders, trying to shed some

of the tension she'd been carrying since the "judgeship" had been thrust upon her.

"What do *you* think is most important? What one thing stands out in front of all the rest?"

When no ready answer presented itself, Mary shrugged and looked away. Yet as her gaze drifted across the quilted cozy on the teapot, the crocheted doilies under the lamps, and the embroidered tea towel on the tray, she realized the struggle wasn't just between quilts and baskets. It was a collision of traditions that, if not handled delicately, could cause ill will throughout Sparrow Island for years.

"Mom, I'm sorry. I think I'd better go see Wilma at The Nature Museum."

Ellen finished replenishing her teacup. "Why don't you call first? Perhaps you could arrange to meet her in a more private setting than where she works."

"Ugh. I should've thought of that."

Happiness dancing in her blue eyes, Ellen offered the cordless phone. "I'm glad you didn't. It gave me a chance to help you for a change."

"You're the best, Mom." Mary took the instrument and called The Nature Museum.

Wilma answered after the first ring and eagerly agreed to Mary's proposition they get together. "I'd planned to take the afternoon off. Ida's covering for me and she came in early, so I can leave now. If you like, I'll meet you at my place, okay? Do you know how to get there?"

Delighted, Mary reviewed the directions, then hung up. "Well, that was easy," she told her mother. "I hope the rest of it is."

"It will be." Ellen retrieved Mary's coat and helped her put it on. "Keep an open mind and love in your heart."

On the familiar admonition, Mary put on her rain hat and

went out to the van. Once inside, she watched Finnegan shake himself before jumping aboard.

"Atta boy," she told him. "Now cover the seat."

He gripped the corner of a waterproof flannel sheet with his teeth and dragged it to his spot. Using paws, teeth and determination, he arranged the sheet over the seat. When finished, he looked to Mary.

"Good boy. You did a terrific job." She signaled him to take his place on the protective cover and he snuggled in proudly. His contented look gave her a little thrill of satisfaction. Once Mary snapped his seat belt in place they were ready to travel.

By Sparrow Island standards, Wilma lived a comfortable distance from The Nature Museum. The phrase always made Mary smile. It meant a comfortable walk in the summer and a comfortably short drive in the winter.

In a matter of minutes, she pulled off Cross Island Road and parked near an older, well-kept home with three good-sized outbuildings. Mary guessed they were used mostly for storage, since the home itself appeared rather small.

She released Finnegan and pressed the button to lower the chair lift.

Wilma bustled up and shared her big multicolored umbrella. "Tell Finnegan to stay. I'll come back for him. No point in him getting wetter than necessary."

Delighted by the thoughtful reception and the time Wilma took out of her busy schedule, Mary obliged. Even with the smell of rain in the air, there was a strong aroma of damp evergreens along with the rich earthy scent from the dark needles covering the ground under their spreading branches. Wafting through the natural perfume was a trace of wood smoke.

Mary glanced up to mark where it came from, but couldn't

see past Wilma's umbrella. Dense drizzle collected and ran in small waterfalls from the brightly colored edges.

Together, they hustled past the house to the second of the three outbuildings. Mary gave herself a mental chiding. Of course, Wilma would be in her workshop. A master weaver, she was a major part of The Nature Museum's big exhibit and demonstration.

"Go get warm by the fire," Wilma ordered. "I banked it before I left this morning and put in a few more sticks when I got back. It's right toasty now."

The "fire" was an old-fashioned cast iron wood stove set out from one wall so the heat could circulate. Steam curled from the spout of a charred copper-bottomed teakettle sitting on the warming plate.

Mary rolled slowly across the flagstone floor. There was so much to look at she didn't really want to move at all. Without conscious thought, she stopped when Wilma left to get Finnegan.

Pegboard covered one section of the wall. On it, arranged neatly in order by size was an astonishing variety of tools. Mary knew immediately they weren't decorations. The grips of the beaters, saws, awls, planes and knives were darkened by sweat and hand oils that attested to their frequent use.

On her left, numerous shelves and long horizontal poles held a wide range of plant fibers. The reeds, raffia and basket willows she recognized right away. Her florist's eye helped her identify the rest: roots, cane, twigs and a variety of grasses including cattail and tule.

Nearby were several tubs. Grasses and other materials soaked in what she presumed was water, although it could have easily been a secret formula known only to the weaver.

Off to her right were several long tables, each nearly covered with an assortment of baskets in various stages of becoming. Although some were more than three feet across, most were more practical sizes. On an elevated shelf, she spotted a row of tiny collectibles.

Realizing her mouth gaped in astonishment, Mary snapped it shut and rolled closer to the stove. She liked the sense of one-ness with nature inside the barn-like building. The interior seemed to glow despite the rain spattering the skylights and windows. Warm, dry air circulated by the heat of the fire in the stove carried the scent of reeds and grasses.

"Welcome to my workshop." Wilma ushered Finnegan inside before closing the door.

The rhythmic clack of his nails on the flagstone floor grew louder as he came to stand beside his mistress. "I'm blown away," Mary admitted, her gaze fixed on the incredible assort-ment of weavings. "Did you make all of these?"

"Only some." Wilma set the open umbrella by the door. "The basket weavers' guild meets here. Many of them helped my husband and me build this workshop a long time ago."

Mary followed Wilma's gaze around the spacious interior. There was something special about labors of love, gifts of the heart between spouses, particularly when one set of the hands that made them were now stilled. "A legacy," Mary murmured.

"I suppose." Wilma took two mugs out of a cupboard near the woodstove. "Legacies and traditions are all wrapped up together for most folks."

"You don't think they are?" *Now this is a surprising turn of subject.*

"I've given it a great deal of thought." Wilma filled a tea strainer with a dark mixture of leaves. "Finally I had to go look up the words. *Legacies* are anything handed down from an ancestor."

"Well now, there's a broad definition."

Wilma chuckled and poured hot water into a stained earthenware vessel before adding the tea strainer. "So broad it's practically useless. *Traditions* on the other hand, are long-established customs or practices that have the effect of an unwritten law."

"Oh my," Mary exclaimed. "There is quite a difference between the two."

"Traditions are also the stories, beliefs and customs—the values a people or a family live by." Wilma shrugged. "For me, a legacy is something you can put in a box and hand over to another generation. Traditional values are passed to the next generation by example, by living them."

"I see." Mary couldn't fault the ideal of living one's values. As to the rest, she'd think about it later. Right now, she wanted to imitate a sponge and soak up every drop of information her hostess was willing to share.

Wilma stirred the steeping tea and a sweet scent wafted into the air. "In basket weaving, tradition guides the weaver's work, provides examples and gives directions. Only by embracing these unwritten rules does a weaver acquire sufficient skill and knowledge to forge beyond them and create a new masterpiece. Yet even this must reflect our values."

"I understand." Mary accepted a mug of hot tea and sniffed the intriguing fragrance. "This smells wonderful."

With a sly smile, Wilma said, "It's Saskatoon."

Realizing she ought to recognize the name, Mary took a sip. It had a sweet flavor, with a hint of rose, reminiscent of the tea her mother served but definitely not the same. She took another careful draught and the answer popped up. Saskatoon was just one name for a very versatile native shrub also known as serviceberry, May cherry and Juneberry.

"Oh my goodness," she said with a laugh. "I have these

growing in my yard. Abby planted them for the birds. I didn't realize we could eat them too."

"Oh yes. Fresh or cooked, they're delicious and ideal substitutes for blueberries. You can make pies, ice cream, syrup, jelly or even wine from them. Many of us collect berries in these." Wilma held out a square basket for Mary to examine. "This is done in the traditional Lummi style. It has twining, twill work, checker weave and a diagonally folded rim."

Tracing an embellishment overlay of coastal sweetgrass that turned the utilitarian item into a work of art, Mary wondered what other delightful treats she'd missed even though they were right under her nose. As Wilma put the basket away, Mary finished her tea and set the mug aside. "Show me more, please."

Wilma motioned to the right side of the room. "Let's start over there."

Mary fastened the leash onto Finnegan's harness and let him pull her across the stone floor. On the way, she noted shelves containing dozens of terra-cotta pots in a variety of sizes. "What are these?"

"Vegetable dyes." Wilma laughed. "We use everything from beets and blackberries to dandelions and onions, plus all kinds of nuts and wild berries."

"Fantastic," Mary breathed. "They all sound edible."

"Most are." Wilma picked up a sheaf of long burgundy streamers. Their rippling movements created the impression they were made of silk. "These began life as reeds." She held them out in invitation.

In Mary's hand, the dyed fibers were cool to the touch and warm to the sight. The deep color reminded her of blackberries and the stains they left on her fingers every August when she and most Northwesterners feasted on the plump fruit right off the bush. With a gulp, she wondered how many hours went into making the dye and refining the plant material just to get it to this point. "Goodness. Learning how to make this must take a while."

With a grin suggesting Mary didn't know the half of it, Wilma said, "Preparing the materials takes much labor and skill. Many times our young ones get discouraged before they get to the actual weaving."

"I think that's true of most arts," Mary agreed and returned the sheaf. "Beginning with raw material is a big challenge. I'm a knitter and naturally curious, so I've looked into what it takes to turn wool fresh from the sheep into the skeins I buy at In Stitches. The answer is a lot of work. And that's not counting raising the sheep."

"So true." Wilma took the lid off a large basket and shook out a flowing cape. "This is a Chilkat potlatch robe. It's made of Merino wool and yellow cedar bark. Here you can see the traditional designs of the whale and grizzly bear." Her fingers hovered over the surface as she outlined a series of brilliant yellow and blue figures.

Stunned, Mary stared at the bold strokes and lavish colors. Though she itched to touch the remarkable ceremonial robe, she kept her hands in her lap. "It's magnificent."

"Fit for a chief." Pride mingled with satisfaction on Wilma's features as she carefully returned the garment to the protection of the basket.

Thoroughly intrigued and wanting to see more, Mary pointed to a row of upside-down baskets. "Tell me about these." Tightly woven in cream, rust and gold, the swirls and peaks of the geometric designs boasted crisp, clean lines.

"Those are women's caps for the Feather Dances, a Siletz tradition."

Caps, not baskets. Recognizing her understandable error, Mary asked, "Siletz?"

"From Oregon. One of their weavers brought a sampling of his works for our display." Wilma picked up an airy cradle and handed it to Mary. "Hazel sticks or switches are the basis of their basketry. Bear grass gives the lovely white color and this artist favors woodwardia fern which he dies with red alder to give it the rich hue."

Mary thought the color looked just like the Turkey red sample Ana had brought by Island Blooms but wisely held her tongue. Now was not the time to make comparisons.

"There's much more." Wilma shrugged. "I don't have time to unpack and repack it all before the men come to take it to The Nature Museum."

"I understand," Mary said. "Don't worry. I wouldn't miss that for the world."

"I'm glad. Whether it's painting, weaving, sewing or something else, the act of creation is a privilege, a way to draw closer to the Creator. When we gather our grasses and our dyes, we are mindful of Who provides them. The same Spirit also gives us our skills. Basket weaving the old way keeps us in touch with the Giver of All."

In her mind's eye, Mary could see her friend harvesting reeds in the marshes at Buccaneer Bay, picking blackberries from the tangled vines alongside the road, digging fat dandelions out of a fallow field. Rain or shine, wind or wet, Wilma had always worn an air of serenity and now, Mary understood why. "I'll never look at a basket in quite the same way again."

"I knew you would understand. This hurry-up world of electronics and automation is not always so good. When an artist stops creating and lets the machines do it, what do they gain? For me, I only see loss."

Mary realized Wilma had just revealed the crux of her refusal to put quilters on the same creative level as basket weavers. "You're referring to the sewing machines with programmable stitches, aren't you?"

Wilma nodded. "And those with computers too. Where is the skill if they do your craft for you?"

Stepping out to the fringe of her sewing knowledge, Mary said, "I don't think they actually do it for you. It's my understanding they are an extension of the craft. They open new doors and take embroidery to a new level."

Resolved to do more research, she continued, "The stitching is just one part of the process. I don't want to lose sight of the fact we all need to express artistry no matter what form we choose."

Wilma slid onto a stool near Mary's chair. "I'm not sure I get what you are saying."

"The medium and the methods are different, but the principles and the goals are the same." The more she'd learned about the two different crafts, the more certain Mary became of the commonalities they shared.

The finished products might be as different as apples and oranges, but both required preparation, processes, practicality and proliferation. More importantly, success only came through love for the art and dedication of self.

"I don't think our goals are—"

Interrupting with a raised hand, Mary said, "Beauty, artistry, functionality—I see it here, everywhere I look. And what you saw at the meeting of the Busy Bee Quilting Society was only the tip of the iceberg."

A spark of triumph lit Wilma's eyes. "Neither have you seen the cream of the weaver's art. I told you, the best items are already packed for transport to The Nature Museum. You just wait until we unveil our display."

"Good."

Wilma's triumph changed to skepticism. "Why do you say good? It won't be good for the quilters."

"Actually, it's good for *you*. I've spoken with a couple of the quilters, Beverly in particular. She and Ana are bringing a group to your exhibit on Friday afternoon."

Clapping her hands and laughing, Wilma jumped up. "They will be amazed and have to concede."

"Possibly. However, you and at least one other basket weaver have to spend equal time viewing what the quilters consider the best of their best."

"Ridiculous. I already did when I attended their session."

"C'mon, Wilma. This time, they'll know you're coming and can bring the things they prize. It's only fair." Mary began to feel like a negotiator during the Pig War on San Juan Island. In 1859, an American farmer killed a British pig for digging up his garden and eating the potatoes.

The conflict escalated so fast that less than two months later, five British warships faced American marines with fourteen cannons. Fortunately, neither Wilma nor Beverly was armed and for that, Mary was grateful.

The Americans and British managed to keep their joint occupation peaceful while diplomats on the other side of the Atlantic took twelve years to resolve the dispute. Mary didn't think the quilters and weavers would last that long. She certainly couldn't. Somehow, she had to get them to see things from her perspective.

"If you insist," Wilma lamented. "I'll go see their works again. After all, you are the judge."

CHAPTER ❦ SIXTEEN

ABBY HIT THE BRAKES
hard to avoid an American coot sauntering across Shoreline
Drive on his way to the sea. His skinny yellow legs balanced a
greenish-black round body. Big green feet with lobed toes kept
a steady, if somewhat ungainly rhythm over the asphalt. All the
while, his short tail flicked and cocked, revealing white under-
tail feathers like a petticoat flashing beneath a skirt.

Thank heaven, Abby thought, she hadn't been driving fast.

Not caring that she blocked one lane of the street, she put
the car in park and jumped out, intending to direct any traf-
fic. American coots were omnivorous and recognized no
boundaries. They fed in a variety of ways—diving to the ocean
bottom, dabbling at the surface, grazing on land near the shore
and stealing from other diving birds. If this one had found a
good food source a little ways from the ocean, he probably
wasn't alone.

She looked back toward the park in the center of town to
see if he had company. "Apparently, you're a loner this morning," she told the coot.

He answered with a series of clucks, cackles and grunts as though lecturing her.

She swallowed a laugh.

The wind tousled her hair and tugged her jacket. Despite a growing feeling of silliness, she continued her vigil. This Thursday morning the road was deserted. She hoped it stayed that way for a few more minutes.

While the coot worked his way toward the rocky shore, she admired his determination and muscle. He finally wiggled into Randolph Bay and she returned to her car to drive the final half block to her destination.

She parked in front of The Complete Boater and shut off the engine. On a whim, she retrieved her binoculars from the glove box. Out on the bay, a lone, chunky coot pedaled furiously across the water. She quickly got him into her sights. It was fun to watch the bird scramble across the surface in his ungainly effort to get airborne. What he lacked in grace he made up for with sheer stamina.

Thank You, Lord. What a delight.

Feeling particularly pleased, she sat back. Talking with Nathaniel Dawkins wouldn't be quite as easy as the other interviews.

Given Hugo's revelations about Digger Dawks, she needed to come up with a very tactful way to approach the con man's son. First, she tried putting herself in Nathaniel's shoes. Just the thought of the island grapevine buzzing with news of the missing ring made her stomach clench.

Rubbing her clammy hands together, she felt a tidal wave of sympathy for the owner of The Complete Boater. There were no easy answers to his dilemma. After all this time, telling his friends and neighbors his father was a swindler would be almost impossible.

Even if folks proved to be initially understanding, whenever something went missing, all eyes would automatically turn in Nathaniel's direction. The business he'd built and the friendships he'd fostered for more than a quarter of a century were all in jeopardy from a past that wasn't his.

She suspected fear of being accused and losing everything he'd worked for was behind yesterday's unexpected closure of The Complete Boater. Whether he heard about the missing ring from Candace or through the grapevine, the news must have hit him like the proverbial fist in the gut.

There was a fine line between her sympathy for his unusual plight and her concern for everyone else at the party. Until the ring turned up, all of them walked under the same growing cloud of suspicion. Determined to take a step toward resolution, she got out of the car and marched up to the door.

Once again, she found it locked. Except this morning, a paper sign hung behind the glass panes. "CLOSED" it said. "OPEN AT 1:00 PM."

Abby went back to her car and drummed her fingers on the steering wheel. She could come up with a slew of explanations for the closed store. She refused to sit and speculate. He was entitled to a presumption of innocence.

After all, he very well could be. Like her, his only "crime" might be that he attended the party. She buckled in, started the car and headed for home.

With time to fill before she could call on him again, she had time to try a new idea. Nathaniel was a single man. He might appreciate some hot, spiced cider and homemade pumpkin cookies. That wouldn't take long.

Back at the house, Blossom eyed her suspiciously and Abby laughed aloud. The sound sent the cat scampering to the seat of a dining room chair tucked safely under the table. Although

Abby cooed and cajoled, Blossom stayed put. The white ball of fluff wasn't accustomed to having anyone home during the day except Mary.

Just after Abby put the first batch of cookies in the oven, the phone rang.

"Hello Abby. It's Bradford."

Surprised to hear from him, particularly during his peak working hours she asked, "What's up?"

"I'm worried about Candace." An edge of desperation frayed his tone.

"What's the latest?"

The lawyer explained, "She's distraught, stubborn as ever, and still insisting on no authorities. I doubt her friends have any idea what it's costing her physically to keep them out of an interrogation room and off the police records."

Bradford heaved a frustrated sigh. "Between that and how rotten she feels for Brandi, I'm afraid she's heading for an ulcer."

"No ring then," Abby said, not needing to phrase it as a question.

"There isn't a piece of furniture Candace hasn't picked up, looked under or turned over. I'm hoping you have some good news for us."

"I wish I did. Sorry to say, I don't have anything yet."

The sound of a deep inhale followed by a heavy exhale came through the receiver. "Confidentially, Abby, right about now, I'm feeling as irrationally angry as some of my clients."

"I'm guessing you're feeling helpless and hating it."

"Yeah. Give me a compromised crime scene, no witnesses and a landslide carrying away my evidence and I know exactly what to do. But one little florist telling me hands-off is driving me crazy. Tell me, Abby, would my presence on Sparrow Island help at all?"

Quite certain his return would only add to Candace's worries and escalate the situation, Abby knew she had to tread carefully. "I suspect your caseload is very heavy and the need for you to be in court is great, or you wouldn't be asking me. You'd be here."

"Correct on all counts."

Hearing the strain in his tone, she decided to smile as she gave him an edited version of her scant progress. It would make her sound more optimistic. Nevertheless, she purposefully omitted certain details. Some he didn't need to know. Others she feared would get back to Candace. In her state, she'd probably reveal them without realizing she shouldn't. "I'm going to see Nathaniel this afternoon, then I'll drop by Laverne Minsky's home."

"You think one of them might have . . . information about the ring?"

Abby noted Bradford's conscious effort to exclude any form of accusation and silently commended him. "I'm hoping they noticed something no one else did. Sometimes those little inconsistencies yield the best clues."

"You do have an excellent mind for deducing possibilities. I'm glad Candace has you on her side."

"Look, I know she took Brandi to work with her today. Candace is going to show her how to put together a Christmas floral arrangement. I'll drop by the flower shop tomorrow morning—when Candace is alone."

"I'd appreciate it. Call me if anything changes . . . if you need anything."

"Sure." They said their farewells and Abby hung up just in time to take the pumpkin cookies out of the oven.

ABBY SPOTTED Nathaniel's battered truck tucked into an awkward parking place on the side of The Complete Boater.

He'd left the best slots near the door open for customers. Appreciating his business acumen, she pulled up and parked.

Al's statement about people, vehicles and self-esteem came to mind and Abby craned her neck to look again at Nathaniel's old truck. Scrapes, rust spots and a crooked fender classified the vehicle as a wreck. A coating of mud and grime seemed to be all that held the yellow and brown beast together.

Funny, she'd never thought of him having a self-esteem problem and decided Al's theory didn't apply. A better test would be Nathaniel's true passion, his boats. They were always shipshape. The truck was just transportation to and from home, work and the marina. Like a number of the vintage cars roaming Sparrow Island, the hard-used vehicle was a rolling testimony to Al's ingenuity and his resourcefulness with a wrench.

"Well, we'll see," she muttered, gathering up the treats she'd made and exiting her car. The afternoon brought blue skies and temperatures reminiscent of late summer. It was the perfect kind of weather for exploring the outdoors and bird-watching.

Unable to resist, she looked toward the bay and spotted a blue heron gliding in for a landing. The ease of his languid wing strokes seemed to taunt her for being an earthbound human.

A loud *wacka-wacka-wacka* sounded as she turned toward the deserted ferry dock and spotted the bright yellow tail feathers of a yellow-shafted Northern flicker. Behind her, another flicker returned the call and she thought about the pair recovering in the laboratory.

A species of woodpecker, they were every picnicker's best friend. The robust birds had a marked appetite for the uninvited guests of all blanket picnics in the wild—ants and beetles.

Watching their typical undulating flight toward the trees, she realized the birds were as giddy for the sunshine and warmer temperatures as the residents. Resisting the lure to follow the birds, Abby entered The Complete Boater.

"Be with you in a minute," Nathaniel called from the back of the store.

Hearing him with another customer, she took her time wandering down the aisle. As a young girl, she'd learned the value of a well-equipped marine chandlery and this one certainly measured up. In one aisle alone, there were paddles and oars, propellers and pumps, floatation devices and purification filters.

She rounded a corner, found the latest in instruments and gauges, charts and navigational aids, and reasoned the store must be flourishing. She credited Nathaniel's attention to detail, the variety of his tack and the spic-n-span cleanliness for drawing steady customers. Pleased for his prosperity, she looped around to another aisle.

"Are you looking for something in particular?" Nathaniel strode past neatly shelved ropes, fasteners and sailboat rigging.

Abby managed a cheery smile. "Not today. I haven't changed my mind about owning a boat. I'll leave that to my father and my friends."

"Considering how busy you are, that may not be a bad idea." Nathaniel eyed the bag she carried. "What brings you here?"

"I brought you something." Abby walked to the back of the store, past the round racks of shirts and squall jackets to the sales counter. She set the cookies and cider on the countertop. "I had the day off and I was in a baking mood."

Skepticism crept across his features. "While I appreciate the thought, I think I know why you came." He peeked into the bag, sniffed and raised his eyebrows. "Spicy pumpkin. *Hmm.* Nuts?"

Abby shook her head. "Afraid not."

"Good." He reached for the steaming thermal cup she offered. After a sniff and a sip, he said, "Thanks, Abby. This is an effective tactic if you're trying to soften me up so you can ask questions. It isn't necessary." He picked up a cookie, took a bite and smiled.

Glad she'd made the effort, she relaxed against the counter. "I stopped by to see you yesterday afternoon."

"I was out," he said in a noncommittal tone. "As it happens, I'm short-staffed. One of my part-timers has decided to stay over in Bellingham until after Christmas. The other one, Horace, won't give out his phone number. Instead, he comes in to check the schedule I post a couple of weeks in advance, then shows up on his days to work."

"For heaven's sake! Don't you think refusing to give your employer your phone number is a bit strange?"

"Since you're asking, I'll admit it's eccentric. But it's one of the things I like about old Horace." Nathaniel's amusement came out as a throaty chuckle. "Having the number wouldn't help anyway. He unplugs the phone when he's not using it."

Abby shook her head in disbelief. Nathaniel's sense of humor apparently encompassed a touch of the absurd. "Did Horace say why?"

"Yup. Often. The phone is for his use. He's not paying for it so telemarketers can call him whenever they feel like it and waste his time. Gotta admire a man like Horace."

If not for emergency reasons, she could appreciate Horace's attitude. Her father would feel the same way.

Chomping on another cookie, Nathaniel drained the last of the cider out of the thermos and into his cup. Abby realized he was getting ready to sweep her out the door. In a minute or two, he'd hand her the empty container and his thanks, and expect her to leave.

Determined to get answers, she took charge of the conversation. "I guess it takes all kinds. Last Saturday night we all became someone different."

Nathaniel grinned. "Yeah. The bee's knees."

The sound of the front door opening announced the arrival of a customer.

"I'll wait," Abby said.

Nathaniel met her gaze, his features suddenly tight. "I rather figured you would."

He knew why she'd come and no doubt wished she'd leave. But Abby had the afternoon to devote to ferreting out answers and the patience of a professional bird-watcher.

Twenty minutes later, Nathaniel rang up a hefty sale and saw the customer out the door. Seeming a bit perturbed to find her still there, he moved behind the counter. "You're the island sleuth and you're checking me out for a reason. Let's get to the point. What do you want?"

"I'm trying to find out if anyone saw something that might help me figure out what happened to Brandi's engagement ring." She crossed her arms. "We need to resolve this before it blows up into a public disaster."

"The ring she put on the mantel ought to be there."

"But it isn't."

"Brandi's a twit. She lacks the good sense to get a valuable piece of jewelry sized, then borders on stupidity by not putting it in a safe place. Or maybe she's just lazy."

Abby raised an eyebrow. Nathaniel sounded as frustrated as Bradford. The main difference was the attorney was more tactful. "I doubt she's lazy or lacking in intelligence."

"If she'd put the thing away, she'd still have it and there wouldn't be all the rumors and gossip running through town." Nathaniel plunged his fists into his trouser pockets.

His gesture said he wanted nothing more to do with this subject and Abby didn't blame him. If Hugo hadn't prepared her, she would've taken Nathaniel's defensive posture as guilt. "You're right. We all wish she'd put it away. Since she didn't and we are where we are, I'm interviewing everyone. I want to find the ring and put an end to the rumors."

"All right. Ask your questions."

"I only have a couple."

His gaze locked on hers in disbelief, but he remained silent.

"Did you notice anyone do or say anything unusual? I'm looking for a behavior or a comment that didn't fit."

"You're kidding, right?"

"No."

Shaking his head on a long sigh, he admitted, "I can't help you. Bottom line, I was at a party having a good time. I saw ten people, including myself, acting out of character."

"You went outside during the festivities," she said cautiously.

"Yeah, so?"

"It was raining."

"I went out for a taste of the briar."

Abby raised her eyebrows, questioning his meaning.

"My pipe."

There had to be more he wasn't telling. His suit might have gotten damp while he stood on the covered porch and indulged in a smoke. The wind could've blown the rain in on him. It would have made him uncomfortable, but didn't account for the mud.

"I understand your cuffs and shoes were muddy when you came in."

"That's right, and my spats were in my pocket," he said gruffly.

"And?" While he drilled her with a challenging stare, she kept what she hoped was a sympathetic expression, although her knees felt a little weak. Maybe confronting him like this wasn't one of her better ideas. Unfortunately, she didn't have another idea. "Why?"

"You're not going to give up, are you?" Without waiting for her to respond, he continued in a milder tone, "You're like a dog chasing a bone. You'll keep chasing answers until you get them, won't you?"

She nodded. "That isn't the most flattering assessment I've ever received, but it's basically accurate."

He rewarded her honesty with a genuine smile, one that reached his eyes. "There was a ladder against the side of the house—for the leaves in the gutters, I suppose. Anyway, the wind had pushed it hard to one side. Another good gust would've knocked it into a window. Rather than let it ruin the night for everyone, I moved the ladder over by the compost pile. It was a muddy trek. End of story."

"It's a good one. Why didn't you want to tell me?"

"I don't like braggarts." Nathaniel leaned back on his heels, then rocked forward and rested his forearms on the counter so he was eye-level with Abby. "For the past twenty-five years I've worked to build this business."

He looked away, his gaze searching the store. "I love this place. The services I provide my customers, the acquaintances and solid friendships that got started over this counter." His open palm slapped the glass top. "Now, because a spoiled mainlander couldn't keep track of her valuables, everyone at the party is suspect. Including you."

Smiling bleakly, Abby met his gaze. "I know."

CHAPTER ✿ SEVENTEEN

FTER HER DISCONCERTING conversation with Nathaniel at The Complete Boater, Abby went to Stanton Farm. A red-tailed hawk tried to kite over the stubbled fields behind her parent's home. The heavy bodied bird had her sympathy. He needed more wind to execute his exceptional hovering ability. She needed more clues to solve her baffling mystery. Or at least a sounding board to bounce them against, a role her father enjoyed, which was why she'd come to see him.

"Sorry, Abby." Sam Arbogast fed unusable bits of storm debris into a small bonfire. Twigs and broken branches too big to compost and too small for the fireplace would make a rich ash fertilizer. "Your folks went over to Friday Harbor. Christmas shopping. Ellen said they had to take advantage of this afternoon's sunshine. George agreed, though I 'spect taking the boat out was more to his liking."

A chuckle gusted out, despite Abby's disappointment. "Well, if they get back early, would you tell Dad I'm down at the dreaming rock? It's nothing earth-shattering. I just could use his advice."

"Sure thing." Wearing a contented grin, Sam stomped a tangled mass of branches into smaller pieces for safer burning. "Enjoy. It's too nice a day to be indoors."

That it was. Abby waved farewell and headed down the path through the stubbled fields to the stand of trees near the shore. Her disappointment ratcheted up a notch and she realized how much she'd counted on hashing over her dilemma with her father.

At the dreaming rock, her most favorite spot in all the world, she decided to do what she'd done as a kid. When her dad was out on a charter and she needed his advice, she pretended he was as close as God and talked to both of them. Even now, as an adult, she was amazed at how much she'd learned from those conversations.

Near the huge rock sat the green plastic storage bin her father had placed there when she returned to Sparrow Island after Mary's accident. How well he knew her, Abby thought. He knew she'd head to the rock, to her favorite place to pray when events seemed too overwhelming.

As she opened the green bin, a warmth and appreciation for her father's thoughtfulness flooded through her. Taking one of the fat cushions, she scrambled up the rock to the top where wind and weather had conspired to smooth the rough edges into a natural seat. However, the passing years hadn't softened the old boulder. If anything, it was harder and the cushion was a most appreciated treat.

Settling in, she drew her knees to her chin, closed her eyes and listened. In a series of harsh *shaark-shaark-shaark*'s, a pair of Steller's jays informed the world they were claiming the upper story of the tall evergreens to her left and she chuckled softly.

Despite their raucous sounds, she liked the noisy birds with the brilliant blue plumage. Believed to mate for life, they often acted like old married couples, chiding each other frequently but always staying close. Above all, like her parents, they were loyal to one another.

Candace too was staunchly loyal. Her determination to stick up for the friends she'd invited to one of the best, and potentially most disastrous parties of the year was admirable. But Abby feared for the young woman's health.

Abby let her gaze wander over the tall spruces, through the thick green needles to the blue of the ocean beyond their sturdy trunks.

The scene seemed to be a reflection of her mystery. Most of the partygoers were like the trees, rooted in the community, growing their businesses and sending out branches of friendship.

Despite Nathaniel's prickliness and Sven's knowledge of jewels, she couldn't count them as the only suspects. Understandably, neither one of them wanted their secrets dragged into the light of an investigation. She couldn't discount Keith either. He had a chameleon-like ability to adapt to circumstances. He also had a wide network of contacts all over the country. One of them probably knew how to fence a diamond ring.

A squirrel darted across the little clearing, around the rock and up a Douglas fir. The jays warned him to take another route. After a bit of chatter, the squirrel started forward, then beat a hasty retreat.

She found herself retreating too, recoiling at the thought that one of her friends took the ring. It was a delusion she couldn't afford. However uncomfortable the truth might be, she had to find it.

Of the three people at the party she didn't know well, two deserved a closer look. Bradford, gifted defense attorney that he was, knew how to make his clients—and himself—believable. His excellent record in the courtroom testified to his persuasive abilities.

From the outset, he'd never included himself on the suspect list. Was it because he knew he was innocent? Or had he fallen back on the strategy that the best defense was a good offense?

The question called to mind an incident during her senior year at Cornell. After watching a less-experienced classmate usurp a position she thought was hers, she'd come to the realization that power assumed often became power granted. But she didn't get that feeling about Bradford.

And if he was innocent, there was no reason for him not to behave as though finding the ring was up to the three of them.

Her thoughts turned to Sven. With his razzle-dazzle discourse on natural and manufactured diamonds, he'd been as adroit at misdirection as Donna Morgan had been at the party. One bump in that road was Hugo, and he was a very big bump.

Even without asking, Abby knew her boss would have checked all Sven's references before beginning a discussion of a landscaping project. The Nature Museum and the conservatory grounds were Hugo's babies, and he guarded their well-being fiercely. Yet, Sven's landscaping references wouldn't include the criminal behavior of his former ladylove. And there was the uncomfortable fact that he'd lied to Abby.

Abby decided to talk to the landscaper one more time—
after she questioned Bradford. With the Laverne Minsky inter-
view set up for later this afternoon, Abby shifted on the pillow
and considered another possibility.

If the ring had been spirited off the island, they'd never find
it and most likely never discover who took it. She recoiled at
the scenario that left nothing for her and the others but soiled
reputations.

THE GLORIOUS, late Indian summer day threw long shadows
across the road as Abby drove through town. Hoping for a
week of this kind of weather, she passed Al's Garage before
turning right on Harbor Seal Road. The Minsky home was
half a block north of the Sparrow Island Medical Center.

The neighborhood was a step back in time. Craftsman style
homes with square-columned porches, big eaves and white
picket fences lined the street. A few had been remodeled—
rooms and garages added—but for the most part the cozy
neighborhood looked the same as Abby's childhood memories.

During grade school and high school while selling candy
bars or subscriptions or collecting box tops and S&H green
stamps for one fundraiser or another, she'd visited nearly every
home on the island. Now, she parked near the low white gate
at the sidewalk and enjoyed the wave of nostalgia.

The dove gray house still had white trim with a burgundy
border on the eaves and around the windows. Pansies in a riot
of color basked in familiar white flowerboxes and in the beds
by the porch. Even the doorbell had the same *br-r-r-r-ring*
today as she remembered.

For an instant, Abby wanted to walk away. The notion that

these people—her friends who poured time and energy into keeping up the only home they'd ever owned—could be thieves was ridiculous. Ludicrous. Out of the question.

Yet to add the Minskys as a couple to her they-absolutely-couldn't-have-done-it suspect list, she needed to speak to Laverne with an open mind. In fairness to Al, Donna, Nathaniel and Keith, the woman who played the chorus girl deserved the same scrutiny.

"Hi, Abby," Laverne said, opening the door. "Perfect timing. I just got home from work."

Mentally, Abby gave her forehead a slap. How could she have forgotten Laverne worked part-time at the Medical Center? "I hope I'm not rushing you."

"Not at all. Come in. Come in." She held the door wide.

Colorful braided rugs shielded the polished wood floor in front of his-and-her chairs. A half-finished fine lace doily sat atop a crochet basket nuzzling the smaller chair. The table between them held a lamp and a stack of magazines, the top one featuring a gleaming automobile engine.

Laverne gestured toward the cheery yellow, white and red kitchen. Clearly, she shared Mary's love of rooster décor. The proud birds pranced across the curtains on the window over the sink and preened on the canisters on the countertop. Ivy, miniature African violets and a couple of succulents sat in rooster-shaped containers on the windowsill.

The kitchen looked like it hadn't changed since the 1950s. Or had it? Abby looked closer and noticed that what she presumed was a cabinet was actually a dishwasher, and the freestanding art deco stove was in reality, state-of-the-art.

"We like the fifties," Laverne said unapologetically. She

picked up a chrome kettle and began to fill it. "I hope you'll stay for some tea. If you're of a mind to ruin your appetite for supper, I've got some frosted sugar cookies I made this morning."

"I'd love some tea."

Laverne gestured to a yellow-topped chrome table surrounded by four chrome chairs with red vinyl cushions. "Have a seat."

"Has Ed Willoughby seen your kitchen?"

Laverne laughed. "Good heavens, yes. He loves it."

No wonder. No one was more 1950s than Ed. He even wore an old-fashioned soda jerk uniform when he worked in his store, Willoughby Pharmacy. "I imagine he feels right at home here."

"He does." Laverne placed a chubby sugar bowl with a leafy cherry design on the table. On her next trip, she brought matching cups and saucers and a plate of sumptuous looking cookies.

Abby eyed the sugar crystals sparkling in the icing atop the goodies. "You really know how to torture a gal, don't you?"

"Hey, Al told me you're investigating. I'm trying to sweeten you up before you bring out the rubber hose."

Relieved she didn't need to explain the purpose of her visit, Abby was still uncomfortable with the idea Laverne had been concerned about their meeting. "Is that really why you made the cookies?" Abby hoped not.

The whistling teakettle summoned Laverne to the stove. "Not really. Al stays open late on Thursday. I usually take him dinner." Pouring the steaming water into a ceramic teapot, Laverne tilted her head toward the backyard. "The cookies are a small way of saying how much I appreciate all he does for me and our children."

Abby rose and looked outside in the direction Laverne had indicated. A brick pathway meandered through dormant shrubs to a back gate. Lilac skeletons peeked over the thick evergreen leaves of several large rhododendrons. Sheltered beneath them, a row of hydrangeas sported giant dried flower clusters on bare branches. Thickly mulched flowerbeds flanked the archway rising up from the picket fence and formed a high trellis over the gate.

Barely visible through a Douglas fir and a red-tipped photinia, was the back of Al's garage. "Your yard must be an explosion of color in the spring."

"Yes, you'll have to come by then and see. I am rather proud of it." Laverne filled their cups with tea. "I have to tell you, Abby, I think Brandi is being very brave and charitable. It isn't as though the girl can afford such a great loss."

"You spoke with her after the party?"

Laverne took the lid off the cute bowl and measured sugar into her cup. "Not the way you and I are talking now."

Hoping to draw out her hostess, Abby said, "I happen to agree with you. The loss of an expensive piece of jewelry would be a blow to anyone. When it's an engagement ring, I'm sure it's staggering." She blew across the steamy tea. "I'm curious why you think Brandi's being particularly brave and charitable."

Laverne put down her teacup. "It must be hard trusting strangers to resolve such a touchy issue. Most people would just go to the authorities and let them handle it."

"Then you think someone took the ring?" Abby probed.

"No. Yes. Oh, I don't know. It's one of those dichotomy things. I can't imagine anyone taking it, yet I can't imagine Candace and Brandi not finding it in the house." Laverne gave a helpless shrug. "The trouble is, the ring's gone and poor

Brandi's left waving in the wind hoping some miracle will bring it back."

"It is a sticky situation," Abby agreed.

Laverne toyed with her cup. "You know, I'm a magazine hound. I love looking at all the advertisements for clothes and jewelry. It's fun to see what the celebrities wear. It might not be smart to admit it, but all that looking gave me a good idea of how much Brandi's ring is worth."

Laverne heaved a puzzled sigh. "Yet she's wearing a fleece jacket worn out at the elbows. It's the only jacket I've seen her in since she arrived."

Abby sat very still. "That's an interesting observation. Maybe it's the only one she packed or perhaps it's a favorite."

"You're probably right."

"The state of her jacket aside, when was the last time you saw Brandi's engagement ring?"

"When she put it on the mantel." Laverne sat back and broke a cookie in two. "Some women are meant to wear jewelry. I'm not. I love to look at it, but wearing it is a pain. Either it gets in my way or I'm afraid I'll break it or lose it. In my marriage, this is a good thing. Al would rather buy me a car than a diamond bracelet. And frankly, the car would get a lot more use than a bracelet I'd keep in a drawer."

"Hi, Mom. Hello, Dr. Stanton." Lithe, dark-haired Eileen breezed into the kitchen. "Oh great. Cookies. Can I take some over to Dad?"

"Sure. He'd love it. Let him know dinner will be a little late, okay?" Laverne popped half a cookie in her mouth then scooped a plastic container off the countertop and handed it to her daughter.

"Sure thing, Mom." Eileen waved and hurried out the back door.

"Our children are our jewels," Laverne said proudly.

Abby smiled her agreement then said bluntly, "There's something I don't understand. You knew about ring guards. You even said you wore them."

Laverne pulled off her wedding ring and handed it over. While Abby examined the plastic insert in the plain gold band, her hostess went to the sink and returned with a ring keeper shaped like a rooster's head. Dangling from its beak were two more rings.

She gave them to Abby before taking the gold band and sliding it back on her finger. "One of those is Al's high school ring. The other belonged to my mother."

The class ring boasted a thick wrapping of string, the original ring guard. The heirloom piece, two diamond chips between three garnets, had a plastic insert.

"Now you've seen the family jewels," Laverne said lightly.

Gazing at the rings, Abby knew their sentimental value far surpassed any monetary value.

"Like I said earlier, my real treasures are my kids. I want to give them the best I can, so I'm still making do and stretching pennies."

Abby swallowed thickly. "But Eileen's always wearing the latest styles."

"You could say her wardrobe is cutting edge."

It was a lightbulb moment and Abby said, "You make all her clothes, don't you?"

"Yup. We save a fortune and everything fits properly. A couple of times a year we go to the big department stores in

Bellingham or Seattle. Eileen sketches what she wants. I look at how it's constructed and then we go to the fabric stores. Guess we're just a couple of material girls."

Abby laughed softly. "When I was at Cornell, I wore the same sweater almost every day for four years."

"So you appreciate how cutting corners helps pay for the kids' college. Ronnie is taken care of with scholarships and grants. And he has job. Of course, Al and I are hoping Eileen will get at least a partial scholarship."

Abby refilled their teacups and took another cookie. This time with Laverne, as awkwardly as it had come about, was in fact a blessing. The woman was generous and loving, with a quality of character that shone whether anyone was looking or not. She could have no more taken the ring than she could walk across the Strait of Juan de Fuca.

"If Eileen has half your dedication, Laverne, I'm sure she'll do very well." Abby nibbled the edge of her cookie. "I've got one last question."

"Fire away."

"At the party, did you notice anyone doing something out of the ordinary? Anything, large or small, that struck you as strange?"

"*Hmm.*" Her eyes narrowed and she bit her lip as she thought. "There was one thing. It was shortly after the bouncer was murdered, and I was helping Candace set up the desserts. I went to the kitchen for serving tools. Bradford came in the back door. I remember being quite startled."

Startled is an understatement, Abby thought. The news floored her. With ten ginger ale guzzlers in a small house, the restroom was a popular destination. She'd presumed that's where Bradford went when he left the living room and he returned as the inspector. "Did he say why he went outside?"

"Not really. He just said it was nasty out there and left his wet overcoat on the hooks by the back door."

"That's it?"

"He washed his hands in the sink and removed his fake scar. He asked me to see if he'd gotten it all. I only got a quick look because he was in a hurry to get back to the party."

Bradford's outdoor excursion was as puzzling as it was unexpected. What could have been important enough for him to leave the party at a point when everything revolved around him in his new role as the investigator?

Deliberating, Abby sipped her tea. Bradford must have been the first to go outside. Until minutes before the bouncer's murder, everyone had been at the table.

CHAPTER ❧ EIGHTEEN

ABBY TOOK HEART FROM the Lord's promise: "He is a shield to those whose walk is blameless" (Proverbs 2:7). With His help, she'd find the answers she needed.

The lights blazing from the windows of the two-story house on Oceania Boulevard were a welcome sight. Mary was home. Tension Abby hadn't been aware she was carrying fell away, softening her shoulders and easing the stiffness in her neck. She and her sister could spend a relaxing evening together, catching up on each other's day.

Abby noticed the sky now looked more lavender than gloomy gray. Streaks of sun-gold laced the clouds on the western horizon, changing them from ominous to breathtaking.

Just as she pulled into the driveway, she heard a familiar voice calling her name. Waving, she parked in the garage, got out and went to greet her visitor.

The sun might be ready to retire for the day, but her young neighbor wasn't. Standing on the bike's pedals, Bobby pumped doggedly up the rise, turned into the drive and coasted to her side. "Hey, Abby."

"Hey, yourself, Master McDonald. What can I do for you?"

"I learned something."

Well, he was ahead of her. Although she'd interviewed Donna Morgan, Nathaniel Dawkins and Laverne Minsky all in one day, Abby had ended up with more questions than when she started. But as she looked into the troubled ten-year-old's face, she put her quandary on hold. "Okay. I give. What did you find out?"

"It's about turkeys." Straddling his bike and holding the handlebars, he wore a scrunched frown of sorrow and uncertainty.

"Let me guess. You learned something you didn't like."

"Sorta. It's bad for me. Good for the turkeys." Scuffing the toe of his sneaker on the driveway, he asked, "Did you know they can run as fast as twenty-five miles an hour?"

"Fully grown wild turkeys are very quick," she agreed.

"And they can fly! They can fly really fast, like fifty-five miles an hour. That's faster than my dad can drive on most of the roads on Sparrow Island."

Wild turkeys can fly. Domesticated birds can't. Abby didn't know whether to laugh or cry. On the plus side, Bobby's interest spurred him into some excellent research. On the minus, his discoveries only added to his culinary conundrum.

"Do the turkeys who get eaten at Thanksgiving get to fly much before . . . you know?"

"Well, I'm not a hundred percent positive, but I doubt they do," she confessed.

"But you're pretty sure, huh?"

Reluctantly, Abby nodded.

"Well, then do you think they get to run a lot? I mean since they probably don't get to fly?"

"I'd say both depend on where the turkey grows up. Some live on what's called free range."

He immediately brightened. "You mean on a ranch? Like cattle?"

"I'm guessing, but it's probably something like that, only on a smaller scale. They're not as big as cows."

"Yeah. That's good. At least they get something. Too bad people don't have steaks for dinner on Thanksgiving. That would be okay, I guess. My friend José Bondevik and his dad have ham." Bobby raised a shoulder in a "go figure" shrug. "I'm sure gonna miss eating turkey."

Just then, his head turned and they both heard the sound of his name in the deepening dusk.

"Mom's calling. I gotta go." He put a foot on the bike pedal, then hesitated. "Can we talk about this later?"

"Sure thing."

He leaned forward, then hesitated again. "You're not gonna . . ."

"I'm not going to what?" Abby prodded gently.

"Eat turkey when we go to the farm." The words came out in a fearful whisper. "I know your mom's making one and that we're guests and everything, but . . ."

A more insistent summons from his mother sent Bobby scrambling for the road. Left standing on the driveway, Abby glanced at the first stars of evening and wondered how she would have answered.

She trudged through the garage, hung her coat in the laundry room and went inside.

"What's up?" Mary asked when Abby entered the kitchen.

"I heard the garage door open and then this big silence. It was weird. I kept expecting you to walk in any minute."

"I was talking to Bobby." Abby put her purse on the telephone table and surveyed the room. Flour coated the special work area Mary used for meal preparation and baking. Judging by the delicious aromas permeating the air, she'd done both.

A pot of hearty soup simmering on the front burner teased Abby's appetite with a bouquet of garlic and rosemary. Coming from the oven, the scrumptious aroma of spicy pumpkin bread made her stomach rumble with anticipation. Another batch of bread cooled on a wire rack on the counter.

"He's been researching turkeys." She went to the sink and washed her hands.

"Oh dear," Mary sympathized. "I ran into Sandy at The Green Grocer. She says he's a very troubled lad these days. The closer we get to Thanksgiving, the greater his predicament seems."

"And now so does mine." Abby leaned against the counter. "He asks tough questions—like, how can a self-respecting ornithologist eat birds?" She met her sister's gaze, saw the amusement in her eyes, and shook her head. "This is serious. To Bobby."

"I know." Mary started drizzling a creamy-white glaze over one of the cooled loaves of pumpkin bread.

Tantalizing hints of cinnamon, nutmeg and clove wafted in Abby's direction. Refusing to give in to the temptation to wheedle a bite and spoil her supper, she quickly offered, "Why don't I put a salad together while you finish up there?"

"Great idea," Mary agreed. "I love to bake, especially at this time of year. When it's cold outside, it just feels right to have goodies in the oven. The only bad thing is how fast a little bite here and a taste there can show up on the scale."

"*Eeek*, that's so true." As she rinsed the lettuce, Abby started counting the treats she'd consumed during her investigation. "Today, I had a mocha with Donna, pumpkin cookies with Nathaniel and sugar cookies with Laverne. I can't understand why I'm still so hungry—besides the fact you're a great cook and everything smells wonderful."

Mary arched an eyebrow. "I didn't hear the word *lunch* on your list."

"Oh my goodness, you're right." Abby plunked the lettuce into the spinner and gave it a whirl. "No wonder I was starting to feel a little cranky." She turned toward the pot of soup and indulged in a deep sniff. "Watch out food, here I come."

While they ate, Abby brought Mary up to date on the investigation. "I've learned at least three people went outside during the party. Toward the end of the evening, Nathaniel went out to smoke his pipe. Sometime during the party, Brandi went out. Donna saw her return carrying an empty trash can."

"Sounds reasonable. The third?"

"Bradford made his foray early, just after he became the victim. Laverne saw him come in before he returned to the party as the inspector."

Mary's brow furrowed. "You're sure only those three went outside?"

"So far, those are the three someone saw. Wandering guests aren't my only problem. We all saw Brandi put the ring on the mantel, but thus far, no one remembers seeing it again. And I haven't learned why Bradford went out."

Mary lowered her soupspoon. "Surely, you don't think he took it."

"He's as much of a suspect as I am." Abby shook her head. "I don't have enough information to say one way or another. Frankly, the one I'm most suspicious about is Sven."

"Because of that terrible woman who changed out the jewels she borrowed from people who trusted her? That must have been awful for Sven."

"Some reporters who watched her trial wouldn't agree with you."

"What do you mean?"

"They think he was in collusion with her."

"If the authorities thought that, they would have investigated him."

"According to the articles, they did."

"Then there was nothing to find." Mary glanced at Abby. "Except maybe a broken heart if he loved her."

"What bothers me is that he lied. He led me to believe he learned about gemstones while looking for an engagement ring."

"Hey, he told you about diamonds and synthetic stones. He didn't have to, you know. Expecting him to tell you his life story while you interrogate him about a missing ring isn't reasonable. You're basically a stranger with no real authority to ask him anything."

"When you put it that way—" Still, he'd intentionally misled her.

"Okay," Mary said lightheartedly. "Tell me about your meeting with Laverne."

Abby complied. Just as she was describing the smart outfit Laverne had made for Eileen, the timer went off in the kitchen.

"That's the third batch of pumpkin bread." Mary started to push back from the dining table.

"I'll get it." Abby went to the stove and selected a couple of toothpicks from the holder on the counter. "Why are you making so much? Are you giving it away or do you have a special event coming up?"

"Both," Mary answered. "It's part of a Thanksgiving tradition Candace and I started years ago at Island Blooms. During the holiday week, we have a table set up where our customers can help themselves to pumpkin bread and coffee. It's become quite popular."

"I'm not surprised." Abby opened the oven and checked the middle loaf. "Perfect." While she transferred it to a large cooling rack, she added, "Traditions are important. People rely on them to keep their world ordered. They're a form of cultural glue."

Noticing a shadow of concern settling on Mary's features, Abby returned to the table. "The situation with Beverly and Wilma will work out. I'm sure of it. Remember the year I spent Thanksgiving in New York with Francine and her family?

"I thought Mom and Dad would be very upset. It truly surprised me they weren't. That's the year they started inviting someone outside the family to the big feast."

The happy memories dancing in Mary's blue eyes curved her lips into a full smile. "We're going to have a farm-full this year, that's for sure."

Abby sat back and took a long drink of water. "The Keatings—Francine's parents—had been inviting outsiders for years. She warned me not to be surprised by what I found on the Thanksgiving dinner table."

Just thinking about that memorable day made Abby laugh so hard her cheeks ached.

"What?" Mary looked around bewildered. "What was it?"

"One of the Keatings' friends was a Korean woman who'd spent weeks making *kimchi*. Another was a Polish lady who made her sauerkraut from scratch, salting it down in wooden barrels."

"Two vastly different kinds of fermented cabbage." Mary's laughter spilled out. "That must have been a, uh, fragrant meal."

"You could say so. Of course you need to factor in three different bean dishes, Mexican, Cajun and a knock-your-socks-off one from the Bronx."

"Oh. My. Goodness. Abby, you didn't eat all that, did you?"

She couldn't help a self-satisfied shrug. "I most certainly did. And it was delicious. But I was told the best part of the evening would come after we ate and it involved the tablecloth. I was rather puzzled. It was big and new, but plain white.

"After an incredible meal, we cleared the food away, and I saw that every dish had left a stain. At first, I felt bad. Then the fun began. Francine handed out indelible markers and we all went around the table writing compliments next to the stains and signing our names."

"I love it!" Mary exclaimed. "What did they do with the tablecloth?"

"Presented it to the newest guest as a memento." Blinking rapidly to hold back happy tears of nostalgia, Abby managed to smile. "I still have it. It's one of my most treasured possessions."

"Go get it," Mary ordered. "I want to see it."

"You will. It's over at Mom's. We discussed Rev. James's little flub on Sunday. You remember, where he told everyone to throw out the old traditions and substitute new ones?"

"Right. Janet had a great time watching Toby while Rev. James went around setting everyone straight."

"Mom's helping. She borrowed my tablecloth to show all her friends the new Thanksgiving tradition she plans to start."

"Why you little scamp. You and Mom. Why didn't you two tell me?"

"It was supposed to be a surprise. I'm telling you now because I thought the story might help you with Beverly and Wilma. No matter how different tastes and cultures are, there's always a way to bridge the gap."

"*Hmm.* Kimchi and sauerkraut. I'll definitely give it some thought, because I do believe you're right."

"Well, I know I'm right about one thing: You make the best bread on the island. The scent alone is making my taste buds tingle with anticipation."

Mary beamed. "Thank you."

Abby slid her gaze to the frosted loaves on the counter. "I'm sure it's even better than it smells."

"Why, sister dear," Mary drawled in her best Scarlett O'Hara imitation, "are you angling for a sample with extra glaze?"

"You must be a mind reader," Abby teased, mimicking her sister's fake Southern drawl. "How else could you know I was so hoping you'd indulge me?"

They laughed, having played this game and reversed roles numerous times since Abby began her permanent residence in Mary's home. Once they cleared the table, they returned with their desserts.

After they'd each savored several bites, Mary said, "By the way, Henry came to see me at the flower shop this afternoon."

At the mention of the deputy sheriff, Abby turned serious. "Was Candace there? Did he speak with her?"

"No. She and Brandi went to Orcas Island. Eastsound, I think. Henry asked about them."

"I imagine he wants to know if they're planning to file a complaint."

"He does. And all I can tell you is the same thing I told him. I don't know. I don't even know if Candace is working or on vacation. The one thing I do know is the shop is her refuge. She finds peace there."

"Ooo-kay. I get it now. I knew you said she was taking some time off while Brandi was here, but then because she's at the store so often I thought I was mistaken."

"You are *not* mistaken. The funny thing is, I'd geared myself to work. Instead, she practically shoos me out. The good news is that I got most of my Christmas shopping done. What I haven't finished are my knitting projects. I'd hoped to have two sweaters ready for the Sweaters for Kids project."

Mary tsked her tongue. "Shame on me for getting so behind. When it comes to traditions, this is an important one. Those children need what we knit."

"It's almost Thanksgiving," Abby mused.

"Tell me."

"Okay. After we finish dessert, go knit. I'll do the kitchen. Heavens, you cooked, so it really is my turn."

Mary cast a glance at the baking mess on her work counter.

"*Mmm,*" Abby hummed around a bite of pumpkin bread. "This is worth cleaning up for."

"Great." Mary wheeled away from the table and retrieved her knitting, but stayed close enough to talk. Blossom immediately grew interested and came looking for an opportunity to play with an unraveling ball of yarn. Finnegan positioned himself strategically between the cat and their mistress to foil the feline's intentions.

Abby began cleaning up. "Thanksgiving is creeping up and you and I need to coordinate schedules. Unless I'll be in your way, I'll make my cranberry relish on Wednesday. It's always better the second day."

"Great. Then I'll have the kitchen Thursday morning to do my marshmallow yams."

"What's Henry bringing?" Abby asked over the running water.

"Cobb salad and a special dressing."

Abby chuckled. "It figures—Henry Cobb, Cobb salad. Hugo told me he's bringing almond truffle green beans. It's an interesting combination I'm eager to try. He's made them every Thanksgiving he wasn't in the bush or on safari since he was a boy."

"Sounds like a culinary adventure. Sam's bringing garlic mashed potatoes. It's his mother's recipe, but one I suspect he's perfected over the years." Mary's knitting needles worked the yarn at her typically fast pace.

Catching a faint glimpse of the lights on at the McDonald home, Abby asked, "Is Mom still making the turkey and stuffing? Or has she changed her mind?"

"She's holding off on the decision." Mary reached into her knitting bag for another ball of yarn. "She and Dad are concerned about Bobby too. Thanksgiving dinner with family and friends should be fun for a ten-year-old, not traumatic."

"I couldn't agree more." Abby finished wiping down the countertops. "I just hope this whole thing with the missing ring doesn't put a damper on the holiday."

"So does Henry, which brings us full circle. He can't do anything until there's a complaint. The problem is, word has apparently gotten out and the news is creating an undercurrent all over the island."

Abby wiped her hands. "I pray the innuendo and gossip don't shred innocent reputations."

"From your lips to God's ears." The staccato clack of Mary's knitting needles betrayed her deep displeasure over the situation.

"Didn't someone once say the only thing a man truly owns is his name—which is his reputation?"

"Yes, but who said it escapes me at the moment." Abby turned a dining room chair toward her sister and sat. "If people are talking, then suspicions are mounting. If the ring doesn't surface soon, real damage will be done."

Mary met her gaze. "Damage that can't be undone. You can't un-know an accusation."

Feeling she had to be missing something vitally important, Abby nodded.

"I'll tell you one thing," Mary said sharply. "If anyone says one word about my sister, I'll . . . I'll . . . I'll run them down with my wheelchair."

Their gazes locked and Abby didn't doubt for a moment Mary meant what she said. A surge of affection welled up in Abby. Her sister was a fierce defender of those she loved. "Being caught in the middle must be hard for you."

"It is. But I'm up to the challenge. Nobody messes with my family and gets away unscathed." She lowered her knitting needles. "Of course, I really don't want to ram anyone. I want the scathing to be legal. Besides, Henry would have my hide. But I'll tell you this: He wants to close the book on this incident, the sooner the better.

"Unfortunately, it isn't that easy. No complaint has been filed, so it isn't a police matter. As difficult as it is to let Candace handle this her way, none of us has a choice."

Upstairs, Abby's grandfather clock chimed the hour. Time was slipping by too quickly.

CHAPTER ✿ NINETEEN

R ED SKY IN THE MORNING,
sailor take warning. The seaman's adage echoed in Abby's mind
as dawn cut a crimson swath across the eastern horizon. The
caution about the weather was the least of her concerns. Far
more important was the storm brewing in Green Harbor over
the missing ring. Already, eddies of distrust swirled in the corners of conversations, clouding the air with speculation.

She rose from the dining table and put away her Bible.
Although Fridays were always busy and this one promised to
be more so than most, she'd gladly spent a little extra time on
her devotions. Starting the day with the Lord centered her,
reminding her of what was truly important.

This morning, she'd gravitated to the book of Proverbs. As
she went upstairs to dress for the day, she thought about the
promise of wisdom and understanding walking hand in hand.
Immediately, the next step in her investigations was clear.

Choosing a tweedy pair of brown wool pants and a forest
green sweater, she completed her preparations in record time.
Downstairs, she checked in with her sister. Although Mary was

already dressed and brushing her shoulder-length silver hair, Abby asked, "Can I help with anything?"

"Nope. Are you going to see Dad?"

"How did you know?"

"Experience. And I heard you come down early while I was reading my Bible in bed." Their gazes met in the mirror and Mary chuckled as she put away her brush. Together they headed for the kitchen. "Talking things over with Dad's a good idea, Abby. He's a great sounding board."

"You'll be okay?"

"Of course." Mary took the cup of coffee Abby offered. "I have Finnegan and my cell phone. Candace is working today so all I have to do is deliver the pumpkin bread. Can you take one to Mom and Dad?"

"Sure, and I'll do the delivery to Island Blooms," Abby volunteered. "That is, if you want me to."

"I'd be crazy to refuse. It'll give me time to finish my sweater projects." Mary put the wrapped loaves in a tote bag. "The one for Mom and Dad is on top. Give the rest to Candace. She knows where to find the platter and the serving equipment."

"Okay, then I'm off." After hugging her sister, giving Finnegan an affectionate scratch and Blossom a friendly stroke, Abby picked up the tote and left.

AT STANTON FARM, Abby went into the house and gave her mother a warm hug while telling her about Mary's gift.

"I'm so glad you girls have each other." Ellen gave Abby another loving squeeze. "And that both of you are here on the island, close to George and me."

Following her into the kitchen, Abby replied, "Me, too, Mom. I had a great time on the East Coast, but there truly is no place like home." She put the foil-wrapped loaf on the counter. "Where's Dad?"

"George is down at the barn." Ellen regarded Abby thoughtfully. "I think a visit from you is just what he needs. And you can tell him about the treat Mary sent."

Wondering why her father needed cheering, Abby went out the back door and straight to the barn. Inside what had once been a storeroom, she found him cleaning and repairing several birdhouses. She recognized them as springtime fixtures on the giant old maple tree in the backyard.

Although she hadn't given it a glance today, she smiled. For nearly half a century, its big trunk and spreading branches had been part of her life, part of her family. Thoughts of home always included happy memories made under the maple's shady canopy.

She settled on a stool by her father's worktable and watched his callused hands tenderly fit a new bottom onto an older birdhouse.

"How's my girl?" He removed the broken perch in front of the house's round opening.

"Stumped."

"I know the feeling." George applied a bead of yellow glue to a short piece of dowel and worked it into the hole.

"Why?" Abby let her gaze wander over his projects. "What's up? Everything in here looks okay."

"Outside is a different story." He led her to the door and pointed toward the trees. "What do you see?"

"Oh no." Abby gasped. From this angle, she could see a tall fir listing sharply to one side. "If it comes down, it'll crash into the old maple." Her thoughts ran ahead to the dangers posed by removing the fir.

At times, her father seemed to forget he was eighty-two.

Although still wiry and in good shape, he wasn't as agile as he liked to think. "Dad! Don't tell me you and Sam are even thinking of—"

"Taking down the fir? Yep. But before you get all riled up, we know it's out of our league. That's what stumped us. Then I talked to the fellows down at Holloway's Hardware. They told me to call that new guy, Sven."

Startled, Abby blurted, "Why? He's a landscaper not a lumberjack."

"Apparently he does both," George said. "It's a good thing, too. A man in business for himself has to be versatile."

Remembering how the fishing expeditions and whale-watching tours were only part of her father's repertoire, she nodded. When times were tight, he'd also used his boat to carry freight and foodstuffs. "Right. Versatile like you were."

He nodded. "Sven has a slot for us this afternoon."

"Thank goodness. But I'm sorry about the tree." Her father loved the stately conifers and the loss of even one struck close to the heart. She looked at the birdhouses stacked beside his work-bench and realized he'd found a way to stay busy so he wouldn't have to watch. "How long has the fir tree been leaning?"

"The big blow last Saturday got it started. Every day since then, it's gotten worse. But don't be sorry. There's always a silver lining. In this case, there are two. Taking it down will give the garden more sun and next winter, your mother and I will have plenty of seasoned firewood."

Abby wrapped an arm around his waist and gave him a hug. "I love the way you always look for a bright side. What do you do when there isn't one?"

"*Ahh.*" George returned her hug and walked her back to her seat by the workbench. "You mean that ring business. Mary told me what you're up against, so I can see why you're asking.

Doubting your friends is a hard thing, Abby. I'd say you need to change your perspective."

"Okay." She leaned a hip on the stool and watched him cut a piece of sandpaper into fourths. "But how?"

"Maybe you're too close to the problem. Like I was." He fitted one of the smaller rectangles into the hand sander. "When you don't like what you're seeing, shift your focus. Ask different questions." He gave her a crooked smile. "Doing that is how I learned about Sven."

Abby felt her chin drop. Of course! She'd been so worried about the potential damage to reputations and businesses she'd lost sight of the obvious. If the ring wasn't inside the house—and no one took it—then by means she had yet to discover, it had to be outside. "Do you mind if I borrow the small garden rake?"

"Take it." He turned toward her. "What's your plan?"

"I want to poke around the outside of Candace's house." She rounded the workbench, reached up and kissed his cheek. "You're a genius, Dad."

He laughed and his brown eyes twinkled merrily. "I must be. My world-famous ornithologist daughter says so."

"And Mary, your world-class pumpkin-bread-baking daughter, thinks you're wonderful too. She sent over a treat."

"Well what are we waiting for?" He put down the sander and reached for Abby's hand. "Let's get a move on."

After a short detour to the tool shed, they went to the house. The fragrance of fresh coffee met them as they entered through the back door. On the stove, a teakettle whistled happily.

"There you are," Ellen said as she moved the kettle and took George's favorite mug from the cupboard. "Are you staying, Abby?"

"I don't dare." She patted her middle. "Mary and I did our

fair share of sampling last night. And I need to check on my feathered patients at The Nature Museum. I'm hoping to release the last of them this morning."

George nodded sagely. "A cage is no place for a wild bird."

After a flurry of hugs and kisses, Abby drove the short distance to The Nature Museum and went in to the laboratory. The pair of Northern flickers fluttered nervously, looking for an escape from their wire prison. Pleased with the return of the birds' strength and energy, she wheeled the cages out to a spot near a stand of red-barked Madrone and opened the doors.

The flickers fluttered out, eager to test their newfound freedom. With a deep sense of satisfaction, she watched them tap the trees for a meal before wheeling the birdcage inside. It was nearly ten o'clock by the time she finished cleaning and sterilizing it.

As she headed out toward Candace's house she viewed the scenery with new eyes. On nearly every road, sawdust and woodchips attested to the industry of the county's work crews. In the woods, sturdy trees supported a host of leaners. Yet in many clearings, at least one tree had lost the battle with the wind.

As she neared the spot where the balloons had marked the turnoff, she heard the deep growl of a chainsaw. Rolling down her window, she listened for the sound's direction. It came from Candace's property. Someone was hard at work and the likelihood of it being Candace or Brandi was nil.

At the end of the long driveway, Candace's home had a new sense of light and airiness. The deep shadows that had cloaked the house were gone, along with the dangerous leaning trees. Candace would be thrilled with the result. Abby parked her car and stepped out.

The growl of the chainsaw ceased. Across the yard, surrounded by a pile of branches, Sven removed his ear protection and looked at her.

As she approached, she saw he was doing more than a good job. He'd not only removed the trees safely, he'd cut the trunks into fireplace-sized lengths. After they seasoned, the big rounds would provide several cords of firewood.

"Hi, Sven."

"Hi." He set down the chainsaw and tossed a shortened branch onto the half-loaded bed of his truck. "If you're looking for Candace, Brandi had to take her to work. Too bad. Brandi's a real worker."

Abby cocked her head.

"She surprised me this morning. Met me when I arrived, ready to help. She said she's coming back. We'll see. I worked her pretty hard for a couple of hours."

"She didn't strike me as the outdoorsy type."

"Me either." He shrugged. "Live and learn. What's with the rake?"

"I thought I'd have a look in the flowerbeds. See if the ring took an unexpected trip outside."

Skepticism tightened his features. "Really."

"I may be grasping at straws, but it is possible it fell into a trouser cuff or got caught in one of our costumes."

"You *are* grasping at straws. It looked like a heavy ring." He grabbed an armful of branches and hurled them into the bed of his truck. "Suit yourself, but make it quick, unless you have ear protection. I've got more cutting to do."

Abby hurried to the porch off the kitchen. On the right side of the steps, a concrete pad held a big green garbage can. She rolled it away and raked through the leaves and needles clustered in the corner.

Nothing.

Mindful of Sven, she ignored her disappointment and kept moving. With short, quick strokes, she raked the perimeter of the concrete pad and porch. Still finding nothing, she turned the corner to the front of the house.

She crouched on the walkway and raked the mulch in the flowerbeds on both sides. "Be here," she whispered, her gaze keen for a glint of gold or anything shiny.

A shadow loomed over her. "This'll be noisy." He held up a reciprocating saw. "Sorry, but I've got to finish this job. People are waiting. And they want me yesterday."

Abby stood, her gaze on the sharp blade. She hadn't found anything, but she had a question only Sven could answer. "Can you give me another minute?"

"What for?"

"I've been thinking about our conversation. Can you tell me how long it might take to create a synthetic stone identical to a real one?"

A storm of emotions darkened his countenance. His gloved thumb flexed over the power switch. "I don't know." Prudence dictated she heed the warning in the hard set of his jaw.

He turned away, pulling on his ear protection.

The whine of the saw chased Abby to her car.

With fresh questions rising faster than the bubbles in a pot of boiling water, she headed for Island Blooms. She couldn't decide if Sven's surly attitude came from an abundance of work, the absence of his helper or the shadows of guilt.

Under different circumstances, it would be a road worth following.

On the way to town, she passed Brandi in Candace's car. Sven was in for a surprise. His helper was returning.

Abby turned her thoughts to the mystery and reconsidered her father's advice. If she followed it and asked new questions, the most logical place to start was with Candace.

Every penny she made was earmarked for something. Even the party had been carefully planned to minimize expenses. The guests brought the food and drinks. Bradford, no doubt, paid for the mystery game.

Maybe the young florist had incurred some other kind of unforeseen debt. Abby's gaze drifted to the dashboard of her hybrid car. Needed repairs or tires could blow a budget in a heartbeat. She could almost hear Laverne Minsky describing ways to cut corners and save a dime.

With a start, Abby realized Laverne wasn't the only one who knew how to cut corners. Candace's distinctive clothing always had an air of familiarity, and no wonder. Last season's skirt was this season's vest. The more Abby thought about it, the more garments she recognized had started out as something else.

Had the young woman tired of such frugal living and seized the unexpected opportunity when Brandi plunked her diamond ring down on the mantel? Abby hoped not, but couldn't ignore the fact the ring would fill out an emergency fund quite nicely. Removing the dangerous trees fell into that category.

To someone counting every penny, the sparkling diamond would have been very tempting, practically a guarantee the next financial emergency could be met. Like a lost and thirsty hiker in the desert finding a sealed bottle of fresh water lying in the middle of the path, all one had to do was pick it up.

CHAPTER ❦ TWENTY

A BBY PARKED IN THE TINY lot behind Island Blooms. As usual, when she entered the flower shop the perfume of the blossoms and the clean scent of soil filled her senses. The shop smelled like . . . Mary—elegant as an orchid, with a touch of earth tones that reflected her practical nature.

"Good morning." Candace rounded the counter, her long strawberry-blonde hair swaying in a loose braid down her back. Although she sounded cheery, her brow had an uncharacteristic furrow and there were smudges below her eyes.

Abby returned the greeting and hefted the tote bag. "Mary sent pumpkin bread for the store. She said you'd know what to do with it."

"Oh goodness, I forgot." Paling, Candace rubbed her forehead. "I'd volunteered to make the bread and it totally slipped my mind. Instead, I went to Orcas Island with Brandi. What must Mary think of me?"

"She knows you have company. She just stepped in to fill the gap. Your customers won't mind who made it. I had a sample last night and it's scrumptious."

"I'm sure," Candace agreed. "I'm also sure no one ever had a better employer than your sister."

"She is wonderful. Why don't we get the tea and coffee started, then set up the table. Afterwards, you can sit down, have a piece of pumpkin bread and relax."

"Yes, yes. Let's get set up."

Between the two of them, it took almost no time at all to put up the refreshment center. A colorful tablecloth in a pumpkin and gourd print and Mary's cornucopia platter proclaimed the holiday. Matching napkins, hot cups and dessert plates invited customers to enjoy the treats.

Candace brought over a small pot of chrysanthemums. The jiggling dance of the orange blooms betrayed the tremble in her hands. "What do you think?"

"It's lovely. I also think you need to sit down for a minute." *Before you fall down.* Abby wondered how long it had been since the young woman had eaten. "Come on. No one's in the store and you look like you could use a break. Have a cup of tea and a piece of bread and tell me about your visit to Orcas."

In the sudden silence, appreciation mingled with apprehension on Candace's features. Abby put two generous slices of the raisin and nut-filled pumpkin bread on a plate and decided to try a different approach.

While Candace rested on the stool behind the counter and nibbled the treat, Abby told her about the leaning tree at Stanton Farm. "The good news is that Dad and Sam realize they've met their match. Sven Dyer is going there this afternoon to take it down."

A genuine smile lifted the corners of Candace's lips. "He's such a nice man. He came by last night because he was concerned about two of my trees. They're going to fall. It's just a question of when they'll hit the house. I knew they were dangerous, but I . . . well, I asked him if he'd do it and let me make payments."

Deciding not to spoil the nice surprise of Sven's labors, Abby put another slice of bread on the florist's empty plate. "What did he say?"

"He's taking them down for free this morning." She gave a relieved shrug. "He called it a friendship favor. He said I'd extended mine by inviting him to the party and he wanted me to know how much he appreciated it."

"*Hmm.*" Abby's estimation of the landscaper shifted. Was it friendship or an opportunity to reclaim the stolen ring that prompted Sven's largesse?

She wished he'd been more willing to talk. Anyone who worked that hard to make a friend must intend to make Sparrow Island his permanent home. "I'm glad for you. And thanks for sharing. It tells me a lot."

Candace started on the third slice of bread and Abby was glad to see healthy color return to the young florist's wan cheeks. Keeping the topic neutral, she asked, "How was Orcas?"

"Every year the shopkeepers seem to start decorating for Christmas earlier and earlier. There were lights and decorations going up everywhere." A heavy sigh preceded a bout of lip chewing. "I'm afraid Brandi's not going to have a good Christmas this year."

"Why not?'

"Oh, Abby, it's awful. We were looking at ornaments and she burst into tears. I was so nonplussed, I didn't know what to say. Brandi's usually practical and professional. I've always admired her. I couldn't believe this smart and polished person I love so much was standing in the aisle crying. She totally dislikes public displays."

"Oh my. It must have been hard on both of you. What did you do?"

"You know the little restaurant in the hotel? We went there and found a table in the back. Her life isn't at all what I expected. I told Mary about Brandi crying in her sleep and she asked me if something had changed recently."

"Has it?" Abby remembered Mary's puzzlement when she relayed the incident. "I thought she had the world by the tail."

"Well, she did and that's the whole problem. The bottom fell out. One month she got a glowing commendation at work. Three weeks later, the company downsized and laid her off. She's taking it very hard. She's so depressed she hardly eats or sleeps."

Candace ate another bite. "The really hard part is Wayne. He doesn't understand how worthless she feels. He's furious that she came here instead of looking for a new job. Even worse, she says all they do is fight and it's tearing her apart."

"Oh dear."

"I feel so bad for her I can hardly stand it. Then on top of everything, her ring went missing." Candace looked up hopefully. "Please tell me you've learned something."

Abby sipped her coffee while deciding how to answer. "Yes and no. Except for Bradford, I've spoken to everyone at the party. All of us had opportunity. When you consider what's at stake for the Minskys, Keith, Donna, Sven and Nathaniel, taking the ring simply doesn't make sense. They'd be risking everything they've worked so hard to build."

"I know." Again, Candace rubbed the center of her forehead as if a king-sized headache lurked just under the skin. "That leaves me and Bradford." Tears brimmed along her lower eyelids. "And I know it wasn't us. I neither need nor want a ring like that, nor would I know how to sell it. Bradford—"

A thin laugh escaped as she closed her eyes and massaged her temples. "Let's just say he's very comfortable financially. He gets upset sometimes because I won't let him pay for repairs to my house. A girl has to have some pride, don't you think?"

Before Abby could answer, Candace continued, "I'll admit there's a limit. If Sven had needed cash up front, I would've asked Bradford to loan me the money to take down the trees."

"There's another person you didn't mention," Abby said softly.

"Who—you?" Hilarity shook Candace's slender frame. When she composed herself, she said, "Thanks, I needed a good laugh." Snatching a tissue from under the counter she dabbed the corners of her eyes. "No offense, Abby, but you and diamonds aren't a fit. You love the birds. The outdoors. Nature. People. Friends. Even if someone gave you a diamond ring, I doubt you'd wear it."

Relieved she'd been pegged so well, Abby tried one more time. "So where does that leave us?"

"I don't know." All traces of mirth faded.

"Think back," Abby prompted. "Who went outside Saturday night?"

"Uh . . . Bradford."

Abby felt her pulse speed up. Since Laverne mentioned his excursion into the storm, myriad questions had hovered over Abby's thoughts. "Do you know why he went out?"

"He heard one of the upstairs shutters banging. Bradford

didn't want to leave me with a repair project on my hands so he went out and secured the shutter before it tore off and took some siding with it."

The explanation was reasonable. Nevertheless, Abby questioned her memory of the night and realized she had been so caught up in the party, she hadn't paid attention to people coming and going. Everyone was constantly on the move, trying to figure out who killed the bouncer.

"Did Bradford mention seeing anyone go outside? Or did he see anyone while he was out there?"

Candace's brow scrunched in thought. "No, and I think he would have mentioned it. If you like, I'll ask when he calls tonight."

"That's all right. I have a few questions for him myself."

"You know, I didn't realize being a hostess required so much work. Between playing the game, keeping the dessert table stocked and my other duties, I'm afraid I didn't pay attention to my guests' movements."

"Other duties?"

Candace grinned sheepishly. "One of my big concerns was the bathroom. It's small and there's no storage space. I had to keep checking the paper and putting out fresh towels." The grin faded to a thin smile. "I mean, we did have a lot of bootlegged ginger ale to drink."

Although Abby's racing thoughts started to paint an unexpected picture, she shared the smile. "That we did."

CHAPTER ❦ TWENTY-ONE

WARM SUNSHINE AND A
brisk breeze accompanied Abby out of the flower shop. The
juxtaposition of warm and cool temperatures mirrored her
thoughts as she walked to the park at the center of town.

The benches near the fountain were deserted with one surprising exception. Clad in a fuzzy white hat, her favorite fleece
jacket, jeans and dairy boots, Brandi chewed her lunch in time
to the music from the compact player on her arm.

Understanding the young woman wouldn't hear a called
greeting, Abby cut across the grass to join her.

As soon as Abby sat beside her, Brandi switched off the
player's tiny earbuds.

"The Green Grocer's deli is hard to resist."

"Yeah. I was starved." Brandi smiled sheepishly.

"According to Sven, you had a right to be hungry. I stopped
by this morning. He told me you worked hard."

"Yeah. So did he. He mentioned seeing you when I got back
from taking Candace to work. I picked up a sandwich for him.
Then, I couldn't stop thinking about it. When he left, I came

back and got one for me." Brandi stowed the music player and earbuds in a jacket pocket. "What are you doing here?"

"I like to come to the park, watch the birds and think."

Brandi took another bite of her sandwich. A seagull hopped hopefully near the toes of her black rubber boots. She swallowed and laughed. "This silly bird likes these boots almost as much as I do. They're ugly as all, but practical. They ought to be issued to anyone who takes up residence in the Northwest."

She popped the last bite of sandwich into her mouth, crumpled up the wrapping and stowed it in a small bag with The Green Grocer logo. "They keep your feet dry and toasty when the rest of the world is chilly mud."

"Right you are." A variety of boots walked through Abby's thoughts. During the party, there were several pairs in the kitchen near the back door. Lined up like soldiers in the rain they'd dripped onto a thick layer of old towels. Only Donna Morgan's bright red pair varied from the usual dark shades of brown or black. Abby wished she recalled which ones were muddy.

She gestured toward Brandi's footwear. "Those are Candace's I presume?"

"Yeah. I'm glad they fit me. I've given them a workout today and there's a lot more to do. I told Sven I'd finish the cleanup around the yard."

"You like working outside?"

"I love it. Maybe I should . . . oh, never mind."

"Maybe you should what?" Abby asked, ready to steer the conversation in a more productive direction. "Look to the outdoors for your next job?"

"Candace told you." Brandi briefly closed her eyes and shook her head. "I should've known."

"She's concerned about you." Abby was too. Brandi looked much thinner, almost gaunt. Despite an exercise glow from her yardwork, she seemed as brittle as spun glass. "I'm sure getting downsized feels terrible, but it isn't the end of the world."

"Easy to say when it's not happening to you."

The point was hard for Abby to refute. She couldn't imagine having to find a new career in another field. Leaving her friends at Cornell had been difficult, but giving up her feathered friends would have taken the heart right out of her. She'd been incredibly blessed with the perfect position the Lord had created for her at The Nature Conservatory.

"Will you tell me about your job, Brandi? It sounds as though you must have liked it very much."

"It paid well."

"What did you do?"

"I was an administrative assistant to a vice president in charge of industrial construction. It *was* exciting. I had an important role in projects that ultimately created good jobs for people." She sighed and stared at her hands. "That is, for other people."

Although several of the partygoers had labeled Brandi as lazy and scatterbrained, Abby saw a much different picture. The woman was an organizer and a planner, a very intelligent go-getter. "What are your plans now?"

"Run away. Stay here. Move to China." Despite her flippancy, she brushed away a lone tear before it could slide down her cheek. "I haven't decided."

Fearing the situation between Brandi and her husband was even more tenuous than Candace described, Abby said, "Interesting choices. What about Wayne?"

Another tear followed the first. "I don't think he wants to be married anymore."

"Right now is definitely not the best time to make important decisions like that. Losing a job is a major blow. It'll be hard to see things clearly for a while."

"That's the real reason I came to visit. I needed time to think. About Wayne. Me. We love each other desperately, but we fight about everything. Big, small, important or not, the subject doesn't seem to matter." Brown eyes filled with fear and pain regarded Abby briefly.

Dropping her gaze, Brandi examined the hands in her lap. "Wayne always knows the right thing to do and when to do it. At least, he mostly does. I just want us to get along the way we did when we got married . . . to be happy like that again."

She tipped her head back and stared at the sky, an odd mixture of hope and defeat in her expression. "I want to roll the calendar back. But I can't. I feel . . . stuck, like there are no answers for me anywhere."

Recalling her morning devotions, Abby said, "Wisdom and understanding need to walk hand in hand. Have you and Wayne shared your feelings and the reasons you think your relationship has changed?"

"Oh, I suppose so. I mean, we've talked. But we always say the same thing. I try to do it his way. Sometimes, he tries to do it mine, but we don't seem to be trying at the same time. It's like we keep misconnecting."

Suddenly Brandi straightened and waved a hand in the air. "I don't want to talk about it anymore. Besides, you've never been married. You don't know what it's like."

Abby's thoughts flew to a certain man she had once loved. "No," she said softly. "But I've been in love. I know what that's like."

"Then you should understand why I don't want to go home

and look for a job." Brandi turned the band of diamonds on her left finger round and round. "If Wayne and I . . . split up, I can't be in the same town. If I run into him on the street or see him with someone else, I'll . . . I'll just die."

Although solving the problems in the marriage was out of Abby's hands, she could point the girl in the right direction. "If I were you, I know what I'd do."

Brandi blotted her tears and leaned forward eagerly. "What?" she asked. "What would you do?"

"I'm a praying woman, so I'd begin by asking God to help me figure out what the problem really is."

Brandi sat back shaking her head. "He won't help me."

"How can you know, unless you ask? He has a wonderful plan for each of us. Don't you think you ought to find out what it is for you and Wayne?"

"I, uh, well, maybe . . ." She snatched several tissues out of her pocket and hid behind them.

Brandi couldn't see a solution until she discovered the right perspective. Giving her a few moments to collect herself and knowing more was at stake than the mystery of the ring, Abby lingered on the bench.

"What else?" Brandi asked. "I mean, you said you'd begin by praying. What would you do then?"

Abby's years at Cornell had taught her easy answers didn't carry much value. Their worth increased when the students had to work for them. "Let me ask you something first. On your job, how often did someone dump a bunch of parts on your desk with the expectation you'd build something special?"

"Well, never."

"Did your boss ever give you half a letter and expect you to draft a reply?"

"No-o-o. I see where you're going." Understanding lightened Brandi's features. "You're saying I can't fix a problem until I know what it is."

Abby smiled. "Exactly."

The younger woman's expression darkened. "But what if it's too big? What if it's spiraled out of control?"

"Get help. Human and divine, you need both."

"But I, we . . ."

Abby raised an eyebrow. "Isn't getting help what your job was all about? The executives at your old company couldn't build a shipping port with their bare hands. Instead, they found people with the right skills to help."

Brandi worried her bottom lip with her teeth. "I suppose it's worth a try."

"I'd say a marriage is worth all the perseverance you can muster." Abby rose and touched the young woman's shoulder. "As I see it, you have two choices. You can wallow in worry and uncertainty, or you can do what's right. Choose well. Your decision affects Wayne too."

Certain she'd given Brandi a great deal to consider, Abby took her leave. With her priorities reordered, her busy day had just gotten busier.

She needed to dash home and get ready for the demonstration by the Northwest Native American Basket Weavers at The Nature Museum. Hugo was counting on her. If she hurried, she might have enough time to contact Bradford. She hoped he wasn't in court and could talk.

WITH THE PHONE pressed to her ear, Abby stood in her office at The Nature Museum. "Come on, Bradford. Answer."

Between getting dressed for this afternoon's event and walking into her office, Abby had put together all the clues and identified the motive behind the missing ring.

Now she needed help in resolving an even bigger problem. Earlier, she'd crossed Bradford's name off the suspect list. By his actions, he'd demonstrated his affection for Candace. His goal was to make her happy. Abby hoped his invitation to call on him for anything included what she had in mind.

She smoothed a hand over the lapel of her black wool pantsuit. The brightly colored parrots and cockatiels clustered on the cloisonné pin hung straight. If Bradford agreed to her plan, she'd contact Sven before she scheduled a regathering of the partygoers.

"Collins here." Bradford's words were quick and clipped.

"It's Abby. I need a couple of minutes. Can you talk?"

"Hey, Abby. Yeah. Let me close my office door."

When he returned to the phone she asked, "Can you come to Sparrow Island this weekend?"

"I can manage that. Have you solved our mystery?"

"Yes. But I need you to do something that might not be easy for you."

Bradford hesitated. "Will it help Candace?"

"Yes."

"Then I'll do it . . . even if I may not want to."

CHAPTER ❦ TWENTY-TWO

Sunshine shimmered on Mary's yellow, red and teal silk jacket while the van's hydraulic lift lowered her to The Nature Museum's parking lot. She adjusted a sleeve and savored a memory along with the feel of the sensuous material. The garment had been hand-stitched with prayers and get well wishes during the long weeks she'd spent in the rehabilitation center after her accident.

At the surprise welcome home party Abby engineered, Beverly had taken Mary aside and shyly presented the quilted treasure. The first time Mary had put it on, she felt like God had leaned down from heaven and kissed her cheek. Since then, whenever she wore the lovely "gift of the heart" she thanked Him for blessing her with such wonderful friends.

Today seemed a particularly appropriate time to wear the gift. The basket weavers' demonstration would start soon and Beverly and the quilters had promised to attend.

Mary rolled off the lift, pressed the remote for it to retract, then ruffled Finnegan's fur while attaching his leash. As they made their way across the full parking lot, she recognized many of the vehicles. The Busy Bee Quilting Society had come in force.

With one last check of Finnegan's service cape, Mary took a deep breath. "Okay, boy. Let's go see the show and hope we're not the main attraction."

Abby met her and held the door for Mary and Finnegan to pass through.

"You look great," Mary said. "Professional, chic and very neutral."

"Thanks, and you look fantastic." She pointed to the basket purse on Mary's lap. "Nice touch."

"Something from both camps," Mary conceded.

"They're all inside—half demonstrating Native American arts, the other half watching and asking questions."

"Gracious, already? I thought I was early and the Busy Bees would still be milling around the lobby."

"You are early, but so was everyone else. They were eager to get started, so we did." Abby gave Mary's shoulder an affectionate squeeze. "Don't worry. It's going to be fine."

"I hope you're right," Mary murmured.

"If you need it, my office is open." Abby winked. "But I'm counting on your level head. You'll have these two groups sitting on a quilt and weaving baskets in no time."

Mary laughed. "I can always count on you to pump me up."

"No blather. All truth." Abby gave her another pat of encouragement before turning to greet the foursome coming up the walkway.

Finding the basket weaving demonstration and exhibit was easy. With Finnegan by her side, Mary followed the crowd and was surprised to see how many of the townsfolk had turned out for the occasion.

Mary was pleased for Abby and Hugo. Those two worked tirelessly to educate the islanders and she was delighted to see their efforts rewarded. While waiting in line to get into the demonstration room, she spotted Beverly waving at her. Praying this day would be a blessing to all of them, Mary waved back.

"I never dreamed it would be this fascinating," Beverly gushed when Mary rolled up. "Wilma's going to teach me about the colorants they use. Since I hand-dye most of my fabrics, I'm always open to new methods. She wants to try some of my recipes too. I haven't been this excited in ages. Just look at those vivid colors!"

Mary exhaled a breath she hadn't realized she'd been holding. Beverly's enthusiasm was a giant step forward. The lines of communication were open and flowing. Even better, the two camps were finding value in each other's crafts. What more could she ask?

The minute she and Beverly moved inside, Mary saw Abby's fine hand at work. Glass cases, laden with extraordinary examples of the weavers' art covered the walls. Instead of a stage, seven tables were strategically placed around the room in a loose ring. Surrounded by avid watchers, a weaver at each table demonstrated a different aspect of the craft.

Dressed in traditional tribal garb, Wilma circulated through the throng, answering questions and directing the visitors. When she saw Mary, her smile broadened. Stepping into the middle of the circle of weavers, Wilma asked the crowd for their attention.

A flurry of hush's and _shhh_'s whispered through the gathering. Standing proudly in her ceremonial costume, she said, "My fellow weavers and I thank you for coming. You honor our traditions, our heritage and us with your presence."

During the applause, Wilma's steady brown gaze lingered on Beverly and Mary, then she spoke again. "Many cultural arts are in danger of dying out. We mean to see ours continue so we invite anyone who wants to learn from a master to raise their hand."

Beverly's shot into the air. Praying her friend would be chosen, Mary watched breathlessly as the weavers hung back, waiting for something.

The eldest of the weavers, a man they obviously respected, rose slowly and ignoring all the raised hands, walked directly to Mary. Bewildered, she looked up at his kind, wizened face. He reached out and touched her shoulder. "You make?"

Realizing he meant her jacket, she reached for Beverly and said, "It was a gift from my friend here. She made it."

"Ah. Then she is the one I want."

The look on Beverly's face declared she recognized the honor she'd been given and she followed the elder to his table. Only then, did the other weavers make their selections from the volunteers.

Thank You, Lord, for taking this coat of many colors and using it to work all things for good. Suddenly, Mary's cheek tingled. She closed her eyes for a long moment while she savored the blessing.

When she looked around again, nearly every table had one of the Busy Bees sitting with a weaver. Leaving it all in the Lord's hands, she became a spectator.

"Each of you has an incomplete basket with a basic weave," Wilma explained from the middle of the circled tables. "Your instructor will walk you through the steps of that basket's technique, then answer questions as you try your hand at making another row or two."

While the volunteers got to work, Mary circled the perimeter of the room, watching and listening.

"Upon my word," the quilter at the first table remarked. "I had no idea it was this difficult."

"Me either," came a second voice. "It looks so easy when *they* do it, but I already broke my bark strip."

At another table, Beverly lamented, "I feel like I have four thumbs." Just then, the softened reed slipped out of her fingers and tapped her chin. She turned to her venerable instructor. "Will you show me again how I should hold it?"

At their table, Wilma's nephew Artie beamed at his pupil. Ana Dominguez had already finished her row. "You're a natural-born weaver, Ana. Maybe you and I can get together at your shop and you can give me a lesson on those great looking wall hangings you make."

"*Sí*. I'd be glad to show you." She picked up a length of gossamer-like fibers. "Will you teach me to make these?"

Henry's deputy nodded. "Good trade."

"You're doing a very good job," Wilma patiently encouraged Rebecca at the last table.

The teenager sat with her arms crossed, scowling at the basket. "But my row is totally uneven and lumpy."

At the table next to her, a quilter known for her appliqués chuckled and said, "Hey honey, if you've already finished a row, you're way ahead of me. The important thing is you're learning something new. If you ask me, that's something we all need to do."

Across the circle, Beverly met Mary's gaze and gave an embarrassed nod. Mary understood it wasn't capitulation.

Rather, it was an acknowledgement of what she'd been trying to tell both sides of the dispute. Creativity only grows in the fertile soil of an open mind.

Wilma came up to Mary and touched her jacket. "You made quite an impression."

"Not me. It was Beverly."

"Yes you. The elder is most impressed that you are worthy of such a gift."

"I've been blessed."

"Indeed. This is a good day."

"A very good day," Mary agreed. "We all have much to teach one another."

"Agreed, but I thought I'd see if you remained true to your stand."

"I haven't budged an inch."

"Good." Wilma gestured to her fellow weavers. "My friends are eager to meet with the quilters, to see the best of their best. It must be soon. Some of our weavers are only here for the weekend. Then they return to their homes on the mainland."

"Tomorrow morning at In Stitches should be fine," Mary said. "I'll set it up with Ana and the Busy Bees and let you know for sure a little later on. And thank you, my friend."

"You're welcome, friend." Her smile turning mischievous, Wilma added, "It's time we made peace anyway."

"ABBY?" DESPITE THE LAUGHTER spilling out of the demonstration room and filling the museum, Hugo's usually jovial features wore a silent plea for help. Accompanying him were Bobby McDonald and his mother Sandy. The boy looked grim and his mother concerned.

"Hey, Sandy, Bobby. I'm glad you two came. Have you seen the weavers yet?"

Wearing the same look of helplessness as Hugo, Sandy nodded. Bobby shrugged.

Uh-oh. Time to talk turkey. Abby held her hand out to Bobby. "Why don't you and I go to my office?"

Hugo shared a glance with Sandy who said, "That's fine with me. Take as long as you like."

Abby looked down at Bobby. Serious matters required fuel. "What do you say we hit the refreshment table first? Get some juice and cookies."

"Okay."

Shortly thereafter, she pushed the office door closed with her hip and carried the drinks to her desk. Bobby carefully put the plate of treats beside them before fidgeting into the visitor's chair.

For several minutes, they munched cookies and drank juice. Bobby seemed to relax a bit, which was good because Abby couldn't. Coming up with the right thing to say felt a little like dancing on a floor covered with old motor oil. One slip and you're down and dirty.

"You know, Bobby, you've given me a great deal to think about this past week."

"You mean about eating turkey and other birds?"

"Yes. I took your questions to heart and found myself wondering how any self-respecting ornithologist could eat poultry."

The boy brightened. "Whoa, am I glad. I was afraid I'd have to stay home alone and miss Thanksgiving dinner at the farm. 'Cause, I mean, if your mom is making turkey . . . my mom will want me to eat it. But if you're not eating turkey either, then she'll probably say I don't hafta."

On a happy sigh, he reached for another cookie. "Maybe

they'll let us eat the other stuff. Like dessert. I hope your mom makes pecan pie, 'cause mine is making pumpkin wonder cake. It's her new recipe."

"Hold on a second. Let's not get drastic here." *Or get distracted.* "You had Thanksgiving dinner at Stanton Farm last year, right?"

"Yeah," he answered wistfully. "Turkey, dressing and all the trimmings."

"It was good, right?"

"Super good. That's why this is so hard, Abby. I'm really going to miss eating turkey."

"So what's the difference between last year and this?"

"I'm older. Wiser. I've been reading. Now, I have insight."

"I see. And this insight—did it come from the poem you read, 'Ode to a Turkey'?"

"Dad wishes I never saw it." Bobby looked down at his sneakers. "I sorta do too. It changed my life, Abby. 'Cause it's so sad. I mean, all those turkeys out there are scared right now. This nice farmer is bringing all this good food, but they know. He's only feeding them 'cause he wants to eat 'em on Thanksgiving."

Abby wanted to lean across the desk and tell the child the silly poem wasn't true, but she knew that approach wouldn't work. Without a doubt, he'd already gotten several variations of the same argument from his parents. Trying a completely new tactic, she said, "It's a good thing the farmer's so smart."

"Smart! I can't believe you said that!"

"Well, it's true. The farmer knows turkeys can't think deep thoughts or analyze a situation the way we do."

"How can you be sure?"

Abby thought of the dozens of articles she'd read and the work scientists all over the globe were doing on the abilities of some birds to use tools. While the debate over intelligence versus adaptation piqued her interest, mentioning it now wouldn't help. "The brain of a bird is very small. It's simply not big enough."

The curl of his lip said he wasn't convinced.

She scooted to the side of her desk. "Drag your chair around here, next to me."

While he did, she said, "Think about Finnegan. He can do a lot of things, but he can't talk, write a book or do your math problems. He's also a lot bigger than a turkey with a much more developed brain."

"But the poem—"

"I'm glad you brought it up, because when you're learning new things, you have to consider the source—who wrote it and why. Is the source reliable, someone you can trust?"

"Dad says a man wrote 'Ode to a Turkey.' That he did it to be funny."

"Your father's a great example of a reliable source. He wants what's best for you. Furthermore, he's right."

Bobby shrugged. "I know he does. It's just . . ."

Abby removed the well-used book from the bottom drawer of her desk. "Here's another reliable source."

"The Bible," Bobby whispered, staring at it.

"God gives us choices. We can be vegetarians."

"No way. Maybe other people can, but not me. I'm not a vegetarian. I'm an antiavian-atarian. That means I don't eat birds."

Abby bit her inner cheek to keep from laughing. "Not even chicken?"

"Well, I like those nugget things and they're chicken, so I suppose I'm an antiturkey-atarian."

Suppressing a smile, she decided they were getting somewhere. "So if you read a poem about chickens being raised for our dinner tables you'd quit eating your mom's fried chicken and the fast food nuggets?"

Bobby thought for a moment. "Giving up the nuggets wouldn't be too hard. I only get to eat those when we go to the big cities. But Mom's fried chicken . . . I'd have to think about it."

Abby opened the Bible to Genesis 9 and read, "Every moving thing that lives shall be food for you."

Abby looked at Bobby. "God didn't say we have to eat meat or that we shouldn't. He said we could." She closed the Bible. "He also gave us the ability to think and make choices. I've made mine."

She waited until Bobby met her gaze. "If my mom is serving turkey for Thanksgiving, then I'm having turkey for dinner. With gravy and all the trimmings. And pumpkin wonder cake for dessert."

He sighed and rubbed the side of his thumb. "What about my mom?"

"I'll explain the situation to her. My mother won't mind if you don't eat turkey. I seriously doubt yours will either if you're committed to not eating it," Abby assured him. "But when you make big choices in life, they work out best if you consider both the information and the source of it. A poem might not provide the best guidance."

Sitting back, Abby allowed him to mull things over. She'd said all she felt comfortable saying. After all, there were some things a wise, mature boy with growing insight had to decide for himself.

CHAPTER ✦ TWENTY-THREE

ABBY GLANCED AT THE dashboard clock. The further the calendar rolled toward the end of November, the later the sun rose. At a few minutes after seven, it was barely a promise on the eastern horizon.

According to the detailed plan they'd worked out the previous night, Bradford should arrive any minute. Candace would meet him at the ferry dock. He'd keep her downtown for breakfast.

Abby pulled up to the Grover home and parked in the driveway. The diversion should give her enough time. After a short prayer for guidance, she squared her shoulders and went to the front door.

"Abby!" Brandi's big eyes got bigger. "I thought you were Candace and forgot something."

"May I come in? We need to talk about your ring."

"Ah, well . . . want some coffee? I do." Brandi led the way into the kitchen.

Abby took a seat at the table and waited for Brandi to join her. "I've spoken with all the partygoers, some of them more than once. Let me tell you what I've learned."

Brandi sipped her coffee slowly.

"We know the ring isn't in the house. It's not in the flowerbeds, not in the fireplace ashes and not in the trash. All have been thoroughly checked.

"I've also learned three people went outside that night. Bradford was one of them. He heard the upstairs shutter banging in the wind. He didn't want it to rip off and leave Candace with a mess she'd have to repair."

Abby knew she didn't have Nero Wolfe's finesse, but she wasn't concerned. Using facts to paint an accurate picture was far more important.

"Between the bouncer's murder and the inspector's appearance, Bradford went outside. He brought the ladder from the side of the house and set it up in the flowerbed under the second-story window. By the time he finished duct taping the shutter to the house, he was wet and cold and in a hurry to get back to the party as the inspector. He figured he could take care of the ladder later and left it where it was. He set the duct tape on the kitchen counter.

"Laverne entered the kitchen just as he was hanging up his wet raincoat." Abby rose and helped herself to a cup of coffee, then returned to the table.

"Nathaniel was the last person to go out. Toward the end of the party, while trying to figure out whodunit, he stepped onto the porch to smoke his pipe. He says it helps him think. The ladder was right where Bradford left it. Now though, it was leaning toward a window. Fearing it would fall into the glass,

Nathaniel removed his spats, stuffed them into his pocket, then took down the ladder.

"Sven saw Nathaniel come in and noticed his muddy shoes and damp trouser legs. Nathaniel didn't mention anything about the ladder to anyone. He doesn't like people who brag about their good deeds and didn't want to be one. However, after we learned the ring was missing, Sven suspected Nathaniel might have taken it. The friendship they'd struck up suddenly cooled."

Brandi winced and stared into the cup she held in white-knuckled hands.

"One other person went out that night."

"It was me. I . . . I took out the trash."

"Donna saw you come in," Abby said softly. "But you took out more than the trash. You took out the ring."

Brandi gasped. Color drained from her face.

"You're the only one who could have. You're also the only one with a motive. In our previous conversations, I got more than a hint of the financial troubles affecting your marriage. This is why I believe you impulsively seized an opportunity masquerading as a short-term solution when you took the ring off the mantel. In reality, the act was a disaster."

A tear rolled down Brandi's cheek.

"At the time, you thought the insurance check was the prize. You've had second thoughts, haven't you?"

Brandi sat rigid and held her coffee cup on the table with both hands. "Since then, I've had third, and fourth and fifth thoughts. I'd give anything to live that night over again and not do something so stupid. So . . . destructive." A second tear followed the first. "What now, Abby?"

She glanced at the window. "The sun's up. We have enough

light to retrieve your ring." Abby rose and went to the back door. "Come, give me a hand."

Dutifully, Brandi followed. After they wrestled the ladder in place, Abby pulled a pair of latex gloves from her pocket and put them on.

With Brandi steadying the ladder, Abby mounted the rungs. When she could look down into the gutter, she saw it was half-full of leaves and fir needles. "Look out below," she called and scooped out several handfuls of debris.

Then her muddy finger stubbed on an immovable lump. She climbed up another rung. A round object was duct taped to the bottom of the gutter. She pried up an edge, then the whole piece of tape and removed the sparkling diamond ring.

Without a word, Abby descended and handed the ring to its owner. "Technically, there's been no crime committed. You can go home and try to forget this ever happened."

"No, I can't."

"Can you stand and face the people you've hurt?"

"I . . . I don't want to." Brandi's gaze met Abby's. "But I think I have to."

"Owning up to mistakes is never easy. The Bible says that when pride comes, then comes disgrace, but with humility comes wisdom" (Proverbs 11:2). "This will take the kind of courage I believe you have." A car pulled into the driveway. "They'll all be here soon."

Terror filled Brandi's face. "Now?"

"The sooner you do it, the sooner it's over."

"Will you stay with me?"

"I won't leave your side." Trusting God's plan for the young woman, Abby gestured to the door. "Let's go in."

As Abby washed up at the kitchen sink, Brandi said, "Give me a few minutes, okay? I need to talk with Wayne."

EARS FLAPPING and tail flying in the warm November morning, Finnegan charged across the front yard after his ball. Laughter filled Mary's chest and bubbled out as he clamped the toy in his teeth and bounded back to her. Dropping the wet red ball on the slobber towel on her lap, he sat and waited for her to throw it again, his whole body quivering with anticipation.

She could relate to his eagerness. She felt the same anticipation over the guest due to arrive at any moment. The tribal elder who'd selected Beverly for his "trainee" yesterday had asked Wilma to arrange a private meeting for him and Mary. Known only as Joseph, he believed the Great Spirit Who Made Everything had blessed her powerfully. Now, Joseph wanted to hear her story.

Mary fondled Finnegan's ears then cupped his muzzle in her hands. "I'll have to tell Joseph about you, too, boy. You're part of my tale. You're a gift from my children and Zack's girlfriend. You bless my life every day."

The whoosh of tires in the drive announced Wilma and Joseph's arrival. The truck was an older model, its dark green paint polished to a high shine.

"Wilma, Joseph, welcome to my home." Mary gestured to the door. "Please, come in. Abby set us up on the back deck so we can enjoy this beautiful sunshine."

Joseph nodded and Mary led them through the house to the wicker chairs on the deck. The thick cushions padding the hard woven seats and backs were another of Abby's little touches. Before she'd left this morning, she'd zoomed around the house, helping set up for Joseph's visit.

Mary prayed silently for her sister and Brandi. This morning would be difficult for all the partygoers. Abby had received the final phone call she'd been hoping for early this morning. Afterwards, she'd given Mary a peck on the cheek and dashed out to her car.

Mary turned to her guests. After removing the quilted cozy keeping the teapot hot, she began to pour.

"Thanks, but none for me," Wilma said. "I need to restock our tables at The Nature Museum and get ready for this afternoon's demonstration. Yesterday was such a success our sign-up sheets for today and tomorrow are full." She turned to the elder. "When you're ready to meet with the quilters at In Stitches, give me a call."

"I'm going there too, Wilma." Mary looked at Joseph. "I wouldn't miss it. You're welcome to ride over there with me, if you like."

"I like." He patted Wilma's hand. "You're a good girl. You do much for your parents and our tribe. Thank you for bringing me. I'll ride with Mary when we finish talking."

With a resigned chuckle that suggested she was quite accustomed to the elder's paternal ways, Wilma said her farewell and left.

Alone with Joseph, Mary wasn't quite sure where to begin the conversation. Instead, she moved the tray with the tea condiments and a plate of cookies closer to him.

He leaned back with his eyes closed and basked in the sunshine for a long moment. Then his dark eyes fixed her with an inquiring look. "Now, we will talk about how the Great Spirit blesses His children."

Mary smiled. It was a subject she knew a great deal about.

CHAPTER ❦ TWENTY-FOUR

ABBY COUNTED THE GUESTS. With the arrival of the Minskys, the assembly of partygoers was complete. However, this was a much different occasion. Instead of wind, rain and laughter shaking the house, sunshine streamed through the window on a somber group.

Abby had summoned them to this inconvenient Saturday morning meeting with the promise she'd solved the mystery of the missing ring. Knowing the proceedings would be difficult, she silently asked the Lord to bless Brandi with strength and courage.

"I thank all of you for coming on such short notice." Abby tipped her head at Bradford. In order to attend, the attorney had to start his trip from Seattle in the predawn hours, long before the others were out of bed. "I know most of you have businesses to get to, so I'll keep this brief."

Pale and quivering, but determined, Brandi rose. Abby took the vacated seat and kept her knee pressed against Brandi's leg as they had agreed earlier. The young woman needed the contact for emotional support.

"I took the ring," Brandi began, her voice quavering. "It was wrong and stupid and what I've put you through was awful. I'm so sorry."

Fannies shifted and knuckles cracked, but no one said a word. Abby gave Brandi an encouraging nod. After all the wrong choices, she'd found the strength to make the right one. The follow-through was a necessary step and the best way to lay a new foundation for her future.

"The night of the party, right before it started, I got a call from Wayne, my husband. He'd just opened the bills for our credit cards and he was beside himself. I'd never heard him sound so defeated. I didn't know where to turn or what to do. Our situation had gone from bad to worse because I'd just been downsized out of my job."

Brandi started twisting the rings on her finger, then caught herself and stopped. "I play with my rings when I'm nervous. I got so upset when I was talking to Wayne, I broke the keeper on my engagement ring."

She took a drink from the water bottle Abby handed her, gave a wobbly smile of gratitude and returned the bottle to the table. "Several of you mentioned my ring was loose and in danger of getting lost. The chance comments gave me an idea. If I could collect the insurance money, I'd have the perfect solution for our financial troubles. I was so wrong. It was dumb and a huge mistake.

"Afterwards, I realized what a mess I created." She turned a sorrowful gaze toward Candace. "Losing my job was no excuse to betray your trust. You've been m-m-my best friend. I feel horrible about the pain I've caused you and for casting suspicion on your friends."

On the other side of her, Laverne Minsky tucked a handkerchief into Brandi's hand. Visibly shaken by the small kindness, the young woman clutched it to her chest. "You've all been so good to me. This last week I've seen what warm and friendly people you are. I hate it that my actions made others look at you with anything but respect. You didn't deserve that."

She took a deep breath and fought for composure. "The thing is, once I said the ring was missing . . . well, it was like a snowball going down hill. I didn't know how to stop it. I just knew I couldn't go through with it. For a while, I thought if I didn't file a complaint, it would be okay. People would forget it happened. I planned to leave the ring where it was. I figured after what I did, I had no right to it."

Although the tremor in the knee next to hers increased, Abby didn't intervene. Letting Brandi finish without interruption would be quicker and kinder.

Brandi looked down at her and Abby gave her a reassuring smile.

"My friend here made me see that running away isn't a solution. I had to identify the root cause of my problems and get to work on fixing them. The first step is taking responsibility for my actions. I couldn't just go back to Seattle and leave all of you with a cloud of suspicion hanging over your heads.

"I phoned my husband this morning and told him." Brandi's voice firmed. "He's ready to face our problems too. All we do is work, but we never get ahead. Sometimes we feel guilty for all the time we spend apart. He buys me presents. I do the same. Then the bills come in and we have to work harder. Longer hours. We know we can't keep digging a deeper financial hole. We have to get help and fix the one we're in."

She dabbed her wet cheeks with the handkerchief. "So that's it. All I have to say, except, I'm so sorry for what I did. I'm so ashamed and mortified. I know I'll never do anything like that again. I hope you can forgive me."

Nathaniel was the first to rise. Empathy writ large upon his features, he said, "Everybody makes mistakes. Owning up to them like you did takes real guts. Trust me, I know. As far as I'm concerned, you cleaned the slate and get a second chance. Now, give me a hug."

Abby breathed a sigh of relief as he enveloped Brandi in a bear hug. Laverne and Donna were next, followed by Al and Keith. After assuring Brandi of their forgiveness and prayers for her future, they headed off to their businesses.

Abby saw them out, then nodded at Bradford. During yesterday's phone conversation, she'd taken him up on his offer of "anything I can do to help." Although her request wasn't what he expected, he'd agreed and followed it up with an excellent suggestion. Now it was time to put it on the table.

Coming forward, he told Brandi, "I want you and Wayne in my office Monday morning at eight."

Already pale, she turned so white Abby feared she'd faint. Jumping off her chair, Abby guided the younger woman onto the seat.

Hastily, Bradford explained, "A friend in my building operates a debt consolidation concern. He's done wonders for couples in the same boat as you and Wayne. There will be no cost. He owes me a favor. I'm using it on you.

"After he gets you on a path to financial health, I advise you and Wayne to go for counseling. Find out why you did this to yourselves in the first place."

Disbelief, then hope shone in Brandi's teary eyes. "I, that is, *we* have it on our to-do list. Thanks to Abby, I understand that asking for help doesn't mean I'm a failure. It means I recognize other people have skills I need to learn. Thank you, Bradford, for your generous offer. I accept. I can't promise to pay you back, but I will promise to do what it takes to get debt-free."

"Good. I'll hold you and Wayne to it. And if you have questions or need help, I'll be there for you."

Sven took a seat beside Brandi. "I know you're a hard-worker. You proved that yesterday when I took down the trees and you helped me clear the brush. I, too, have a good friend in Seattle." He looked up at Bradford and grinned.

"Mine's in the nursery business. The guy has a green thumb with plants but a red one in the office. He desperately needs help organizing and running the business. If you want me to, I'll talk to him. Nathaniel was right. Coming clean like you did has convinced me you'll make the most of your second chance. A go-getter who doesn't mind spending part of her day outside is exactly what my friend needs."

"You'd really give me a recommendation?" Brandi asked in amazement.

"Yesterday, maybe. Today—absolutely. Coming clean shows me you're a person who owns up to her mistakes. This is not a handout. It's a hand up. Someone gave me one once, now I'm passing it on to you."

"Thank you, thank you, thank you both. I know I sound like a scratched CD but I'm just so overwhelmed. You guys are so wonderful, helping me put my life back together after what I did, I don't know what else to say."

Sven gave her his card then looked at his watch. "Sorry. I've gotta go. I have several appointments today. Give me a call later this afternoon and we'll talk about your résumé."

The landscaper passed Abby on his way out, murmuring, "I need to catch Nathaniel. See if I can buy him a cup of coffee." He hesitated. "I better get him a Danish too."

Thank You, Lord, for Your perfect timing. And for giving us another generous man with a discerning eye.

"It's time for me to leave too." Abby nudged Bradford as he moved toward one of the empty seats. "Walk me to my car. We'll give these two a chance to talk."

At the front door, Abby paused and looked back. Candace put a hand on Brandi's shoulder and she looked up hopefully.

"I'm proud of you." Candace sniffed and swiped at a tear. "This was the hardest thing I've ever seen you do."

Confident they were on the way to reconciliation, Abby stepped out into the bright sunshine. "What a gloriously beautiful day."

"Thanks to you it is," Bradford marveled. "If there were more people like you, Abby, there'd be fewer lawyers like me."

She smiled up at him. "We'll always need strong, caring men like you. I truly appreciate what you're doing for Brandi and Wayne."

"I want them to succeed as a couple, not just because of the bond between Brandi and Candace, but because I believe Brandi's sincere. She could have retrieved the ring at any time and followed through on her original plan. Instead, what happened this morning has opened my eyes. I'm beginning to understand why those two are so close."

"Solomon would be proud of you," Abby teased. "A man who understands his girlfriend's girlfriends is rare."

"Understanding is the beginning of wisdom," he bantered back. "Maybe there's hope for me yet."

She grinned. "It's one more thing to be grateful for on Thanksgiving."

"If I've learned anything about Sparrow Island," Bradford turned serious. "It's the generosity of the people who live here. Their openness is a breath of fresh air. They're willingness to help one another is humbling. They don't measure a person by how much money is in his pocket or theirs—either too much or too little."

"Money's a poor yardstick," Abby agreed.

"I'm still amazed the Minskys invited Candace and me to their house for Thanksgiving dinner. I'm honored. They're genuine folks."

"Yep. That's Laverne and our auto mechanic."

"Al's not a mechanic." Bradford put his fists on his hips in a pose of mock indignation. "He's a motor maestro and a great guy. He tuned my car up last weekend and now I'm getting better gas mileage than ever."

"Be sure to tell him. He'll be glad to hear it." Abby moved to her car.

Muffled laughter floating from the house brought a relieved smile to Bradford's lips. "Thanks again, Abby." He opened the trunk of his car and retrieved a pair of work gloves and a well-used windbreaker. "I think I'll make myself useful and give them a bit more time."

With a farewell wave, Abby turned her key in the ignition and watched Bradford ascend the ladder and begin cleaning the gutters. He'd come a long way and not just in miles. Yesterday, at the beginning of their conversation, he'd been an angry attorney determined to protect his sweetheart from further harm.

Fortunately, he'd also been open-minded enough to see the best way to protect Candace was to help Brandi.

Abby sent up a prayer of thanks and added, "You do work in mysterious ways, Lord. Whether Bradford knows it or not, he's turning into a Sparrow Islander. I'm happy for that too."

CHAPTER ❦ TWENTY-FIVE

Aт тне твıттеr оf нer cell phone, Abby reached down to the floorboard for her purse.

Mary finished backing out of the garage and put the van in park. "Must be Mom. Good thing she caught us before we left."

The sisters shared a knowing grin. Practically every Thanksgiving, their mother thought she'd forgotten something she needed for the big feast. The item was usually in the refrigerator, the pantry or not on the menu.

The twittering birdsongs Abby had programmed into her phone sounded again as she pulled it out of her purse and glanced at the screen. "Whoever it is, it's not Mom." Hoping there were no injured birds needing her to rescue them on this special day, Abby answered with a cheery, "Happy Thanksgiving."

"And to you too," Brandi said. "In fact, that's why I'm calling. Wayne and I want to wish you a happy Thanksgiving and tell you we're using another one of your suggestions."

Delighted with the upbeat lilt in Brandi's voice, Abby asked, "Which one?"

"We've always gone out to eat on Thanksgiving. Today we're starting a new tradition. From now on, we'll be celebrating at home." Her voice took on a dreamy quality. "Counting our blessings over a candlelit dinner."

"Brandi, that's wonderful."

"You're wonderful. Thank you so much, Abby, for your advice and support and . . . everything."

"You're very welcome." After they said their farewells, Abby shared the short conversation with Mary.

"I have to agree with Brandi." Mary hit the button to close the garage door, finished backing the van out of the driveway and headed for Stanton Farm. "You are wonderful. The first time I knew for certain was on another Thanksgiving. I think you know which one."

Abby met her sister's gaze and the years fell away. For a moment, they were two little girls again, gathered at the holiday table. An enormous golden brown turkey steamed on their mother's special platter.

Not quite four years old, Abby had scrambled up to kneel on her chair, get as close as she dared and stare at the amazing sight.

Her father put down the carving knife and asked in a concerned tone, "What is it, honey?"

"It's big meat! Can't you see, Daddy? God gave us big meat."

With a whoop of laughter, he swung her into his arms and twirled her around. "Yes He did, Abby." Bringing Mary into his embrace, their father held them tight. "My precious girls. Someday, you'll know how mightily He has blessed us."

Returning to the present, Abby reached over and touched Mary's arm. "You're the best sister in the whole world."

"Listen to us," Mary said huskily. "We sound like the Stanton sisters' mutual admiration society."

Basking in a warm glow, Abby said, "The last two weeks have been hectic, but I wouldn't trade them for anything. Your escapade with the weavers and the quilters proves God has a great sense of humor."

The quilt show at Ana's shop had been a smashing success. With Mary's guidance and Joseph's encouragement, the two groups finally realized they shared the same desires and challenges. Gaining respect for their crafts and passing the traditions on to the next generation were too important to waste time feuding. Joining forces made much more sense and promised to be a lot more fun.

"God isn't the only one with a sense of humor," Mary said as they neared their destination. "We've been so busy I forgot to tell you about Wilma and Beverly."

Her curiosity rising, Abby studied her sister. "I know several of the quilters and the weavers are having Thanksgiving dinner together. Is there something else?"

"After Beverly invited the Washburns and they agreed to come, Wilma said it was about time. How could you promote traditions if you don't have any Indians at a Thanksgiving feast?"

"Oh dear." Despite her concern, Abby chuckled. "I have to admit that sounds just like Wilma. I hope it's not the start of another silly feud."

"Not this time. Beverly figured out Wilma has a wry sense of humor. Beverly told her if they planned to d-y-e together in the spring, she'd have to bury the hatchet." Satisfaction seemed to sparkle around Mary. "Wilma thought it was hilarious. It looks like those two are on the way to becoming the best of friends."

"I'm so glad." The joy in Abby's heart grew when she saw her father in the drive waiting for them. After she released Finnegan and they exited the van, she and her father shared a hug. Then the three of them stood back while Mary's lift descended.

"I'm glad you girls are here," their father informed them. "Helping you gives me something to do. Your mother banished me from the kitchen."

Abby saw the merriment under his thinly disguised poor-pity-me performance. "Did she catch you trying to sample everything again?"

"Of course." He winked at Abby. "It's my job. After all, it is Thanksgiving."

Mary wheeled off the lift and reached up to return his hug. Then, she warned, "Don't mess with my marshmallow-topped yams, Dad. They're right-out-of-the-oven-hot and I don't want you to get burned." On her hand command, Finnegan opened the van's side door.

George reached inside for the insulated case. Carrying it like it contained the crown jewels, he shot a hopeful glance at Abby. "What did you make?"

She picked up the basket she'd packed and moved aside for Finnegan to close and latch the van door. "Your favorite cranberry relish."

"Oh no. You girls are making this tough on me. To do the relish justice, I'll have to wait for the turkey." He gave a theatrical moan, then stiffened. "Whoa, Mary's right. I'd better get this inside. The heat's starting to come through the bottom."

While he hurried up the stairs, Abby and Mary went up the ramp. Cool, crisp air swirled around them.

"Ah, there's no place like the Northwest in late autumn," Mary said.

Puzzled, Abby glanced at her sister. "I wasn't aware you'd spent any autumn outside the Northwest."

"I haven't." Mary laughed mischievously. "That's why there's no place like it."

A horn toot heralded the arrival of the McDonalds. The sisters turned to wave and Abby was glad to see Hugo pulling into the yard behind the young family.

"Everyone's here except Henry." Abby held the front door for Mary and Finnegan. Delicious aromas wafted from the kitchen.

"He'll be along shortly." Confidence filled Mary's tone. "Trust me. He won't miss Thanksgiving dinner with us."

After shedding their light coats on the bed in the guest room, Mary and Abby went in to their mother's domain.

Ellen tossed her hot pad on the counter and rushed to greet her daughters with the loving affection Abby knew they could always count on. On this Thanksgiving Day, she felt particularly grateful for the parents God gave her.

Their unconditional love and guidance had molded her and Mary's character. The values they lived and instilled in their daughters had influenced their choices and shaped their lives. Abby wished every child had such positive role models.

Sam caught her in a warm hug and said, "I know what

you're thinking, 'cause we do this every Thanksgiving. You get all misty-eyed wanting everybody to have what you do. There's always hope. I'm living proof. If people are breathing, God isn't finished with them."

"Thanks for the reminder."

"Anytime." He released her and stepped back.

"My, oh my. You and Dad look down right dapper today. I haven't seen you in a tie since last Christmas."

"I haven't worn one since then." An easy smile deepened the crags on Sam's weathered face. "Today's a special occasion. It calls for our finest, right George?"

"Right." He glanced down at the apron covering his dress shirt and gave them a sheepish look. "Right after I take care of business here."

He rolled his sleeves to the elbows and removed the turkey from the oven. Ellen fluttered at his side as though she could actually catch the big, steaming bird if he dropped it.

"Hold it right there," Mary called.

When he turned, a camera flash lit the room.

"It's going to be one of those days, huh?" Sam asked.

"You bet," Mary said cheerfully. "I have plans for these pictures."

"What kind of plans?"

"You'll see."

The sentimental project Mary planned for Christmas made Abby grin. If Sam thought she waxed nostalgic, he was in for a big surprise when he opened Mary's gift.

Bobby entered the kitchen, followed by his parents. Sandy greeted everyone, then took the giant box her husband carried so Neil could join in the hugs.

"It goes over here, Sandy." Mary directed her to the vacant spot on the dessert table next to Ellen's pecan pie.

After Sandy put the big box down, Abby couldn't resist peeking inside. Shaped and decorated like a turkey with its tail feathers spread, the ingenious cake made her gasp.

Sliding up next to her, Bobby peered over the edge of the box. "Cool, huh?"

Abby bent down and kissed his cheek. "Very cool."

"Happy Thanksgiving," Hugo boomed from behind them. "Henry's hot on my trail."

"Looks like we're going to eat on time," Ellen cooed. She clasped Abby's hand. "Come, I need your help."

They went into the dining room where Sam and George had put the extender in the table and gathered additional chairs. Each place was set with Ellen's best china. Pairs of candles shaped like ears of corn guarded the spot in the middle reserved for the turkey.

"Oh, Mom." Abby touched the plain white linen tablecloth.

"Rev. James had a good idea about adding new traditions." Ellen twined her arm around her daughter's waist. "So did you. After you explained his mix-up, I decided to take your tablecloth with me and help him and Janet spread the news. I think the number of Sparrow Islanders adopting this tradition will surprise you."

"It's one more treasure to remember." Abby returned her mother's hug.

"Because of you, Abby. You're one of my treasures." Ellen handed her a small box of wooden matches and went back into the kitchen.

Abby lit the candles and thought of Brandi and Wayne.

They'd gotten help, human and divine, even if they didn't quite recognize God's hand at work. Yet. The forgiveness, mercy and restoration they'd experienced came from Him. She and the other partygoers had just been conduits.

A sudden realization made her smile. She'd plumbed new depths with her fellow partygoers and they'd all grown closer as a result. Each of them had come away from the mystery of the missing ring with a new appreciation for each other.

Mary placed the cranberry relish on the table. A serving spoon overhung the cut glass bowl. "Are you okay? It's time to bring out the food."

"I'm fine. Just indulging in a case of my traditional Thanksgiving misty eye." Abby headed for the kitchen and took Hugo's almond truffle green beans. They smelled much better than they sounded.

When the table was practically groaning under the steaming serving bowls surrounding the golden brown turkey, Ellen announced, "We're ready to eat."

For reasons known only to stomachs and ears, even the men in the living room heard her and began gathering around the table. Abby watched her friends and family take their places and her heart swelled with gratitude.

Henry stood beside Mary like the pillar of strength he was.

Eight decades of living sat lightly on George and Ellen. The happiness they found in each other and the love they freely gave away came full circle, blessing them with vibrant health.

Neil and Sandy were at either side of Bobby, one of Sparrow Island's best hopes for a bright, shining future.

Then there was Sam, steadfast, loyal and always willing to lend a helping hand. He'd become a part of the family while

Abby was still in New York, but there was no question of his status as a family member.

Finally, there was Hugo, fellow nature lover, flexible employer, stalwart friend and generous philanthropist.

Abby's thoughts leaped to the friends not at the table. Rev. James and his family were joining Janet's, along with a cadre of friends.

No doubt, the quilters and weavers bantered over a table full of culinary specialties. The same scene probably played out at The Bird Nest with the Chois and their guests, Sven, Donna, the Dominguezs, and any wandering guests.

At the Minsky household, Al and Laverne and their children would sit down with Nathaniel, Bradford and Candace. Instead of football after dinner, car and boat engines would be the hot topic.

Abby's reverie ended when her father asked the gathering around the Stanton table to join hands before he led in prayer. They all had much to be grateful for this Thanksgiving.

When he finished, Bobby spoke. "Before we sit down, I'd like to read my poem." He unfolded a piece of paper, cleared his throat and began to read.

Ode for a Thanksgiving Turkey
by Bobby McDonald

I read about turkeys and I felt bad.
My Thanksgiving dinner was gonna be sad.
Cuz reading the poem caused me grief
It even changed my eating belief
Til a wise lady showed me The Book
And I had to take another look.

God said all He created was good to eat
And that includes turkey meat.
I'll thank Him for you when I sit down to dine
With family and friends and a meal so fine.
And be grateful for them and their patient love
Because we're gifts to each other from God up above.
Now that we're all standing in position
Let's sit down and have a taste of tradition.

A NOTE FROM THE EDITORS

THIS ORIGINAL BOOK WAS created by the Books and Inspirational Media Division of Guideposts, the world's leading inspirational publisher. Founded in 1945 by Dr. Norman Vincent Peale and his wife Ruth Stafford Peale, Guideposts helps people from all walks of life achieve their maximum personal and spiritual potential. Guideposts is committed to communicating positive, faith-filled principles for people everywhere to use in successful daily living.

Our publications include award-winning magazines like *Guideposts, Angels on Earth* and *Positive Thinking*, best-selling books, and outreach services that demonstrate what can happen when faith and positive thinking are applied in day-to-day life.

For more information, visit us online at www.guideposts.org, call (800) 431-2344 or write Guideposts, 39 Seminary Hill Road, Carmel, New York 10512.